FEDORA III

Even More Private Eyes and Tough Guys

Other books by Michael Bracken

Fiction

All White Girls
Bad Girls
Canvas Bleeding
Deadly Campaign
Even Roses Bleed
In the Town of Dreams Unborn and Memories Dying
Just in Time for Love
Psi Cops
Tequila Sunrise

Anthologies

Fedora: Private Eyes and Tough Guys
Fedora II: More Private Eyes and Tough Guys
Hardbroiled
Small Crimes

FEDORA III

Even More Private Eyes and Tough Guys

edited by

Michael Bracken

BETANCOURT
& COMPANY
Doylestown, Pennsylvania

Fedora III
A publication of
Betancourt & Company, Publishers
P.O. Box 301
Holicong, PA 18928–0301
www.wildsidepress.com

FIRST EDITION

For Sharon.
Always.

Table of Contents

Monkey See Monkey Do

Tom Sweeney

Kidnapping works.

Odd statement coming from an insurance dick, but 1933 was a tough time in the insurance business. Money for premiums was tight and anyone who thought they might not need the insurance stopped paying the premiums, leaving us stuck with only the policies likely to pay out. Fraud rates skyrocketed.

You might think this situation would make claims investigators like me in high demand, but jobs were few and far between during the depression. People worked for rock-bottom wages, and any mug, no matter how good, got the can if the company didn't like him.

1933 was a tough time for the underworld, too, a transition time. With Prohibition on the ropes, organized crime saw its major source of revenue — bootleg liquor — evaporating. State after state plumped for repeal, and with near beer already for sale under Roosevelt's executive signature, the underworld twisted and churned. Lots of shaking up in the ranks and lots of creative crime, with kidnapping emerging as the odds-on winner to replace bootlegging as the cash cow.

Kidnapping works. Gangs already had the manpower, a series of hideaways in the form of hidden, unused liquor warehouses, and a desperate need for money. The number of kidnappings grew, and as long as everyone kept their heads and returned the victims safe and sound, the kidnapping industry would keep growing.

Allied Insurance had already stopped insuring people against kidnapping, but there were a lot of policies still in effect. I've studied the kidnapping MO. I know the mistakes that can be made, and I'm the only guy Allied has who is tough enough to face down organized goons. Allied needs me to head up their kidnapping department here in Kansas City.

So where was Morris sending me?

"You heard me right. Oklahoma."

"To find some hayseed setting fires."

"To keep another one from starting and getting more people killed." He raised his hands in a gesture of surrender. "You're my arson guy, Pete. What can I say?"

I looked at the sheets in my hand. "Three fires in three years. Gimme a break."

"Three fires within thirty miles of each other. One in each of the past three Septembers."

"So?"

"So it's the end of August and I don't want to pay another claim for damages and loss of life. And I don't want this type of thing to become one of those Monkey See Monkey Do crimes."

"Still, kind of a waste, isn't it? Say I do go down to West Muleshoe or where ever —"

"McPherson Junction."

"— and live with those cornhuskers and their pigs every year for a month or two, sort of a company-sponsored vacation."

Morris gave me a look from under his thick eyebrows but I kept talking. "How am I supposed to stop something that I won't know will happen until it's over? Some things you can't stop beforehand. Besides, this Monkey See Monkey Do stuff is a lot of crap."

I threw the case sheets on the Boss' desk. "If some half-wit farmer is going to ape this guy and set a fire every September, we're screwed. Best I could do is catch the guy after he sets the fire."

"Well, that'd be something, wouldn't it?"

"Where's the payback for Allied? Put me in kidnapping and forget these fires. Pay off the policy if this annual fire of yours ever happens, and next year's too. Who cares? I'll save Allied a hundred times that fire policy in two weeks on one kidnapping case alone."

"It isn't just the money, Pete." Morris looked at me sort of pained, like he was going to cry or something. I sat up straighter. "You've worked for me since I've been with Allied. You're like a son —" I started to speak but he held up a hand. "No, you are, and I'm worried about you."

Oh, Christ. "Am I busting up too many fraud cases for you, Morrie? Afraid I'll get your job?" I squirmed a bit in my chair. Maybe I overdid that a bit, but he was asking for it.

Morris went on like I hadn't said a word. "Your results are fine, Pete, and you can have this job as far as that goes. It's your methods. Too many complaints about rough stuff."

"Getting soft, are you? I never hit no one that didn't deserve it. And how the hell do I get onto these guys if I don't think like them, act like them?"

"You can't, Pete, and that's why you're going down to Lafayette County Okla-homer. You been working the rackets so long, you're starting to act like a racketeer. I seen it with the G-men and I see it with you."

There wasn't much I could say to that, so I kept quiet. Morris stood up and looked out his window at the hazy-gray

Kansas sky. He spoke without turning around. "I didn't pass any of those complaints up the chain, Pete, but some day you'll step over the line. I'll have no choice." He turned around and son of a bitch if his eyes weren't wet. Jesus, what a nance. "One of these times, Pete, you'll turn it on and won't be able to turn it off."

I grabbed the sheets off his desk and stood. "All right, I'll go. Just don't expect me to make friends with these hayseeds."

"You could use a few friends, Pete."

"I got you, don't I? At least I used to."

"I'm your boss — you need friends." He spread his hands and shrugged. "Hey, I was just like you before I got married." He plastered this stupid smile on his face like some undertaker. "I know. Trust me, Pete, guys like us are in bad company when we keep to ourselves."

"I said I'd go."

"This'll be good for you. You'll have to go incognito, and have to mingle with people. They're good folks, these farmers." He waved a hand toward his window, to the squat city beyond the streaky glass. "Cities are killing us."

I held back a yawn, waited to see if he was done. He wasn't.

"You'll work undercover as a hired hand. Just listen and get along. Have some fun. Stop this Monkey See Monkey Do stuff before it gets started."

"Monkey See Monkey Do! I'm telling you people commit crimes for a reason, not because someone else did the same thing."

"There you go, then. Go out and find the reason three fires were committed a year apart. There's a federal marshal down there, says some farm hand name of Billy something-or-other worked for two of the outfits that burned down. Billy's working for Ellie Roberts' ranch now and the marshal got you a job there. Check out this Billy mug. We've got big paper on Roberts, on a lot of those farms. Do this right and I'll try to get you assigned to the kidnapping group."

"Promises, promises."

"The marshal's name is Jasper Gordon. He says don't make contact unless you have to."

"He's probably the one that started the fires."

Farm work was tough for a few days, but nothing I couldn't handle. I fit in with most of the guys okay and took a real shine to Miz Roberts' daughter Helen.

I found that Billy was well-liked — hell, *I* liked him — and that he functioned more or less as foreman at the Roberts ranch. He went to town for supplies every Saturday with the old geezer who ran the blacksmith shop. I got the old man in a poker game and cleaned him out so I could give him ten bucks for the right to go to town in his place. That's a month's pay for him, not something he could turn down likely.

Then I won the ten bucks back off him in fifteen minutes of cutthroat poker.

The blacksmith was a booze hound and Billy had a bad case for the moving pictures. When I got Billy back to the ranch after only one matinee and I came back sober, Miz Roberts sent me to town with Billy regular.

That allowed me to telephone Morris each of the last three weeks. Morris okayed the long distance charges because we couldn't pass more'n one or two wires in a single afternoon while I was in town. Working undercover, making long distance telephone calls, if this was a taste of what the kidnapping team was going to be like, then I couldn't wait for it to happen.

Making telephone calls without Billy catching on was easy. After warning me not to get drunk, he headed for the Bijou like clockwork.

It only took a few minutes to raise KC, even from a public phone in a place like McPherson Junction. And today for a change it took only a few seconds for Morris to get on the line. He must have been talked to about long distance charges. "It's been three weeks, Pete," he said. "What have you got?"

"You told me take a month."

The chuckle came distorted over the line. "You starting to like being a farmer?"

"It has its good side."

The chuckle stopped dead. "You ain't falling for some dame, are you?"

"No," I lied. If I told him about Helen Roberts, I'd be hearing farmer's daughter jokes for the rest of my life. "But it is kinda nice working out here." That last was no lie. Three squares a day, every day. Damned good food, too. And people were different here, open and honest, I could get used to that. Makes 'em easy to trick.

"You leave the skirts alone. You find that arsonist and get back here. McAddams is rounding out his kidnap team. You want in, you better get back damn soon."

"Yeah, yeah." I rang off and sauntered over to the Bijou to wait for Billy. *Tarzan the Fearless* was playing, so I didn't have to worry about fighting with Billy about not staying for the second show. He likes to see movies twice, but prefers musicals. A big guy like that, too. No accounting for taste.

We went to town in a wagon pulled by a horse. Hard to believe, but whole sections of this country are stuck in the last century. It made for a long trip, though, and gave us a chance to talk.

Generally Billy is quiet enough to make Silent Cal sound like a blabbermouth, but he was talkative enough this afternoon. Mostly about the movie, but it was an opening. I played along, hoping to sneak something good out of him.

"So you like this guy Crabbe, huh?" I asked.

"Night and day," he said. "I mean, Weismuller makes a good Tarzan, don't get me wrong. He may even look more like Tarzan. But Buster Crabbe — now he can *act.*"

"Well, that's important."

"Sure is, if you want to tell a story. Just like dancing is important for musicals. Ruby Keeler about ruined *42nd Street* for me. Whatever made *her* think she could dance?"

"Bet you dance a lick yourself," I said.

Billy smiled. "I've been told that. Would have won the dance contest last year at the State Fair, weren't for McCarran."

"What he do? Wasn't your partner, now, was he?" I reared back, pretending to be shaken. Lloyd McCarran was the swamper, cleaning the outbuildings and doing anything too dirty or menial for the regular farmhands. I'd been hired to be his helper, but had as little to do with him as possible. He's the kind of guy makes your skin crawl. Anyway, I had more on the ball than any of these farmers and within a week was working for Mrs. Roberts direct.

"Naw," said Billy. "He was just mad. Put a small nail in my boot, he did. Lifted the insole and drove it in. I didn't feel it until I got to moving real good, dancing, you know, but once I knew it was there I couldn't ignore it. I danced like a lumberjack."

"What the hell he do that for? You two have problems?"

"Naw. He wanted to bring Katie, and she went with me."

"Katie Miller? Didn't she die in that fire last year?"

"Yeah." Billy stared out beyond the horizon.

I stuffed down the sympathy I felt for him and said, "So you took her to the fair. Doesn't seem like much to get mad over."

"It ain't," Billy said. "But I guess he was still mad over the year before."

"What happened the year before?"

Billy clucked the reins and looked sideways at me. I pretended to be interested in a small dust cloud on the horizon. "You sure do ask a lot of questions," he said.

I'd pushed too hard. I took a minute before looking back at him. "What? Oh, sorry. Just making conversation, learning about what's going on in the country."

"First thing you oughta learn is don't ask questions."

Sometimes you work your tail off, unraveling twisted threads of a case and chasing down the wrong trails, and sometimes the blue bird of luck lays an egg right in your lap. I was working on the same farm, bunking in the same barn, with the mug that I'd been sent to look for. Lloyd McCarran, the swamper and general helper I was hired to help.

A week after I'd roused Billy's suspicions, I was talking with Helen Roberts under the cottonwood off by the stick corral. I was waiting for Billy to bring the wagon around for the trip to town, but wasn't about to pass up a chance to chat up Helen.

Twice while we talked I saw McCarran walk by. The second time I wondered where he was going, walking between the barn and the machinery shed. I sensed Helen shiver next to me and caught her staring at McCarran.

"Weird fella, huh?" I said.

"Gives me the creeps," she said, and hugged her arms tight around herself. I wanted to do just that thing myself, but held back. These farmers do everything slow. Anyway, she was kind of sweet on Billy, even though he acted the chump with her. I'm ten years older than Billy, probably fifteen years older than Helen. Give me enough time and familiarity will blur the age difference.

Give me enough time. Don't push, that's the key.

Just before McCarran reached the barn, he looked around and caught us staring at him. He hesitated, then slipped inside. All my hackles went up. I may not know farmers, but I know guilt when I see it.

"McCarran bother you?" I asked suddenly.

"No. Yes. I mean, well, I shouldn't let it bother me."

I stepped between her and the barn. "How's he bother you, Helen?"

"He keeps asking me to go to the fair with him. I don't want to, but —"

"But he's kind of wearing you down?"

"Yes. No. Not wearing me down, but I'm getting afraid. He's so intense. I don't know what will happen when the fair comes along."

"Want to go with me?" I tried to keep the eagerness out of my voice. "McCarran wouldn't dare fool with me."

"I — No, I'm going with Billy. Oh, don't mind me. I'm just like a little girl sometimes. Afraid of shadows, I suppose. Oh, here's Billy."

Billy came around the corner of the barn in the wagon and pulled up in front of the wide doors. Helen walked up to meet him and I followed. So she was going with Billy, huh? Well, if he continues to play the chump with her, and I get to stay here a few more weeks, she'll be mine, not his.

She stopped in front of Billy, who looked over her to me. "Ready?" he asked, ignoring her.

Fool. "In a minute. Want to check the barn."

"What for?"

"Be out in a minute." No need to tip his hand and let him play hero with Helen. McCarran's days of bothering her were over, and I was going to get the credit.

The barn was empty. "McCarran," I shouted. No answer. I opened the makeshift door leading to his small room.

It was empty and damn good thing, because I might have beat him to a pulp right then.

It was a disgusting hole of soiled clothing and dirty blankets and raw pictures of naked women on the walls. A box of biscuits and a quart of hooch sat on an upturned crate next to the bed. Light from the barn behind me glinted on something under his bed and I knelt down to see. More hooch. A row of pint bottles lined the wall under the bed. I stood, then looked again. The booze was dark, even for homemade stuff. Bastard was lucky he didn't go blind drinking that crap.

I sniffed. The room smelled of something besides McCarran's dirty scent. I moved around a bit, sniffing, trying not to gag on McCarran's sour body odor that permeated the room. Then I caught it. Kerosene. I went back into the room and searched as well as I could without touching anything. No kerosene.

I searched the barn and off behind the tall wooden-slatted stalls where Miz Roberts milks her cows, a five gallon can lay half-hidden behind some old tack. I unscrewed the top and sniffed.

Kerosene.

This can had been in McCarran's room. No doubt of it. And if Helen hadn't been spooked by him I'd never have known. At least I could report something to Morris today, maybe even extend my stay here. The State Fair was in two weeks. Billy was sure to hang around the guys, leaving Helen to be rescued from embarrassment by me.

Billy was silent most of the way into town, and I wondered if he was suspicious of my always happening to be near where Helen happened to be. In town, he hung close to me at first, but the minute we had the wagon loaded up, he headed for the Bijou. I watched him buy his ticket. He took it from the girl, then turned and waved it at me. As soon as he went inside I headed for the phone in the Western Union office. It only took a minute to raise KC.

"No, I ain't got proof, Morrie. Proof's for the DA. My job is just to shine the light on the right mug."

"This one's a little different, Pete. I —"

"Shush!" I said. A shadow stretched out from around the corner of the depot from where I was making the phone call.

"Someone's eavesdropping."

I set the receiver on the hook and quickly rang off. I spun quickly around the corner and bumped straight into Billy.

I grabbed him by the shirt. "What're you spying on me for?"

A moment of fear crossed his eyes before he remembered how strong he was. He shook off my hands and pushed me backwards. "What're you doing using the telephone? You ain't paid enough to make no telephone calls."

"None of your business."

"I'll make it my business," he said, then crunched up his face. "I'll make it Miz Roberts' business. She'll want to know what you're doing making telephone calls."

I let it drop, and we rode back to the ranch in silence. I don't know if his threat to tell Miz Roberts was real or not, but I couldn't chance it. After being caught on the phone like some rube, I knew I'd have to be more careful around him. He wasn't the hayseed he appeared to be.

We were passing through a shaded hollow, almost in sight of the ranch, when I spoke to him. "Billy, I'd appreciate it if you didn't tell Miz Roberts about the telephone call."

"Why? What are you hiding?"

"I'm an investigator."

Billy stared at me, chewing his lip, digesting this information. "A cop?" he asked. I could have told him anything, but stuck with the truth, in case this went to trial and Billy had to go up before a jury. "I work for an insurance company," I said.

He looked disappointed. "You ain't a G-man?"

"No, just an insurance investigator. Look, you know the fires you been having this time every year?"

From the blank look on his face, I realized he was like all the other hicks around here, so busy living today that they don't see what's been happening all around them. "The Sweetgrass Farm," I said. "The Miller place, the Orwell place?"

"Oh, yeah, they all caught fire."

"Well, Lloyd set 'em all." I clamped my jaws. Damn, I wish I hadn't said that. I was so used to speaking to Billy like he was an idiot, it just slipped out.

Billy surprised me by not going *oh gee whiz* on me. He chucked the reins a bit, making the pair of horses do a slip step, and rode silent for a few moments.

"Figures," he said finally.

Now it was my turn to look in wonder. What did Billy know? I waited for him to continue, and when he didn't, I said, "What figures, Billy?"

"Never did like McCarran, chasing after those girls like he done."

"Girls? Besides Katie that time with you and the dance?" Billy seemed more laconic than stupid. A quiet guy will fool you sometimes. I ought to know, it was my best ruse.

He looked at me like you'd look at a dog too stupid to find his food bowl. "Helen Roberts."

Yeah, Helen. That bastard. I was so pissed I almost missed Billy's next words: "Suzie Orwell."

"Katie Miller and Suzie Orwell both?" I asked. Well, there's some proof for Morris. Suzie died in the Orwell fire.

I had studied the sheets enough to know the names. Both the Millers and Orwells were small families. They all died in the fire. I forgot their ages, though.

"How old were Katie and Suzie, Billy?"

"I dunno, fifteen, sixteen."

"And Lloyd McCarran was sniffing after them?" Lloyd was at least thirty, and hardly had the job to impress a young girl.

"Yeah. He's an old bronc rider. Tried to get them to go to the Fair with him."

A tingly chill spread up my spine. Now I knew why the fires had been set. "Fires happen near the time of the Fair, Billy?"

He had to think about this. "The Miller's did for sure, 'cause I remember they'd just taken first in Draught Horse, then the horse went and died in the fire. Burnt up. Dunno when the Orwell's fire was."

"What about the Sweetgrass Farm? That happen around Fair time too? They have a young girl?" Another thought struck me. "Lloyd work for Sweetgrass before their fire?"

"They's a big outfit. I didn't have no truck with Sweetgrass."

I had to go back to town. Call Morris and have him set the dogs on McCarran. Before he does another fire, with Helen in the house. "Pull up."

"What?"

"Stop the wagon. I need to go back to town."

"We ain't more'n a mile from the ranch."

"I have to go back and call this in. You don't want McCarran to get away, do you?"

"He won't," Billy said, but he pulled the horses to a stop. "You go back," he said. "I'll walk from here." He jumped off the high seat and moved past the horses.

They started to move, keeping pace with him. I grabbed the reins and gave a tug. Nothing happened. "Billy!" I cried.

"I haven't driven a team before."

He looked back over his shoulder. "Easy," he said. "Slap 'em to go, pull back to stop. Hard." He turned and ran off before I could tell him to stay away from McCarran.

I should have known Billy would spook McCarran. Everyone thought he'd left the country, but I knew better. I knew the way eggs like McCarran thought.

I missed the Fair, sticking close to the ranch, staying up most of the night, every night. Lloyd never showed, but I knew it was only a matter of time. I stayed away from town and the telephone so Morris couldn't tell me to come back. He wired me. I wired back that something big was about to happen, that I couldn't leave now. Christ, he's the guy that wanted me to have friends.

I was tired during the day and slept a lot, but Miz Roberts never fired me. I doubt the marshal told her the truth about me. I think she just felt sorry for me.

Everyone else thought I was a drunk. What with being tired all day, red-eyed from lack of sleep, who could blame them. Only Billy stuck by me, and him I avoided until I could sort out my intentions toward Helen. I let slip something about Helen to him, and I think he suspected the truth. Anyway, he left me alone.

Helen was distantly polite. She knew something was wrong but didn't hassle me. I loved her for it, for her faith in me. I could see what Lloyd saw in her, that bastard.

Two weeks after the Fair she gave me a Bible. "This belonged to my Uncle Ned," she told me. "He kept it all through the Great War."

I wanted to reach out and hold her. I took the Bible to occupy my hands. "He died," she said. "Flanders Field."

"Helen, I'm sorry, I—" I stepped forward, but my tired

feet barely cleared the clumps of sod beneath me. I stumbled against her, pulled back, almost fell to the ground.

She balled both hands into tiny fists. "I hope they never repeal Prohibition," she said. "I hope . . . I hope I never have to see men like you and Lloyd again. Ever." She turned and ran to the house.

It took an effort to get back to my feet. I thought for a minute about following her into the house, but what was the point? I'd lost her.

I carried the Bible back to my room in the back of the barn. This was McCarran's fault. If he'd left her alone, if he'd stayed to face the music, if he'd just died. I went into his room. I don't know why.

Nothing had changed since the last time I'd seen it. I kicked over the crate by his bed. The biscuit box fell onto the floor and broke open. The bottle of booze fell, too, but it didn't break. I grabbed it and left the Bible on the floor in its place.

The barn was empty, but I climbed into the loft anyway, and started to work on the hooch.

Sunlight coming through the spacing between two warped barn boards woke me. I crawled out of the loft and stumbled outside. Must have been close to noon. I could hear voices in the house. Miz Roberts and Helen and Billy, most likely, getting the noon meal ready for the hands still out in the fields.

To hell with this. To hell with Billy and Helen and Lloyd. I knew more about how the kidnapping racket worked than anyone in Allied, and here I was on this glorified pig farm.

I'd go back to Kansas City, with electricity and flush toilets and women who wore makeup. And I'd make Morris transfer me to kidnapping.

I knew more about it than Jake Factor or Boss Shannon or any of those other stiffs Allied was using. I oughta kidnap Helen is what I oughta do. With what I knew, I'd never get caught.

'Cept with her, I don't want the ransom. I ran a hand over my face. I had to get back to KC.

I went inside and packed my bindle.

Just before I walked back through the open barn door, I saw something slide around the corner of the house into view. A hunchback. No, a man leaning over. Lloyd McCarran, with a five gallon can.

I yelled and he looked up. I pulled my gun from the bindle I'd dropped on the ground. I was afraid to shoot at McCarran, afraid the bullet would go through the house. I fired a shot high into the air.

Lloyd looked up, saw me, and ran around the corner of the house. I took off after him. Just as I rounded the house, he disappeared into the cedar brake bordering the creek. I ran down the slope. From behind me, someone yelled — Billy? — but I kept on, gun in hand.

Something crashed in the underbrush. I fired off three shots and heard a yelp.

No more sounds of movement. I went forward slowly, gun ready.

McCarran lay against a blown down cottonwood where he'd dragged himself.

He grimaced when he saw me. "What'd ya shoot me for?"

"I guess you can figure it out."

"I was chasing that guy, same as you."

"What guy?"

"The guy pouring kerosene around the house. I came back looking for my old job and saw him. I yelled and took after him. What'd ya shoot me for?"

"Nice try, McCarran. You'll hang when I'm done with you."

McCarran shifted himself. "Don't think so. I got alibis for those old jobs. Nothing to tie me into this one, either.

My word against yours, and from the smell of your breath, you're still drunk."

"We'll see." Someone was crashing around down by the creek. "Over here," I yelled.

"My word against yours. Even if I go up, might as well be in jail as living in a barn the rest of my life. Which will be longer than that damn Billy's if I don't get sent up."

"I'll kill you if you do."

"A little late for Billy, don't you think?

"Won't matter to you — you'll be dead."

"You call this living?"

I wanted to shoot him then. I couldn't stop him except by killing him now. Only one way to deal with guys like him. The rage built in me, roared in my head.

Except I'll never get Helen or anyone like her that way. Morris was right in a way. There's a line you can't cross and still keep certain company.

I'd almost settled down when he lit my fuse again. "Maybe it ain't Billy I'm going to get," he said. "Maybe it'll be the girl."

He started to get up, and I hit him on the side of his head with my pistol. Hard. "You die if you lay a hand on her."

McCarran just laughed at me. "I'm a walking dead man, same as you. The girl's mine." He licked his lips. "Some things you can't stop, not even you, brother."

I aimed the gun at his forehead, and clicked back the hammer. McCarran shook his head. "You're tough, brother, but not that tough." He sucked on his lower lip. "I think I'll take her over to the brakes. Keep her a few days. May as well make it worth dying for, eh?"

The gun bucked in my hand, sending a roaring lance of flame reaching out to touch McCarran's chest.

I looked from the spot of red that had appeared on McCarran's chest to my gun, still smoking. I hadn't meant to shoot.

I don't think I meant to shoot.

I sensed someone behind me and whirled, gun ready. Billy held up his hands. "Don't shoot."

I lowered the gun and turned back to McCarran. The bullet had knocked him back against the tree trunk and he sat spraddle-legged on the ground. The spot of red on his shirt had widened to fist size.

McCarran coughed. "Guess I went too far, huh, brother? Maybe I was wrong. Maybe you are tough enough. Least, you are now." He coughed again, and red spittle formed at the corners of his mouth. His eyes widened for a minute, and I wondered what he saw.

His eyes cleared and just for a second the slackness left his face. "See you in hell, brother."

A pair of undercover dicks had my apartment house staked out by the time I made it back to Kansas City. I called Morris from a drug store. "I can't help you, Pete. They got a warrant on you for doing McCarran."

I hung up and walked toward the stockyards. I had a cousin in Baltimore could put me up until I could raise a stake somehow.

The east-bound passenger pulled into view around the makeshift corrals of milling steers, the setting sun framing it blood red through the dust. Heading in the opposite direction, a long freight slowly gathered speed.

West. A man could lose himself in California. Make a quick stake, do pretty much anything he wanted. Cops and crooks both ain't so wise out there.

With what I know about kidnapping, I should do okay.

An open boxcar slid by and I hauled myself in.

A handful of bindle stiffs huddled on one side, the fraternity of the open road. "Hi, Brother," said one.

"Shut up," I said, lifting my shirt to show the gun stuck in my pants.

Bumsickle

Lee Goldberg

Detective Bud Flanek used a plastic knife to scrape the last bit of strawberry jelly from a tiny Smucker's tin, smeared it on his hot, cheddar cheese bagel, and took a big bite.

He didn't really like the bagels in this place much. The only way he could eat them was to smother them with anything that had some flavor, which is why he ordered a bagel that was covered with cheddar cheese to start with. What Bud Flanek liked was the hot, heavy, onionized air that filled the tiny shop all winter long.

Every morning, he left his city-owned Crown Vic idling at the curb, and while the worthless heater struggled to warm the icy, cracked-vinyl interior of the car, ate his breakfast at one of the chipped linoleum tables. Just for the heat and the smell.

It was pathetic, Bud knew that. But it wasn't like he was squandering any great promise. By his own reckoning, he wasn't much of a cop and even less of a man.

Bud became a cop because the perky recruitment officer who visited his community college had the best pair of breasts he'd ever seen. He thought he might get laid if he signed up and showed some enthusiasm.

He didn't, and twenty years later here he was, a pot-bellied, 38-year-old Spokane homicide detective with thinning hair and nicotine-stained teeth, hemorrhoids and perpetual rhinitis, all packaged in a polyester suit from Walmart's distinctive Perry Como collection.

Bud accepted the gradual hair loss, learned to live with the sore butt and runny nose, and didn't care about his suits, as long as they were cheap, didn't wrinkle easily, and didn't cut off his circulation. The only clothes he really shopped for were Hawaiian shirts because they had some artistic merit.

He gave up the cigarettes when he and Diane were trying in vain to have kids, and managed to stay away from them even after the divorce, but couldn't bring himself to have his teeth bleached, or whitened, or whatever the hell they called it. People would know immediately what he'd done, and figure he did it to get laid, which would be true, since he hadn't had any action in a couple of years and his prospects weren't good.

As far as being a cop went, Bud had managed to achieve mediocrity. He cleared cases, but nobody was going to mistake him for Lt. Columbo. Luckily for Bud, in reality very few murderers had the smarts of Patrick McGoohan, Robert Culp, or even a reasonably intelligent goat. Catching killers was easy. It was the paper work that was difficult.

Bud's cell phone chirped. He didn't have to answer it to know that someone was dead.

Every winter Bud Flanek inevitably found himself stomping through the snow in the park, taking off his nice wool mitts and swapping them for a tight, thin pair of plastic gloves to examine a frozen corpse.

More often than not, they were natural deaths, the natural result of being broke and homeless in a big city with brutally cold winters and even colder politicians.

The deaths were sad but simple cases, nothing that could qualify as a homicide, not unless the laws were changed, and the city council members who voted to slash shelter funding could be arrested for premeditated murder.

The park was virtually deserted; it was too early and too cold for anyone to be out, except for a couple of uniformed officers and Erno Pender from the coroner's office. Erno was the only person Bud knew professionally who made him feel superior by comparison, if only because Erno weighed thirty pounds more than Bud, had half as much hair, and the pock-marked skin of a kid who picked his face through adolescence.

"Did you think to bring me a bagel?" Erno asked.

Bud pulled a cheddar cheese bagel out of his jacket pocket and dropped it into the evidence bag Erno held open in front him.

"Thanks," Erno said.

"You gonna eat it or analyze it?"

"I'm saving it for later," Erno waved towards his meat wagon. "I'll eat it in the car on the drive back."

"Too bad. I was hoping you could tell me what passes for cheese on those things."

"You bring any cubes of butter, maybe some breakfast spread?"

Bud shook his head no, shivering in the icy wind. "What's breakfast spread?"

"The stuff that's not butter or margarine." Erno sealed the bag, stuffed it inside his coat, and led Bud off the jogging path into the shrubbery.

"I appreciate you putting that in layman's terms for me," Bud said. "Can you do the same on this stiff?"

"A bumsickle."

"I'll need a little more than that."

"Female Caucasian, mid-to-late-30s, no apparent signs of trauma. Looks to me like she just curled up under a bush with her bottle and froze to death."

The woman was bundled up in a ratty, men's overcoat that was at least two sizes too big for her, hugging herself, her face turned to the ground. An empty bottle of Scotch lay at her feet.

"Any ID?" Bud asked.

"Pockets were empty," Erno replied. "We'll roll her prints when we get back to the morgue."

Bud leaned down and looked at her face. She didn't die peacefully, she died defiant, her eyes closed and lips drawn tight in an expression of stubborn refusal. Her skin was chalky white and perfect, her black hair short and ragged, like she'd cut it herself in a frustrated hurry with a pair of rose shears. It was probably the kind of thing she'd do.

He hadn't seen her in two years. Nobody had.

"You know her?" Erno asked, reading his face.

Bud nodded, overwhelmed with sadness and dread and unanswered questions. Where had she been? Did she just come back from somewhere else, or had she been living in the city all along, managing to hide from them all?

"I got to give the Chief a call," Bud said, his voice a barely audible rasp.

Erno looked at the corpse, then at Bud. "She's somebody that important?"

Bud turned up his collar against the cold, shoved his fists into his pockets, and trudged off towards his car, mumbling into the wind.

"Just his wife."

When Lissy Masters woke up during the night, wanting a smoke and not finding one, she'd get out of bed, grab some change off the nightstand, and walk a couple blocks to the Stop-and-Go on the corner.

It wasn't the hour, or the walk, that unsettled people on the streets. It was that Lissy didn't bother getting dressed to do it.

The first time she showed up naked at the Stop-and-Go, demanding a pack of Marlboros, the startled clerk didn't know whether to sell her the cigarettes, call the cops, or drag her behind the counter for his interpretation of how the market got its name.

He sold her the cigarettes and let her walk out, a decision all the more astonishing considering the clerk was a paroled sex offender who only took the job so he'd have free access to girlie magazines.

When the clerk found out later that she was the wife of the deputy chief of police, he considered her naked, nocturnal visits a divine test of his character, proof of God's hand at work. Later, some time after she disappeared, he would credit her for leading him to Jesus.

Lissy was blessed in that way. She didn't have to adjust to the world; it twisted itself all out of shape to adjust to her.

At least, it used to.

Bud Flanek sat in Chief Masters' office, trying to look anywhere but at Fred Masters, who stood with his back to him, staring out the window in deep contemplation.

Chief Masters was a big, muscled man in a tailored suit who looked like he'd be much more comfortable in a loincloth, letting his abs and glutes flex in unfettered glory. No matter how well-fitted his suits were, Masters' body always seemed to be straining at the seams to break out.

But if Chief Masters was uncomfortable, he didn't show

it. He was a man who prized control, over others and over himself, which was why it was so important for him to hide his pain from Bud, and why it was so important for Bud not to show he saw it.

So Bud concentrated on the badges, awards and commendations on the walls and the one, small photo of Lissy Masters on her husband's spotless desk.

There was something disturbingly erotic about the picture, although it was nothing more than an innocent head shot. It was a rawness to the smile, and a mischievousness in the eyes, that seemed to promise trouble, and a lot of fun making it.

Lissy often disappeared for days at a time, only to show up again in a big way, like the time she took a Mercedes Benz on a 230-mile test drive, abandoning the car and the salesman on the side of the road in Idaho when she finally ran out of gas. Masters ended up buying the car, taking out a second mortgage on his house to pay for it, just to smooth things over as fast as possible.

At the time, even the officers who were snickering behind Masters' back at his embarrassment felt sorry for him.

Once, Bud picked her up at a McDonald's, where she was sitting naked, casually eating a Happy Meal, at 3 a.m. Bud sat across from her, sharing her fries, before he drove her home and dropped her off outside her door. He didn't want the Chief seeing him.

A few hours later, she walked back out into the sunrise and wasn't seen again. That was two years ago.

"You know I tried to help her," the chief finally declared. "I put her into rehab three times, though drugs and alcohol were never her problem. I wish they were, at least I could have understood that."

"I'm afraid you'll have to come down and identify the body, sir."

The chief turned around and looked at Bud, who immediately straightened up in his seat.

"I'm aware of what I have to do, Flanek," the Chief said.

Bud swallowed. "Yes, sir."

During his entire career, such as it was, Bud was careful to go unnoticed, a feat he accomplished by showing absolutely no ambition or initiative whatsoever. Everybody took him for granted, a familiar piece of squad room furniture, and he liked that. Now here he was in the Chief's office, where he couldn't help but make a resoundingly bad impression. Why couldn't some other cop have found Lissy Masters?

"Any idea where she's been," the Chief asked, "or how she ended up in the park?"

"No sir," Bud replied, "but I've got officers questioning the homeless to see if any of them knew her."

"She wasn't homeless," the Chief snapped. "She had a home, a good home."

"Yes, sir." Bud felt beads of sweat rolling down his back.

"If she was living on the streets in my city, don't you think I would have known about it? That we all would have?"

"Of course, sir."

There was no way this could turn out well for Bud, but at least it would be over soon. He thanked God that it was clearly an accidental death, something that could be wrapped up in a day, as opposed to a protracted murder investigation, which could drag on for weeks and give the Chief ample opportunity to be dissatisfied and disgusted with him. With luck, in a couple days the Chief would forget Bud Flanek ever existed.

"You're sure about how she died?"

"There's nothing at this point to indicate a homicide, sir. The coroner is pretty certain she froze to death, but we'll have the results of the autopsy this afternoon."

The Chief nodded, as much an acknowledgement as a

dismissal. "Go down to the morgue, wait on that report, I don't want the press getting it before I do."

"Yes, sir."

Bud rose from his seat and gathered his overcoat from the adjoining chair. "I'm very sorry, sir."

"So am I." The Chief turned back to the window.

Bud glanced one more time at Lissy's picture and left.

He had no desire to see someone he knew dissected, so Bud waited in the hall, eating a bag of chips and staring at the diagram of the building's emergency exits on the opposite wall.

By the time Erno Pender finally emerged in his blood-streaked lab-gown, Bud had memorized the ingredients of Nacho Cheese Doritos and knew how to get out of the building in any situation.

"How did it go?" Bud asked.

"As hard as I tried, I couldn't revive her." Erno held his palm out to Bud. "You got some change for the vending machine?"

"I meant were there any surprises?"

"Low blood sugar makes it hard for me to recall."

Bud dug into his pockets and scowled. "You make at least twenty grand more than me."

"But you have pockets and I don't."

He handed Erno a handful of assorted change.

"Thanks." Erno shuffled up to the machine. "She froze to death."

"Is that all you've got to tell me?"

"I thought you'd be relieved."

"I am, but with the Chief involved, I need all the details."

Erno scrutinized the selections. "Besides being a little

drunk, there were no drugs in her blood stream, no needle marks, no suspicious cuts, bruises or abrasions. All that's left are corn nuts."

"What corn nuts?"

Erno wrapped a knuckle against the glass. "*Those* corn nuts. Nobody wants to eat corn nuts. You cleaned the machine out. You ravaged it. If you gave a damn about any of us down here, you'd have the courtesy to leave at least one bag of chips."

"Does that mean I can have my change back?"

Erno angrily jammed coins into the slot. "She had sex before she died."

Bud immediately looked at the nearest emergency exit. "She was raped?"

"I didn't say that." Erno punched a button on the machine. "There was no physical signs of force, but I got enough seminal fluid for a DNA match if you think you'll ever need it."

Bud wondered if this was information the Chief really needed to know, because if he did know, then he probably would want the poor guy hunted down, and he'd want Bud to do it. That wouldn't do anybody any good, particularly Bud, who knew he'd never be able to find the guy.

All of this ran through Bud's mind in the time it took for Erno's bag of corn nuts to drop from the shelf into the slot. Bud was working out a way to ask Erno to do him a big favor, and omit the semen findings from his report, when Erno spoke up.

"Whoever he is, he never has to worry about child support."

"What do you mean?"

Erno shook his little snack. "There are more corn nuts in this bag than sperm in his, if you catch my meaning."

Bud did and immediately wished he didn't. "Can you tell me the time of death?"

"No."

"Can't you take a guess?"

Erno tore open the bag of nuts and spilled a few into his hand. "A few months ago, a couple of hikers in Spain found a guy frozen in a block of ice. They called the police. Turns out the guy had been missing for a while. A couple thousand years, in fact. Maybe it was more like a hundred thousand. I don't know. The point is, they wouldn't have known how long ago he froze to death if wasn't for certain evolutionary changes, and the clothes and tools they found near him. Since we haven't evolved much since Lissy Masters died, and we had a pretty warm summer, I'd say she died some time this winter."

Erno popped the nuts in his mouth and crunched on them, using the loud crack they made to punctuate his point.

Bud thought for a long moment and decided to ask Erno to do him a big favor before sending the autopsy to the Chief.

It took the security guards fifteen minutes to respond to the break-in, hardly the instant, armed response promised on the sign in the front lawn. But Bud Flanek was thankful for the extra time; it gave him a chance to find the freezer in the basement and a comfortable chair to sit in.

The two rent-a-cops appeared in the open doorway at the top of the stairs striking dramatic poses they learned from TV. One stretched his arm straight out, twisting his wrist so his gun was aimed sideways, a grip that looked cool, but was about as useful as trying to shoot the weapon with his foot. The other security guard held his gun straight up, right in front of his face, a stance that might be effective if his target happened to be levitating directly over his head.

"You guys ever fire those guns, you're gonna hurt yourselves worse than the person you're trying to shoot, so why don't you put them away?" Bud sat at the bottom of the stairs in a folding chair, one arm resting on top of the padlocked freezer, the other holding up his badge to Crockett and Tubbs.

"Bud Flanek, Homicide."

"Where's the perp?" Tubbs asked, reluctantly holstering his gun.

"In the time it took you to get here, he could almost be at the airport. In another five minutes, he could be on a plane to Jakarta," Bud said. "But as luck would have it, the perpetrator is right here."

"He's in the freezer?" Crockett asked.

"No," Bud replied. "He's sitting in this chair, putting his badge back in his pocket."

"You broke into the house?" Tubbs asked. It was more of a statement than a question. Bud nodded. "I assume you've got a search warrant you can show us."

"I couldn't get one, even if I'd tried, which I didn't, because whether I have a warrant or not isn't going to matter," Bud glanced at his watch. "What I really need is for the two of you to wait here with me for a while."

"Wait for what?" Crockett asked suspiciously.

"Assistance in a homicide investigation. Did your dispatcher notify the homeowner that there'd been a break in?"

"Yeah," Crockett replied.

"Then it shouldn't be much longer," Bud motioned to some folding chairs propped against the wall. "Take a seat, relax. You might learn a few things."

The two rent-a-cops shared a confused look, then went over and took some seats, unfolded them, and sat down.

Bud glanced at his watch again and felt the two guys staring at him. "So, you guys ever try to join the police department?"

"I didn't meet the height requirement," Tubbs groused. "Or the weight."

"And you?" Bud asked Crockett.

"The department doesn't recognize the high school equivalency exam certificate of completion as a valid diploma," Crockett explained bitterly. "It's jealousy, that's what it is. Anybody with half-a-brain can see that someone who graduates early is smarter than someone who takes four years to learn the same stuff, right? So rather than have any intellectuals around who'd make them look stupid, they don't let us in."

"Sounds like you've both got legitimate grievances. You ought to take it up with the Chief of Police." Bud motioned to the stairs. "What do you say, Chief?"

Crockett and Tubbs looked up and were stunned to see Police Chief Fred Masters standing at the top of the stairs, his face rigid with anger and contempt. The two security guards turned to Bud in shock, but his gaze was on the Chief, who came slowly down the stairs.

"What the hell is going on here, Flanek?"

Bud knocked on the freezer. "The three of us were just sitting here wondering why you keep your freezer padlocked. Do a lot of frozen dinners get stolen in this neighborhood?"

"You broke into the police chief's house?" Tubbs stared at Bud. "Are you crazy?"

"No, I just haven't had sex in two years."

"Two years?" Crockett repeated incredulously.

"And when it's been that long you don't forget the last time," Bud looked back at the Chief. "It was the night your wife disappeared."

"I don't know what your problem is, and I don't care. You're fired. Surrender your gun and your badge, now." The Chief thrust out his hand for them, but Bud didn't move.

"Lissy made one of her naked, late-night trips to McDonald's and I got the call. We shared some fries and I offered to take her home. I was driving her back when she climbed in my lap and started kissing me. I had to pull over or crash. Once the car stopped, I was a goner, she had me. I knew Lissy was doing it to embarrass you, to get your attention, just like everything else she did. But she was beautiful, and she was naked, and she wanted me. I couldn't help myself."

The Chief lifted Bud out of his seat and threw him against the cement wall, knocking the air out of him. As Bud slid to the floor, the Chief pulled out his gun and jammed it against the detective's forehead.

"You miserable excuse for a man. I ought to shoot you right now."

Bud grimaced, trying to catch his breath as he spoke. "Then it's a good thing I invited witnesses."

The Chief looked over his shoulder, suddenly remembering the two security guards, who sat dumbfounded in their seats, their eyes wide and unblinking. He backed a few steps away from Bud, holstered his gun and regarded him with disgust. "You're finished. I'll see you go to prison for this."

Bud rose awkwardly to his feet, bracing his back against the wall for support. "What happened that night? She have a few drinks and fall asleep? How long did you wait before you locked her in the freezer and let her die?"

The Chief spun around, driving his fist deep into Bud's stomach. Bud doubled over and dropped to his knees, coughing up blood. The Chief turned back to the guards.

"Get him out of here," he told them. "I'll have officers here in five minutes to arrest him."

The Chief started back up the stairs. The guards moved like sleepwalkers, trudging over to Bud and lifting him to his feet. They'd never had a call anything like this before.

"You know why my wife left me?" Bud sputtered, barely able to speak. "I make $37,000 a year and I'm infertile."

The Chief froze on the stairs.

"That's how I knew Lissy didn't die last night, last week, or even last year. That's how I know she's been in this freezer with your fish sticks and meat pies."

The Chief slowly turned around, his gun in his hand again and aimed in Bud's general direction.

"She was an embarrassment to you. There was no way you'd ever become the Police Chief with her around," Bud spit out more blood and wiped his mouth with his wrist. "So you made her disappear again, only this time for good."

The Chief came down the stairs. Crockett and Tubbs dropped Bud on his knees and moved away from him.

"Once you were Chief, and enough time had passed, you dumped her in the park. You knew it wouldn't be possible for the coroner to determine when she actually froze to death. You should have gotten away with it."

"I still could." The Chief walked behind Bud and aimed his gun at the back of his head. "What's to stop me from executing you, shooting those two, and saying the intruder did it?"

"The blood sample I left with the coroner. He's already having a DNA comparison done between it and the semen sample. It's going to match, whether I live or die tonight."

The Chief raised his gun and stepped back from Bud. "When did you get so smart, Flanek?"

"I'm not smart," Bud replied. "Just unlucky."

"Not half as much as me." And with that, the Chief put the gun in his mouth and pulled the trigger.

The sound of the gunshot reverberated off the cellar walls like a bomb blast, jolting the two security guards off their feet and knocking Bud face-first onto the floor.

After a moment, the shot still ringing in his ears, Bud sat up and looked at the two guards, who staggered to their feet, their faces ashen.

"So," Bud said, spitting out another gob of blood, "either of you guys have any job applications on you?"

Ordained Sin

Carol Kilgore

I picked myself up from the sidewalk, straw hat in hand, just in time for Becky's fist to land in the center of my gut again. This time I didn't go down, but I should have. It would have saved me a lot of pain and Becky a lot of trouble. I never should have taught her how to throw a punch.

She shook her index finger in my face. "And another thing, you lying, scheming, boozing, two-bit dick. Don't ever think you can spend the weekend with a rodeo whore and expect to sleep in my bed come Monday."

She paused and took a deep breath. Her breasts heaved inside the bright yellow tank top she wore. It was a delectable sight.

"Ain't gonna happen. Not in this lifetime or any other one." She punched me again, then hit me over the head with the jackhammer she called her purse.

When I came to, the clothes from my closet hung from the limbs of the big oak tree in Becky's front yard. The back of my neck felt sunburned, but at least the fire ants had left me alone. They're bad in the spring.

My underwear was draped over the bushes, and my

shaving gear and other toiletries stood like toy soldiers inside my hat. All except the shaving cream. She had used it to write *Sorry Bastard* on the back window of my ten-year-old Ford pickup.

I tried to recall what the rodeo queen looked like. We'd hooked up midway between the steer wrestling and the first-go bull riding. The old arena had seen better days and better cowboys, but it was the place to be on Saturday nights. Loud music, cold beer, and people looking for a good time.

The lady had been flirting with the bull riders, I'd been looking for a cowboy who owed me money, and we'd wound up with each other. Her breasts were bigger than Becky's and her ass looked damn good in Wranglers, but that was all I remembered. Maybe Becky was right, and I didn't deserve to share her bed. I pushed myself up, dusted off my jeans, and watched the world spin.

After reclaiming my clothes and other gear, I climbed in the truck and headed for my office. I'd be sleeping there for the next few nights at least. Then I'd see about wheedling my way back into Becky's good graces. She'd come around. She always did.

In the meantime, what I needed was a client who would pay me real bucks as opposed to stiffing me for everything I wasn't paid up front. I had plenty who came crying to me for help, then didn't pay. With a little extra cash, I could move my office to the other side of town and maybe gain some respect.

River Springs was the soul and spirit of the Texas Hill Country, but my work took me beyond the natural scenic beauty of the surroundings, beyond the pricey camps and even pricier dude ranches that dotted the local hillsides. And way beyond the River Springs Resort, a huge rambling structure built of cedar, limestone, and river rock out on the San Antonio Highway on a bend of the Guadalupe River just past the rodeo arena.

People came from all over the country and spent a lot of money there. They also dropped a wad in town at restaurants and the Old Towne shops. It was good for everyone's business except mine.

Occasionally one of the camps or ranches hired me to find out who was making off with their gear. Or an attorney over in the county seat would pay for my services in a defense case. But by and large, my clients lived under rocks like the local rattlesnakes and sought me out to find deadbeat dads and cheating wives, or vice versa. They were the people who shouldn't be allowed to breed and pass on their piss-poor gene pools.

Two blocks later, I bounced over a dozen potholes in the parking lot of a rundown shopping strip and pulled up in front of my office. Douglas Investigations was sandwiched between Juan's Taco Stand and a cowboy gin mill called Boot the Bull.

I had just unlocked my door when a big white car driven by a blue-haired old lady entered the parking area, carefully dodged all the fucking potholes, and pulled up behind my truck. A young woman emerged from the passenger side and told the driver thank you. She waved goodbye and the car pulled away. The luscious vision walked my way.

Becky must have whacked me harder than I thought, so I blinked. No, the woman was as delicious as ever, with curves in all the right places, heavy make-up, and a tumbling-down blonde hairdo. She wore black bicycle shorts and a bright green halter top. I pushed my hat to the back of my head and smiled. Couldn't help it.

"Are you Nolan Douglas?" Her soft voice reminded me of the rustle of satin sheets, but her hollow eyes haunted my soul.

"Yes, ma'am. What can I do for you?"

"I'm Crystal Carpenter. I need your help."

Crystal Carpenter? That was another punch in the gut. My first inclination had been to drag her inside my office, bolt the door, and call the police. But I hadn't acted on that impulse. Instead I stood aside and allowed her to enter.

Even so, I did lock the door. Not because Crystal Carpenter sat facing my battered-to-hell desk, but because last week Bobby Duane Larkin rode his old mare up to my door and burst inside waving a gun. He threatened to kill me unless I found him a new dealer since his old one had been busted and he needed to score. Then he crashed on my floor, and I had to go catch his damn horse to keep her out of the traffic.

I pulled off my hat and dropped it on my desk before sitting down. Seated behind my desk, I felt more in control. But as I looked really hard at Crystal, I felt my control slipping. I first saw her face on television almost two years ago, but that face looked little like the one across from me now. Then it had been scrubbed schoolgirl fresh, with laughing eyes and a wide smile. Her dark hair had been pulled into a ponytail, not bleached and teased like today. Crystal had been a high school senior, gone missing three days before her prom.

Police had questioned the usual suspects, all the family, and all the neighbors. News broadcasts, all-day searches. Zilch. The whole town of River Springs — all of Ingram County, actually — was involved in trying to locate the missing teen. Nothing. The family had no history. No run-ins with CPS, no domestic violence reports. And her father was the Ingram County District Attorney.

Now here Crystal Carpenter sat in my office, looking for all the world as if she belonged with the hookers over in San Antonio or up in Austin. Except I caught a glimpse of fear in her eyes.

"Mr. Douglas, do you know who I am?"

Everyone in River Springs knew Crystal Carpenter. I nodded. "Of course. But I didn't know you had been found." I must have missed more than I thought over the weekend.

"I haven't been found. Please let me stay here."

So she had run away. I leaned back in my chair. "How do you know about me?"

A quick flash of her wide smile. "Everyone knows about you. Well, at least we knew about you two years ago."

I didn't understand, and I felt my eyebrows draw together in puzzlement. "Excuse me?"

"At school. Mr. Fenwick told us about hiring you to find out who kept stealing his trashcans full of trash."

Graham Fenwick. A prissy little man, but he had paid my full fee without quibbling. And promptly, too. The boys who had been searching for exam questions had been properly dealt with. "What did Mr. Fenwick say?"

"He said if any of us ever needed a private eye, you were the best. I don't have any money, but I'm hoping you'll help me, anyway."

What else was new. She sounded like most of my clients. Fifty cents down and the rest if I ever found them. Maybe. I sighed. "Why do you need a private investigator, Crystal? Why don't you go home to your parents? Or to the police?"

She looked down, then back at me. "Because I need you to prove what I'm going to tell you is the truth. My parents would say I'm lying, and the police would put me in jail."

I knocked on Becky's door. "Open up, Becky. It's important."

Silence. After everything Crystal had told me, I knew

I needed a woman's help.

"I know you're in there. I hear you breathing."

More silence.

I shifted the old saddlebag I carried for a briefcase to my other hand and knocked again. Sometimes that woman infuriated me. "Becky. It's not for me. I need your help. More important, someone else needs your help."

The silence continued.

"Becky, I'm sorry. Come to the door and listen to me. That's all I ask."

The deadbolt clicked and the door opened, secured by a chain. I'd told her those damn things were useless, but right now I was glad she never listened to anything I said. Otherwise, the door would have remained closed.

"Thank you, Becky." I smiled at her.

"Don't make me sorry about this, you lousy bucket of crap."

She knew me well. I ran my hand down my face. "You won't be sorry, Becks, I swear."

Becky rolled her eyes. She had heard those words from me too many times. Why she still put up with me, I didn't know.

"I need you to babysit."

The door would have closed, except for my foot. That's why I always wore boots with thick soles that stuck out past the flesh and bone of my feet.

"Move your foot, shithead."

No way in hell. I whispered, "Listen to me, Becks. Sweets. It's Crystal Carpenter."

The pressure on my foot eased.

"Crystal Carpenter? *The* Crystal Carpenter?"

I nodded. "One and the same." I still didn't move my foot.

"Spill it."

That was Becky. A woman of few words. "When I left

here, I went straight to my office. I barely had the door unlocked, when she pulled up and asked if I was Nolan Douglas. Said she needed help. You won't recognize her, Becks. She's been through hell."

"Why didn't she go to the police? Hell, why didn't she go the fuck home?" Becky was quite a woman, one who never spared her thoughts.

"Because the police are the ones who've had her for the past two years, and her daddy was the one who gave her to them."

Becky released the chain and let me in.

I'd barely begun relating Crystal's tale when Becky interrupted, hands on her hips. "Where is she now?"

"Outside in my car."

"You stupid asshole." Becky jumped up and ran outside. Less than a minute later, she and Crystal sat on the sofa across from me, Becky with her arms around the girl, cuddling her as if she were her own long-lost child.

I knew better than to say anything more. George Strait's latest CD played in the background, and not too softly, so I listened to Texas swing while the drama played out across from me. Becky would let me know when she was ready for me to continue. As for Crystal, she let Becky coddle her, but her eyes were blank and she looked as stiff as a day-old corpse in the middle of winter.

Becky spoke gently to her, and every once in a while Crystal nodded or shook her head. I couldn't overhear their whispered conversation, but once Crystal wiped at her eye as if brushing away a tear. I took that as a good sign.

Minutes ticked by on the old mantle clock. I crossed and uncrossed my legs as I watched the long minute hand creep slowly downward.

Finally Becky said, "Okay, Nolan, here's the deal. I'm going to the store, and I'll be back in less than an hour. You stay here with Crystal. Don't fuck up and leave her alone again. And give me your credit card." She held out her hand.

True Becky. She glared at me while I pulled a card from my wallet and handed it to her. "I don't suppose asking you not to buy too much will work?"

She cocked her head and stared at me with a look of disbelief. "Not if you know what's good for you."

The door slammed behind her.

"She loves you."

I whipped my gaze around to Crystal and shook my head. "No way. She hates me, and I don't blame her. Every time things are going good with us, I fuck it up."

Crystal smiled. "Becky's trying to make you see how what you do hurts both of you. She may think you're stupid, but she loves you. I can see that. Anyone could."

I didn't want to talk to Crystal about my relationship with Becky. Hell, I didn't understand it myself. And Crystal should not have been able to see anything about us. She should have been interested in college boys and passing her next exam and wondering what to wear to the frat party on Saturday night. "You wanna play gin or dominoes or something?"

She shook her head. "I want you to tell me what happened here in town after . . . after I went missing."

I thought back over the months. "Everyone was stunned, of course. Searches. House-by-house canvassing and distribution of flyers with your photograph. Billboards. People put yellow ribbons around everything, some even on the grills of their cars and trucks. Someone reported seeing a van — black, I think — but no one located it. They talked to your boyfriend. Probably made his life pretty miserable."

"Poor Tyler. Did he go on to college like he planned?"

My fists balled at her loss of innocence. I shrugged and

made myself unclench my fingers. "Sorry, I don't know."

"Not that we would have anything in common any more."

I leaned across and clasped her hands in mine. "Listen to me, Crystal. What happened to you was *not* your fault. I will do everything in my power to make sure those bastards pay for what they've done to you. And to the other girls."

Crystal stared at the floor.

"You escaped, Crystal, as soon as you could. As soon as you were capable, mentally and physically. Those two go hand in hand. If the accident hadn't happened, you would have figured out another way. You're a strong person. Show the sons of bitches what you're made of."

"I'm not strong." She continued to look at the carpet.

Crystal needed more help than I could give her, but right now, I was all she had. I sighed and went on. "Yes you are. God knows I wish to hell I could take away what happened to you. But it was no more your fault than if you had been struck by lightning or mauled by wolves or ravaged by leukemia. Do you understand me?"

She nodded, then looked up. "I was a virgin before my father raped me."

Rage surged through me. I vowed to make that man's life holy hell. "Honey, you don't have to tell me all the details. It's enough you gave me the names of those involved."

"There's more."

My gut knotted again. I should have told Becky to pick me up a bottle of Super Pepto while she was out.

"I didn't tell you how the whole thing worked. They called us Gideon Girls."

"Gideon . . . like the hotel Bibles?"

She nodded. "All the guest rooms at the resort had them."

I wanted to grab my deer rifle and hunt down the

animals that had done this to her. "Crystal —"

"No, let me finish. They used a pink highlighter to mark page numbers and chapters and verses in those Bibles. Those told the room number and the time for the holder of the Bible to show up at one of our rooms. I was in room 512."

Her matter-of-fact tone chilled me. I swallowed the sour taste that rose into the back of my throat.

"The resort was nearly always full, but they handed out the Bibles only to the guests who paid for them. And plenty did."

And paid plenty, I imagined.

"Most nights I had two or three guests visit me. And so did the other girls. Always men. Mostly guests, but our keepers made regular rounds, too." She paused for a few seconds. "And our fathers."

"Crystal, I need to record this, too." I pulled out my recorder from the saddlebag and identified Crystal and the time. It took maybe thirty seconds. "Go on."

She repeated the Bible information with no prompting from me. It tore me up inside to listen to her soft sweet voice tell of such cruelty, but it was important for her words to be recorded. She must have dreamed of this day for a long time.

My thumbs worried each other, as my grandmother used to say. An old habit that reappeared whenever life closed in.

"I feel better telling you, Mr. Douglas."

"We'll get them. And we'll see to it they pay for what they did. I promise you that."

She gave me a sad smile and went on. "Besides the highlighted numbers, they inserted a bookmark into each Bible. A Bible verse and a picture of a man and woman having sex were printed on the bookmark."

People could do most anything these days with a computer.

"The girl had to please the guest in some way that

related to both the picture and the verse. The men told us we were pure, and because we were pure, they would have a closer communion with God by having sex with us. They believed that."

I wondered, and not for the first time, how some people could so intertwine not only the Bible and sex in such perverted ways, but also throw pain and humiliation into the mix.

"If we didn't do a good enough job, we always heard about it the following day. And we paid. The guests were never shy about complaining about the service."

I could imagine. And that was the problem. I didn't want to imagine any of this. As soon as I figured out what to do with everything Crystal had given me, I was going to personally go over and beat the living crap out of her father. If I ended up doing time because of it, so be it.

Crystal interrupted my thoughts. "Is it all right if I take a nap?"

"Sure. Lay down right here." I stood, pulled one of Becky's hand-knitted throws from the back of the sofa, and covered her. "When Becky returns, I'll be leaving. She'll take good care of you."

"Thank you, Mr. Douglas."

Not many people called me Mr. Douglas any more. I smiled at her. "It's my pleasure to help you, Crystal. You stay safe with Becky until this is over. These people are already looking for you. They have a lot to lose, and they'll be dangerous. But Becky's a crack shot and mean as a snake. She'll take good care of you. You just do what she says."

In my office, I made a pot of coffee and tried a few pushups while it brewed. My Glock and a small Beretta Jetfire were locked in a file drawer. I pulled them out and checked to make sure they were loaded, then placed the Glock on my desk and shoved the Jetfire in my boot.

With a mug of fresh coffee in hand, I played the tape, then opened the list Crystal had made of everyone she knew who was involved. I made my own computer report and named it the Gideon file.

The first name I typed in was that of Crystal's father, Vance Carpenter. I added the other information I knew about him, what I remembered from when Crystal disappeared, and the things Crystal told me he had done or caused to be done to her and the nineteen other Gideon Girls.

I followed suit with the other names, the sheriff, the River Springs police chief, a few street cops, attorneys, one judge, one doctor. The guards she called their keepers. Two men whose names anyone in America would recognize — the brains and money behind the whole operation as well as the silent and well-concealed owners of the resort. One of them had liked Crystal and had liked to talk. And, of course, the names of the fathers of all the girls. Crystal thought there were others involved, but these were all she knew.

One of the cops on Crystal's list, a skinny jackass named Martinez, had always pissed me off. He had squinty little bird eyes and a mean-looking mouth. I knew he was dirty from the first time I saw him lean on a bartender down in Old Towne, but I hadn't known exactly how dirty he was until now. I'd take real pleasure in bringing him down.

Next I listed all the girls and the information Crystal knew about each of them. They came from all over the country, and they had formed a pact. Each one memorized all the facts about the other girls they met — their names, hometowns, mothers' names, and something particular about each girl, something only someone close to her would know. In Crystal's case, it was a small blue birthmark high on the inside of her right thigh.

The background and court record databases I subscribed to were next. It didn't take long for the names to come up. I printed the records and saved the search. What I accumulated was the ugliest mess I had seen in a long time. I wanted to personally round up each one of those bastards, those miserable excuses for humanity, and bury them alive. But not before I hurt them, and hurt them as bad as I could. Crystal's father would be the first.

All the terrible crimes these men had perpetrated on their own daughters were beyond my comprehension. Or at least I *wanted* them to be beyond my comprehension.

Each of the girls had been taken by her father on or shortly after her eighteenth birthday. The men were careful about that. Most of the girls had been virgins. I could imagine the sort of shit fed to them over the years by their fathers to make sure they remained that way.

The ones who were not virgins had been severely beaten by their own fathers in order to return them to a pure state, according to Crystal. She had witnessed one such assault. I had other thoughts. They culminated with me taking a cattle prod to the balls of those sorry pieces of shit.

The girls were kept cloistered on the top floor of the resort, which was reached only by a keyed elevator. On the night a new girl arrived, she was taken to what the girls called the Blue Room, where a large padded blue exercise mat was permanently secured to the center of the floor. Forty blue chairs, one for each girl and each father surrounded the mat. All of the girls and all of the fathers, each dressed in a blue silk robe, were present for each new induction. Crystal had witnessed six besides her own.

The new girl was introduced to everyone, given a glass of champagne laced with Valium, then undressed by her father. Each man then took a turn at fondling her, kissing her. If she became violent, she was restrained, spread eagle, on the mat. All watched as the father raped his daughter.

After it was finished, the new girl was turned over to

the other girls to take her to her new room. Twenty girls were always present, and Crystal did not know what happened to the older girls when they left. But I knew.

Crystal had also provided names of the six girls she had known who had vanished. The body of one girl had been found outside of her hometown in Ohio a few months ago. I was fairly certain the girl had been murdered by her father while the other fathers watched, or even participated in her killing. As they were all present at her initiation into their society, it made sense they would all be present at her farewell, too.

Crystal's escape had been a fluke. One of those things the bad boys couldn't have guarded against even if they had thought about it. An underground tunnel ran from the resort to a large enclosed outdoor area about half a mile away from the main building. Beyond the pool, beyond the tennis courts, beyond the back nine. I'd seen the fence myself, an eight-foot high concrete block and stucco enclosure marked with signs of *Private Property — River Springs Resort and Conference Center.*

The enclosed area was for the girls to use and contained a pool, hot tub, jogging track, and chairs shaded by large umbrellas. They spent time there every day, weather permitting, under watchful eyes. Closed circuit cameras hung at each corner, and they were always accompanied by a keeper.

Yesterday, while the girls were there, a tractor-trailer rig had plowed into the corner of the concrete fence. The left front bumper and wheel crashed through first, followed by the rest of the truck. The broken concrete blocks scraped the skin off the trailer, and the whole rig came to rest inside the exercise yard with the right front wheel of the truck hanging into the pool.

As Crystal and the other girls watched, men, women, and children poured from the truck, human cargo smuggled from south of the border a hundred miles or so away. The guard grabbed the radio, and Crystal knew the entire event had been caught on the cameras.

She didn't know if any of the other girls would grab this opportunity, but she had to. Freedom lay only yards away. She had minutes, if that. But she had to try. If all the girls were punished for her actions, she would fully accept the blame. There was no other choice. She wanted freedom enough to accept any risk, and it had paid off for her.

Because of the local law enforcement involvement, I didn't know who to call. I had been monitoring the news, and while there was a big hoopla about the accident, the truck driver's fatal heart attack, and the illegals still running free, there was nothing about anything Crystal had shared with me. But I believed her story completely. All I had to do was look into her eyes.

I pulled the computer print-out on Pino Martinez, thinking I could verify police involvement from him. He'd never struck me as being smart, just as being a bully. The only thing that jumped out at me was a write-up on him in the San Antonio paper last year. He had been caught in a sting operation at one of the city's gentlemen's clubs. There was no further news, and I was pretty sure money had changed hands along the way to get the charges against him dropped.

I looped a holster on my belt and shoved the Glock into it, then I slipped the recorder into my shirt pocket. Martinez would be a good place to start. He worked the night shift, and I knew if I went to Old Towne I would find him before too much time passed. Sure enough, he was on the sidewalk outside the second place I went, hassling three young women about their identification. I switched the recorder on.

I walked up and shooed the women inside. "Go on in. I need to talk to Officer Dickhead."

They giggled, but Martinez didn't think it was funny.

"Hey, asshole, who you think you are interfering in police business?" He shoved my shoulder.

"Lay another finger on me, jerkoff, and I'll break your fucking arm. Come over to the parking lot where we can talk without being in the spotlight." I grabbed his upper arm and pulled him along with me. This felt good. I was itching for a fight, and I wanted to wipe that smirk off his face with my fist. Practice for Crystal's father.

We rounded the corner, and I shoved Martinez back against the wall.

"What the shit's the matter with you, man?" He stood straight.

I wanted to make him hit me first, and I didn't think it would be hard to do. I figured he would want to beat me to a pulp rather than haul me in or shoot me and be bothered with the paperwork. He reached for his radio, but I grabbed the front of his shirt with both hands and pushed him against the wall again. "It's over for you, Martinez."

"I always knew you were a crazy gringo." He brought his arms up between mine and pushed them apart.

I stepped back, and Martinez jumped at me quicker than a duck on a June bug. His right hand came at my gut, and I stepped back just in time to keep it from making a solid hit. I could have done that with Becky earlier, but I deserved everything she wanted to hand out.

"Let's see who's gonna push who around this time." Martinez came at me again.

This time I hit back. I felt my fist sink deep into his gut, as if I could grab his spine with my fingers. He staggered. "You ever hit girls, Martinez?"

Anger burned his face. "I only hit assholes like you, Douglas." He came at me again.

I sidestepped and we did a little dance. "You ever fuck girls, Martinez, or do you fuck boys?"

This time he flew at me, fists flying. One caught me on

the left cheekbone and I spun away.

"How's it feel, cocksucker? You think I could hit like that if I fucked boys?" He came at me again.

Warm blood dripped down my cheek. "News is all over town about those boys, Martinez." I caught him in the chest.

He bent double, breathing hard. I stepped back far enough not to be caught off guard. Sure enough, he straightened up swinging.

I shook my head. "Thought you had more street smarts than to think I would fall for that. Then again . . ."

"Go ask Chief Riddles you think I fuck boys. He'll tell you different." His fist damn near broke my arm, but I knew his hand was numb after that blow.

"Chief Riddles, huh? How would he know? Does he watch?"

"Sometimes —" Martinez stopped in mid-sentence. Fear and anger flashed again in his eyes. He knew he'd been tricked.

I crooked my finger at him. "Come on. You want a piece of me? Let's get it on."

Martinez didn't know what to do, but it didn't take him but a few seconds to decide. I'd been prepared for most anything, including the big gun attached to his hip, but in the end, he came after me one-on-one. He had his macho image to maintain.

He was so focused on me, he forgot to protect himself. My left fist caught him on the side of the jaw, my right in his solar plexus, and I elbowed the back of his neck on his way down. Pino Martinez sprawled on the asphalt, out cold. I grabbed his cuffs and secured him to the only thing handy, the gas meter. Somebody would find him in a few hours. I took his radio, gun, pepper spray, and keys and locked them in his squad car parked at the curb.

I felt better now. Beating up someone who needed it wasn't usually my style, but I had to start somewhere. I had all the proof I needed to steer clear of the locals. Next I would call the Rangers. As far as Crystal knew, none of them had been involved. I picked up my hat, shoved it on my head, and walked toward my truck. My phone rang. "Douglas."

"Get over here." It was Becky. "Crystal's gone."

"When?"

"Now. Maybe two minutes ago. I must have dozed off. The back door squeaked."

I knew it cost Becky to admit she'd dozed off. But she knew that back-door squeak well and it would wake her from the dead. That was why I never used it any more.

Crystal could be headed to only one place. "It's okay, Becks."

"Find her, Nolan. She's a sweet kid."

After I hung up, I headed straight to Vance Carpenter's place and parked down the street. On this side of town, the houses and yards were larger, but that didn't make the people any better.

I figured all the people involved were crazy scared about now and the operation had been moved elsewhere. But Crystal's testimony would go a long way in eventually finding the bastards and, with luck, some of the girls. I started up the driveway when a familiar crack split the quiet night. A gunshot. And it came from behind the Carpenter house. I ran toward the sound.

When I rounded the corner, I came face to face with Crystal. She held a large revolver with both hands and pointed it at her father who sat on the ground in his pajamas holding his right shoulder. In the glow from the porch light, I saw blood oozing through his fingers.

"Stop right there, Mr. Douglas."

Becky had done a fine job with Crystal. She had restored her hair to its natural dark color and cut it to shoulder length. Crystal shoved the left side behind her ear. Her face was scrubbed clean of makeup, and she wore a pair of jeans with a T-shirt. She looked like a high school girl, except for her eyes.

But my second worst fear had come true, the first being there would be no trace of Crystal or her father. "Don't do this, Crystal. Will you let me call for an ambulance? You and I can leave so you won't be here when it arrives."

She shook her head from side to side. "No. No ambulance."

"Call them," Vance Carpenter said. "This girl's crazy. She stole that gun from my nightstand. Woke me up and forced me out here. Everything she says is a lie. Thank the Good Lord her mother is away visiting her sister. I wanted my little girl back. Not this . . . this harlot. Look at her!"

Anyone looking at Crystal would think no such thing. I shook my head. "I think you can be quiet, Mr. Carpenter. Crystal has been very cooperative. And your daughter is a lovely person."

"She's a raving lunatic." He tried to stand.

"Don't get up, Daddy."

Carpenter ignored her, and she fired again, this time hitting his left kneecap. He shrieked and sank to the ground. Blood spread over the thin fabric of his pajama leg.

"Don't you wish you hadn't taught me how to shoot, Daddy?"

I should have rushed her and forced the gun from her fingers. But this was her moment. No jury in the world would convict her. No jury in Texas, anyway. Instead, I reached for my Glock.

She glanced my way. "No, Mr. Douglas. Don't make me shoot you, too."

"Crystal, one of the neighbors will call the police about the shots. They'll be here any minute."

Although she still trained the gun on her father, she faced me and I saw for the first time her red, swollen eyes and the tears streaming down her cheeks. "I'll make it quick,

Mr. Douglas."

She turned back to her father. "Goodbye, Daddy." She fired, and a red stain filled Vance Carpenter's groin. He screamed in agony.

I ran to Crystal and she turned the gun on me. "Back up, Mr. Douglas. I don't want to hurt you."

"Crystal, please stop. I can help you. You came to me for help. Please let me help you."

Her father moaned and curled into a ball. Blood soaked his clothing. "See what it's like to hurt, Daddy? But I won't keep you in pain like you kept me." She fired again. The slug hit him square in the side of the neck. His head jerked violently, then was still. Vance Carpenter would never visit his particular brand of godlessness on anyone ever again.

Sirens wailed in the distance, growing louder. They would arrive within minutes. I had no way of knowing who it would be.

"Crystal, come with me. I hear the police, and we don't know who it is. I won't let them take you back."

"No."

"My car is down the block. We can go around back, but we have to leave now."

Crystal backed up a few steps. The sirens were close now, only blocks away.

I held my hand out to her. "Please, Crystal."

She raised the gun to her temple.

"No, Crystal. Don't do this. Don't let the sons of bitches win." I stepped toward her.

"It's too late, Mr. Douglas. They won a long time ago." She pulled the trigger.

The case had made headlines worldwide for over a week. But I didn't really think much about that now, standing beside Crystal's grave. I hunkered down and placed a yellow rose on the fresh dirt, then sat and pulled my knees up, wrapping my arms around them.

"Crystal, I came to tell you they're all behind bars with no bail. Thanks to you, the court has the ammunition it needs to put them away. Well, most of them are in jail. Judge Sorrells hung himself, and Sheriff Harden is missing. Somebody will find him one of these days. But the important thing is all the girls are safe.

"The men had them packed and ready to move, but the place was crawling with cops — plus Border Patrol and Texas Rangers and who knows who all else. Some of the illegals went inside the resort and the manager wouldn't let anyone in to find them. The Feds obtained a warrant, and they found the girls inside the tunnel.

"I wish I could have helped you more, Crystal, I surely do. God knows I did a piss poor job. Maybe you should have found somebody else besides me and Becky. But we did the best we could.

"When I leave here, I'm going to go talk to Becks. With a lot of luck, maybe she'll take me back. We'll see if you were right about her loving me. You taught me a lot. And I wish there was some way I could repay you."

I stood then, brushed the dirt from the seat of my jeans, and smashed my old straw hat back on my head. "I'll be here again next week, Crystal. I won't forget."

Coronas N Crawfish

George Wilhite

"What the hell was he doin' like that, Tib?"

I shook my head and twisted my mouth a little before answering Falls County Justice of the Peace Robert Chominski.

"Pregnancy testin' that mare for me, Bubba. I found him like that when I got home from the feed store."

Bubba moved his 425-pounds into the horse stall to examine the body a little closer, his 64-inch Tony Lama belt touching both sides of the three-foot-wide doorway. Inside the 10x10 stall, the 6-year old broodmare moved nervously within the confines of her cross-tied halter, trampling straw everywhere. Between her rump and the front wall of the stall, the skinny body of a man dangled, bumping against the 2-inch-thick wooden walls every time the mare shuffled.

"But with his arm up her ass?" Bubba asked, his face wrinkled up at the smell of horse manure and death.

"Up her vagina, Bubba, not her ass. He was palpating to see if he could feel a foal in there."

Bubba took a bunch of pictures with the Polaroid camera the county provided him for just such situations — well, maybe not *exactly* just such situations. Once the sixth picture was done, he nodded toward me, his face still twisted against the smell.

"Let's get him out of there," Bubba said, trying to steady Benny Wilson's prize mare, Freda's Fredericksburg Folly, to keep her from moving and doing any more damage to the body. I stepped up to her head and calmed her down, rubbing her forehead lightly. I looked back at Bubba and indicated with my chin that he move to the horse's rear.

"Just grab him under the armpit and lift slightly, Bubba. He should come right out of there."

Bubba did and, with a plop, the late Lawrence Capshaw Davis, DVM, fell to the ground of the stall and didn't move.

"Okay to move the mare out to the pasture?"

A white-faced Bubba just nodded, his face even more twisted now as he backed away from the body and out into the hallway. I unclipped the mare from the cross-tie and led her out of the stall and into the 10-foot alley that ran through the center of the 8-stall, corrugated tin barn. At the end of the alley, I opened a gate to an outside pasture, slipped the halter off the mare, and let her go before turning back to the Justice of the Peace.

"Bubba, you look a little under the weather, there. What say we go into the house and get a beer? Larry ain't goin' nowhere for a while."

"Yeah, sounds good," Bubba said as he took one last look at the thin corpse of the vet before his massive belly overruled his dedication to official duty. "But that's a hell of a way to die — your arm up a horse's ass."

"Vagina, Bubba, vagina."

Sitting at the kitchen table with a Corona in his hand, Bubba actually began to get some color back in his face. At the stove, Maria Anita Sanchez-Thibadeaux wiggled her ass in her short sundress in time to the strains of Tejano and Zydeko music escaping from the wireless headphones she wore as she cooked. Across the table from Bubba, I took a healthy swig of Corona and looked over at my wife, noticing how nice her ass looked when she did that erotic butt-shake. Must be *La Bamba*. It was our wedding song.

"What ya makin', Maria?"

Without missing a step in her impromptu dance and continuing to stir the pot, Maria turned. The left earpiece of the headphones was slightly off center of her ears so she could hear what was going on around her. She hunched and dipped her shoulders with her eyes closed for a couple of bars as the song ended, then she reached up and shut the earphones off.

"Crawdad etoufa menudo with Polish sausage and cabbage."

Bubba practically licked his lips and drained his beer. He'd eaten enough of Maria's cooking to know that her combinations of Cajun, Mexican, and Slavic cooking might sound horrible, but they always tasted fantastic. She ladled a couple of bowls of the steaming stuff and set them in front of us. Bubba dropped his empty beer bottle into a Coke crate in the corner and grabbed another Corona from the fridge with one hand while spooning etoufa-menudo into his mouth with the other. Good thing for him his chair backed up to the refrigerator or he would have had to make an ethical decision between getting a beer and eating. Maria brought her own bowl to the table and sat down.

"You out here social or official, Bubba?" she asked, adding a dollop of salza to the top of her stewlike concoction.

Bubba made an admirable attempt to get part of his mouthful swallowed before answering.

"Official, ma'am. Got a call from Tib about a body."

Maria raised an eyebrow at me underneath her square-cut, Betty Page black bangs. I finished my beer and put my own empty in the Coke crate.

"The vet. Died while pregnancy testing that mare the Wilsons brought down to breed to Excalibur's Edge. I found him when I came back from the feed store. Called Bubba on my mobile."

She nodded as if such things happened everyday. But then she'd been married to me for 10 years now and nothing much surprised her. She'd known I trained tracking dogs for South Texas Prison when her father had introduced us. She'd been 18 and just starting Palo Alto College on the south side of San Antonio. I'd been 26 and working at the prison for about three months after a two-year stint at a Louisiana prison farm. Her father had been impressed with me, not just because of how well I cared for and trained the dogs, but by the fact that I had actually been through the police academy and worked for the New Orleans Police Department before moving into the dog training business. Unlike some of the redneck, let-'em-tear-'em-apart dog trainers Andy Sanchez had worked with before, I showed some of the professionalism I'd learned at the academy and on the NOPD, and I trained my dogs to an even higher degree than was necessary for tracking purposes. It wasn't until after he'd learned I'd been a K-9 narcotics officer in New Orleans, though, that Andy introduced me to Maria.

About that time, the lowered engine sound of a slowing vehicle on the farm-to-market road in front of the house, followed by the crunching of gravel under tires, signaled the arrival of the sheriff's department that Bubba had called when we'd come into the house. Rousing himself from the table, Bubba managed to look as official as he could get, strode out the door with a nod to Maria in passing, and started issuing orders to sheriff's deputies. I stepped out onto the cedar board porch and leaned up against a stripped cedar post supporting the roof. Together, Bubba and I watched as deputies directed an ambulance driver to the barn, a body bag folded neatly on top of the gurney they had to carry instead of roll over the dry, fine sand that made up that part of Falls County.

"No Ludy yet, huh?" I asked.

"Nope, like that's unusual. All the cases I've worked, I've only seen him at the crime scene first once. That crazy woman that was naked on Highway 6, stopping cars, and asking the drivers if they wanted to fuck, remember?"

We both grinned, remembering how it was only after there were 10 or 12 cars lined up on the shoulder that the call had come in. A Baptist preacher on his way from Franklin to Waco had thought there was an accident, pulled over, and found guys lined up waiting for their turn with the Texas A&M college junior they later found had been drugged with that date-rape drug by her boyfriend. He'd left her on the side of the road when she started freaking out and wanting more once he'd finished with his pleasure. When she started stopping pickups and asking the drivers for sex, he'd taken off and left her there.

Maria stepped out onto the porch.

"Did Ludy really get in line and drop his pants but couldn't get it up?" she asked.

"Naw," Bubba said, "but he did stand there and watch three or four of them go at it before he stopped it. Sorry excuse for a sheriff if you ask me."

He stepped off the porch and put his palm-leaf straw hat back on his head. With a nodded goodbye, he directed the ambulance drivers on the handling of the body. Since Falls County was a poor county — median income of about $12,000 — the county did not have its own medical examiner or coroner. If there was any suspicion in a death, the JP had to have the body sent off to Dallas for an autopsy. That rarely happened because the same lack of money that kept the county from having an ME also kept it from being able to pay for the work in Dallas. Consequently, JPs looked at the body, determined cause of death, and filled out their death certificates. With no blood at the scene, Bubba would probably rule the Davis case a heart attack. Nothing to do with ethics; everything to do with finances.

Chief Deputy Walter Howell came in to get my statement. Usual stuff. Name? Juan Bautista Thibedeaux Jr. Nicknames? Tib, Juan Two. Occupation? Dog and horse trainer and breeder. I'd had to ask the same batch of questions myself enough to have the next answer ready even before he asked the question. When he finished, he put his pad back in his chest pocket, added the pen, thanked Maria for the coffee, and left.

As the deputies finished up their work and piled back into their vehicles, I stepped off the porch to go feed my dogs. Like the autopsies, trackers and tracking dog services were jobbed out by the county. As the only tracker-trainer within an hour's drive, I handled tracking chores for the state prison in the Brazos River bottom just outside Marlin, for the county, and for all the towns within the county, not to mention drug searches for all the schools. I also received calls from all over the state to track for escapees, do drug and weapons searches, and occasionally to find missing children or adults. From behind me on the porch, Maria called out quietly.

"Died with his hand up a horse's butt, huh?"

"Vagina, Maria, vagina," I said without breaking stride or looking back.

"I got your vagina."

That at least got a smile and a turned head from me as I headed for the barn.

"Yes, ma'am, you do. And I'm planning an inspection as soon as I get back in the house."

Maria turned and bounced back into the cedar board-and-batten house, a grin of her own on her face.

"Aaaaghh!"

I tensed, then relaxed, a light film of sweat pouring off both our bodies after two hours of sex with Maria. Sex that had started in the twilight after I'd fed the dogs and horses and that had lasted until I couldn't see anything else but my wife's face framed with black hair. I lowered my shoulders back down to hers, kissed her lightly on the slight upturned part of her already small nose, and then buried my face in the long, silky black hair at her neck, nibbling at the base of her throat. A few minutes later, I rolled off her. She turned on her side and played gently with a curl of hair on my neck.

I was just getting ready to roll on my side and kiss her when a low howl that felt more like a deeper black in the night than really a sound made me sit straight up in bed, my left hand going immediately to Maria's shoulder and my right to the Springfield Armory .45 in the holster attached to the side of my nightstand.

"That's Phydeaux," I whispered.

"Why the hell would a drug dog start howling in the kennel?" Maria whispered back. "Somebody slip him some coke in his feed?"

I reached behind the bed's headboard and pulled out the shortened pump shotgun, handing it to Maria.

"Just make sure it's not me before you use that thing. Anybody else, you blow the hell out of 'em."

I slipped into a pair of Wranglers, eased my feet into a pair of sneakers, and crept out of the bedroom door. Because I knew she didn't hear the back door open or close, I moved across the grass and stood in front of the bedroom window, the dim illumination of the vapor light from the other side of the barn silhouetting me in the opening for her. I waved my hand so she'd know it was me.

Phydeaux — the bloodhound with the huge, sad eyes

and the massive drooping jowls that dripped drool almost continually — continued to howl lowly. I'd found most of my dogs at animal shelters. It seemed like I had a sixth sense that guided me to certain dogs. But Phydeaux had been busted out of the K-9 program in San Antonio about five years back. He'd been scheduled to be a tracking dog based on his bloodhound lineage, but he'd fizzled horribly. I had picked him up when the K-9 officer called me to see if I wanted the dog. He was useless tracking a person, and he couldn't find bombs for shit, but I had found the dog had an uncanny sense for drugs. He could smell marijuana, cocaine, or heroin at twice the distance most dogs could. He'd immediately become my main drug sniffer.

I knew sitting in the dark holding the shotgun made Maria anxious, but she'd been in a similar situation or two in the past with me. And she'd held her own. She'd learned to breathe quietly, counting her breaths to keep track of time so that she didn't have to look at a clock.

It didn't take long to find what Phydeaux was howling at. He'd found drugs, a kilo of cocaine, within 20 feet of his kennel. The kilo, though, was half in and half out of the vagina of the mare the vet had pregnancy checked earlier that day. It had come open inside her. No telling how much she'd absorbed. I hit the button on my Maglite to take a closer look. And there, right in the middle of the white powder, was a pin with a rust-color residue on the end of it. Looked a lot like dried blood.

Half an hour later, I was sitting in my recliner that separated the living room from the kitchen, cell phone in hand, as Maria handed me a steaming cup of fresh chicory coffee, with enough molasses and rum to make it almost another drink entirely. On the other end of the line, the Justice of the Peace picked up his phone.

"Hello, Bubba," I said, taking a scalding sip of coffee. "You may want to get ahold of the ambulance boys and have them ship that body to Dallas. I thin' you got a murder on your hands."

The deputies came back, took my statement, looked at the dead horse with no idea of what to do. Maria and I went to bed but didn't sleep much that night. Twice now in one day, our peaceful little existence here had been shattered. Neither one of us said anything, but we were both wondering what the hell was going on.

Next day, hauling two mares back to their owners, I called Bubba, who stammered a lot and said nothing for quite a while. Finally, he told me he talked to the sheriff and they determined that there was no foul play there. That the lab said the pin in the coke had nothing on it. I asked him if he'd ever heard of a lab making a call that quick. Bubba said no; I nodded and hung up on him, trying to figure out how the hell I could slam down the receiver of a cell phone.

When I got back, I went straight to the stable and pulled out the tape from the security recorder. The cops never saw the cameras because I use the little board cameras that surveillance people hide behind ties, in purses, or in ball caps. I took the tape in the house and rewound it. Then I ran it forward at fast speed until I saw someone entering the barn. In black and white video, Sheriff Ludy Wallace walked as stealthily as an overweight, 63-year-old man can into the barn and into the mare's stall. He was carrying a package. When he came out of the stall eight minutes later, the package didn't come out with him.

A phone call to Texas Ranger Dave Fellows in Waco got me an appointment. Once he saw the tape, a call from him to Bubba got us a warrant. I went along to identify Sheriff Wallace for Dave. We arrested him about 9:30 p.m. in his home alone, a 63-year-old bachelor without even a parakeet for company. His place was secluded out in the country, down in the live oaks and cottonwoods of the Brazos river bottom. I left Dave with soon-to-be-former-Sheriff Ludwick Wallace and headed home in time to catch the 10 o'clock news on Channel 10.

Maria woke me up with her best imitation of a flute player the next morning even before my alarm went off at 5. She went in to start coffee, and I headed out to feed horses and dogs. When I came back, she had the coffee done, so I grabbed a cup and sat down in the recliner to flick on the early local news. I listened dully to the piece on public school students not scoring high enough on their test scores and something about a local shindig at the Heart O' Texas Coliseum on Saturday night. The third story woke me up. I punched up the volume on the remote.

" . . . Ranger Dave Fellows was pronounced dead at the scene by Falls County Justice of the Peace Robert Chominski. Sheriff Ludwick Wallace said that the cause of the fatal automobile crash is under investigation and will take highest priority."

I couldn't believe my ears. When I called the SO, they told me the sheriff was on vacation. Then, I couldn't get hold of Bubba. I had to get in touch with someone. Ludy and Bubba had to both be in this thing together. And I was the only one who could tie them together!

It was too early to make a call to the Ranger office, but I had the card of a captain I'd worked with a month before, cell phone number neatly written on the back. When Capt. Brent Dalton answered, I gave him the whole spiel. He asked if I had any evidence. Fortunately, I'd made a copy of the original video for Dave. I agreed to meet him in Waco with another copy of the tape. Texas Rangers don't take it lightly when one of their own is killed. I left Maria with the shotgun and brought the three attack dogs — Rottweilers named Larry, Moe, and Curly — in from the kennel. They listened to her just like they did to me. She'd be safe enough. I gave her Capt. Dalton's cell phone number.

Within an hour, we had a warrant based on the tape, and we went to Bubba's office. The captain made short work of the door, but the docket we found showed no arrest warrant issued the night before. We both expressed the same thought at once — Bubba had been keeping two sets of official documents and without the original, it would only be my word against his in court. A quick search of the place didn't reveal anything, so the captain got on his phone and called the Texas Department of Public Safety office in Waco to get some help.

Meanwhile, he let me slip off to check on Maria and promised to send someone around to stake out our place. I was on the Falls Road going past the prison when I remembered that Bubba's parents' old farm was on the way. I stopped off at what was now Bubba's deer lease. Bubba wasn't there at the cabin that had been the place's old smokehouse, but he had been. Cans of food and a sleeping bag were thrown in a corner. But there was nothing else inside and few places even to hide anything. Under the sink cabinet, I found a piece of fairly fresh plywood, but that's not an uncommon place to have to replace because of water leaks. I checked it anyway, but it was solid and I couldn't find any way to loosen it without prying the nails out. I was checking outside when I found the two pieces of old clapboard that had bright shiny nails holding them on instead of the rusted ones everywhere else.

They were directly below the window above the sink. Probably for access to pipes, I thought, but I tried them anyway. There, nestled into a nice little compartment whose top was the fresh plywood, was a big rectangular bundle wrapped in a double thickness of black trash bags, the kind with the yellow plastic drawstrings. I unwrapped them enough to see the edges of a Justice of the Peace's docket book, big and heavy and burgundy, and another smaller, green cloth ledger book. I got back in the truck and got out of there, but I pulled over a mile or two down the road and checked the docket. Sure enough, there was the warrant for the sheriff's arrest. There were also a whole lot more entries that I was sure weren't in the public docket book.

Maria and the Remington shotgun met me and the trash bags at the door. A snarling dog flanked her on each side. The third kept watch at the back door, legs spread. Their tails wagged once when they saw it was me, but they went immediately back on alert.

"What happened?" I said, getting into the house and away from the door.

"Two suits came up while you were gone. I didn't answer, just sat here with the shotgun aimed at the door. They heard the dogs and left."

"Well, they've got us pinned in. They're sure now that we have dogs and they know they can't get to us without the dogs letting us know. So their only options are to wait for us to leave here or to come at us from a distance. I don't like either of those options."

I moved to what looked like the hall closet. It had been, and it still was, sort of. But it was only three foot deep and the back wall pushed in to reveal our panic room, a six- by eight-foot metal-lined room taken partly from the living room and the guest bedroom. In it were some emergency rations, water, and most of my guns. I reached in and took out the bulletproof vest I'd bought as a New Orleans narcotics officer. I started strapping it on and moved Maria and the three dogs into the room.

"I don't like the looks of this, Tib," she said. "What are you going to do?"

"I'm going to try to get them here when I know they're coming. Capt. Dalton is staging some troops for a search near the county line, about 20 minutes away. I'm going to call him on my cell phone and tell him to get over here right away."

"But you always told me . . ."

I put a finger to her lips and shushed her.

"Don't worry. I'm counting on it."

I took one last look at her beautiful Latin face — the short nose, the Betty-Page hair, the red lips — then I kissed her and shut the door.

Immediately, I grabbed my cell and dialed the captain's cell number. He answered on the third ring.

"Capt. Dalton, don't talk. I'm on my cell phone. I'm at my house, the phone lines have been cut, and I have the proof you need. I know it will take you about 30 minutes to get here, but don't use the local police. Some are dirty. But I need you here as fast as you can make it."

I punched the "end call" button and shut the phone's power off, too.

I got down low halfway between the front door and the back with my Springfield out. I'd sent the gun to a bullseye pistol gunsmith when I'd bought it. He'd tuned and tweaked it. Guaranteed to shoot a 2-inch group at 50 yards, mine shot a 1-inch group consistently. At 30 feet, it would put one .45 slug on top of another as long as I could keep pulling the trigger. I had seven shots in the magazine and two more clips on the two magazine holders on my belt.

At that point, all hell broke loose. Three or four shots came through the window, but I wasn't falling for it. I figured the shots were just cover for the guys coming in the door. And I was right.

One suit busted in the front door with his shoulder and went down when my Springfield's slug took out a chunk of his neck including his jugular. Blood spurted to one side and he went down. At the same time, Suit No. 2 came through the back door, but he was watching for dogs and that slowed him down a bit. I had a perfect side shot. He lost his right ear and a major portion of what was behind it.

The only trouble was that I had to turn my back to the front door to catch the second thug. Maria had said there were two. I'd not counted on a third. Someone whacked me on the head from behind and I went to my hands and knees on the floor. I fought to stay conscious and watched a size 13 crepe-soled Justin kick my Springfield away from me behind the recliner.

I looked up through a red haze and saw Bubba and Ludy standing over me. Bubba had a Baretta 9mm auto aimed at my head. In fact, he was trying real hard to push a hole through my left temple. Ludy was by the door with a Mossberg riot gun aimed at my head, a fat cheap cigar clenched between his teeth.

"Tell Maria to come out of the panic room and leave the dogs in there. I'll have my shotgun aimed at the door and will kill anything that comes through it unless it's her. If she doesn't come out, I'll kill you right here," Ludy said.

She did as I said, coming out in only her sundress with both hands held shoulder high. Bubba made her turn completely around to make sure she didn't have a gun. He was leering the whole time.

"You look at her, that's one thing, Bubba. You touch her, I'll kill you."

The fat JP knew he was in control with his pistol and Ludy's shotgun on me. But he also knew I meant what I said. His leer faltered for a minute. Maria noticed it, too.

"Will you quit with the broad, already?" Ludy said.

He poked me in the ribs with the shotgun.

"You know why we're here. You're the only one can connect us. You got to die."

Bubba moved to one side and motioned Maria to stand between him and me. She stepped beside me with her hands still up, glancing down at me on my hands and knees. When a man tells you you're going to die, you got to either act or talk. Action was not an option at the moment, so I talked.

"Like the Ranger, Ludy? Be hard to make this one look like an accident."

He glanced at the two suits lying inside the doors.

"Horrible scene me and Bubba happened on here. Musta been drug related, you reckon?"

He laughed around his cigar. Bubba laughed, too.

"You really threw me a curve that night the mare died," Bubba said, standing closer to Maria and trying to look down the top of her dress. "I couldn't figure a way to get the coke out of the mare with everyone around, especially after you turned her out. Ludy was gonna call you in the next morning for questioning and I was going to get it then. Never figured the shit would bust and kill the bitch."

Maria drew her shoulders back slightly, pulling the sundress tight across her chest where Bubba couldn't see anything.

"Yeah? Well, her dying interrupted a great night for us," Maria said.

Without turning, she looked down at me again, using her eyes to point down, then at the panic room door. I could see it wasn't closed completely.

"I wish we could have one more night like that," she said to me. "One more night with your hand sliding up the inside of my thigh, holding my tit. I have to hand it to you . . . well, I guess I can't hand it to you with my arms up," she said, lifting her hands a little higher and turning them back and forth as if to highlight the joke.

The movement caught Bubba's eyes and allowed her sundress to ride up a little higher, high enough for me to see .357 titanium revolver that we'd nicknamed the "Tit gun" in its holster, taped to the inside of her upper left thigh just below her crotch with duct tape from the panic room.

I acted like I was still groggy. With my right hand, I caught Maria's knee and pulled myself into a kneeling position beside her.

"I guess you want the docket with the warrant in it," I said wearily, motioning with my left hand toward the couch. "I didn't have time to hide it. It's right over there on the sofa."

"Wha. . . ?" Ludy said as he looked toward the couch. Bubba looked, too.

While they were still bewildered that I had their secret, I ran my hand up Maria's thigh, my hand unlatching the thumb break and drawing the gun swiftly, but behind her leg.

"How'd you. . . ?" Bubba started to say, but I cut him off with a short command.

"Attack!"

When the two men had turned toward the couch, they'd taken their eyes and guns off me and Maria. Now they started to bring them back to bear as I hollered and shoved Maria behind the recliner. But a blur of black and tan flung the panic room door aside and hurtled at Bubba.

"The dogs, you idiot, the dogs," Ludy yelled and tried to swing the Mossberg back around to me.

I'd cocked the hammer of the Tit gun as I'd raised it. The little lump of blaze orange that served as a front sight on the end of the stubby 2" inch barrel was in the middle of Ludy's chest when I pulled the trigger and felt the heavy recoil jam into the heel of my hand. I didn't see the bullet hit, but I saw Ludy double over as I pulled the trigger a second time.

Bubba had turned toward the attacking dog and actually had his gun halfway up before Moe hit his arm. I had three shots left in the Tit gun and I waited until Moe's weight carried him and Bubba's arm out of the way before pumping all three into the big man's chest. But at 400-plus pounds, there was a lot of Bubba between the impact area and his vital organs. I was out of ammo and he was still moving, shaking the dog like a mouse as the other two came out of the doorway. The big man was strong enough to reach over with his other hand and grab the Beretta. Left-handed, with a 125-pound Rott hanging from his right arm and blood going everywhere, he backed up against the wall to steady himself. I saw the muzzle looking right at me when three explosions deafened my right ear and I watched him crumple to the floor with three more neat, round holes in his chest.

Through the smoke to my right, Maria was crouched behind the recliner, my Springfield smoking in a two-handed grip braced against the arm of the recliner. I called the dogs off and sent them back into the kitchen area with a sweep of my hand.

Maria straightened up and looked around, taking her left hand off the .45 long enough to sweep a stray curl of black hair from her red lips and heave a sigh.

"Well, this place is a mess. Guess I'll be cleaning up all afternoon."

I grabbed her with both arms and held her close, wanting to tell her so many things, but several nervous nickers from the horse pasture and the sound of running hooves allowed me just enough time for a quick, but real, kiss.

The horses were running around in circles, milling, even before the helicopter could be heard. Capt. Dalton stepped out of the DPS copter a couple of minutes later in the middle of the horse pasture.

"Thought it'd take you 30 minutes at least," I said as I shook his hand.

"I got the emphasis on cell phone, so thought someone might be monitoring it. The DPS copter in Waco was already on its way here. Got to my staging area in five, took us ten to get here. Looks like you couldn't wait."

"I figured if they were monitoring the calls, it would make them act. If they weren't, I'd just wait for y'all."

I motioned over to the sofa.

"There's the docket. Lots of stuff like the warrant we

couldn't find. Lots of others just like it that Ludy and Bubba used to blackmail folks. There's also a ledger that I didn't expect to find. Vet was in there, so was Billy Wilson, who owned the mare the coke was found in. Drug charges. Coke. From the amounts, I'd say they were both recreational users."

"But neither one could afford word getting out in the circles they ran in," Capt. Dalton said. "Lots of horse people would have quit them both immediately."

I nodded.

"Yep, I guess Ludy and Bubba were holding that over Billy. I've known him quite a while, even back when I was in South Texas. He'd never hurt one of his horses on purpose or even take a chance on something hurting them. Ledger showed a couple of big payments to the vet recently. He was probably making some noise lately; they paid him a couple of token blackmail payments, then Ludy planted the coke with the poisoned needle in the mare. I'd say they were using the mares to transport coke to different places throughout the state and had people picking up the coke. Might have been stable hands or other vets on the take. I don't know and I don't care. That's your job."

The Ranger glanced at the docket and ledger on the sofa.

"Well, our job is just starting, then."

Two weeks later, Capt. Dalton called to tell me the drug smuggling ring had indeed been state-wide. In fact, it even extended into Oklahoma, New Mexico, and Louisiana. Ludy had used the folks with drug contacts to find other horse industry workers — vets, stable managers, etc. — that had some dirty laundry, mostly recreational drug use, and blackmail them. The Rangers found several of the sheriff's deputies, a couple of local police officers, and even a DPS trooper involved in the scheme. Retribution was swift and hard. Billy Wilson had his charges dismissed for cooperating with the Rangers.

I hung the phone up and watched Maria swinging her hips to the Tex-Mex rhythm of Little Joe & La Familia's "Mira Juanita" while she was rolling out the dough for kolaches dulce, another of her Czech-Mex recipes. For about the hundredth time since she'd slipped me the Tit gun, I realized how lucky a guy I was. I walked up behind her and snatched her up, heading for the bedroom to give her another one of my patented duct-tape-burn thigh rubs I'd gotten so good at over the last two weeks. She put both hands on my head and kissed me long and hard. Neither the flour handprints on my hair and ears nor the headphones we never quite got off her neck bothered us for the next hour, but the kolache dulces didn't come out so good this time.

One Hit Wonder

J. L. Abramo

I found myself alone.

The telephone on my desk had beckoned four times.

I was waiting for Darlene Roman to pick up the call. My able assistant was much better at offering salutations, and Darlene had a knack for making it sound as if she were transferring the caller to someone important. On top of that, I might have reminded her, answering calls was one of the things she was being paid to do. But then Darlene might have reminded me that the last time we brought in enough business to earn her a decent paycheck, we were still pounding telegraph keys.

I finally realized that I was alone. I grabbed the telephone receiver, guessing that Darlene had ducked out for a quick drink. A carrot smoothie at the health food bar across Columbus Avenue.

I was trying to decide which of the standard greetings I would use; "Diamond Investigation, Jake Diamond speaking" or "You have reached the offices of Diamond Investigation, please leave a detailed message. We will return your call as soon as possible, beep."

Before I could utter either, the caller spoke.

"Do it tonight. You know the address; the studio is on the second floor above the market. The last class lets out at ten. By the time all of the students leave and she gets into her street clothing, it could be close to eleven. She always makes a stop at the newsstand, out toward Jersey Street, for a newspaper, and then she goes to her car. The car will be parked behind the school that I mentioned. It should be the only vehicle back there, and it will be dark. Make it look like a mugging, and make fucking certain that she's killed. You'll get the other twenty-five grand when the job is done."

I might have told him that he had the wrong number, but the line went dead.

I tried remembering how to get the caller back, how to find out who had dialed our office thinking he had reached his hired assassin of choice. I punched star 80, nothing happened. It was the only number that came to mind, then I realized that I was thinking of a Bob Fosse film.

A woman had been marked for death. I had six hours to find her. Somewhere in San Francisco.

"It's in Noe Valley, Jake," Darlene said confidently, examining the wall map of the city, "Jersey is between 24th and 25th and only runs between Douglass and Dolores."

"We're looking for a studio of some kind. Art class?"

"Could be anything," said Darlene, "ceramics, acting, dance, photography."

"Second floor above a market," I said, "north or south of Jersey Street."

"It could be Douglass, Diamond, Castro, Noe, Sanchez, Church or Dolores," Darlene said, rapidly listing street names.

"That'll narrow it down."

"C'mon, Jake. Stop whining. Excuse me for being melodramatic, but a woman's life is at stake."

"The hit-man didn't get the instructions, Darlene."

"We don't know that, Jake. Maybe the man who called realized his error. And the woman needs to be warned, one way or the other. Sooner or later the guy is going to get her killed," Darlene said, "he must be determined if he's putting up fifty thousand dollars."

"Why don't we just call the police?"

"Think about it, Jake. By the time the SFPD gets into gear, this woman will be pushing up daisies. And that's if they even take you seriously."

"Pushing up daisies?"

"Give me a little slack, Jake. It's almost five, we have to do something."

"Give Vinnie Strings a call, and Joey Russo. Ask them if they can get over here, as soon as possible; we'll split up the area between the four of us and hit the streets."

"I can't help feeling it, Jake, but this is really exhilarating."

"Just what I needed on a Friday afternoon," I said.

We gathered around Darlene's desk, looking down at the Castro District map she had printed off the Internet. Don't ask me how that's done. Joey Russo was out somewhere doing business. His wife Angela sent their son-in-law, Sonny the Chin, in his place.

We decided we would comb the area between Douglass and Dolores Street, from Alvarado to Clipper. We each selected a quadrant, choosing the intersection of Noe and 24th Street as the starting point.

Darlene, Vinnie, Sonny and I climbed into my Toyota and headed for Noe and 24th. Once there, we would all go out into our sectors on foot and come back together after two hours. If any of us found the studio, it would leave two more hours to decide on a plan of action before class let out at ten.

We avoided considering the possibility that the place wouldn't be found.

I took the southwestern quadrant, nine square blocks. There were small markets everywhere, and newsstands up and down from Jersey Street. I walked into each of them, and other businesses along the way, asking about local studios and public schools. A number of visual and performing arts studios were identified, but none which sat directly above a deli or market. The nearest schools were the James Lick Middle School on the north side of 25th off Castro and the After 6 School opposite, but there were others within the boundaries of our hunt.

Undaunted, I plodded on, grabbing a slice of sausage pizza on Douglass Street for sustenance. I could picture Darlene working on a falafel sandwich as she walked Castro. Vinnie would be searching for a double bacon cheeseburger, and Sonny the Chin would be enjoying a moveable feast that his mother-in-law had brown-bagged for him.

I glanced at my Timex. Nearly half past seven and no luck.

I could only hope the others were having more success, and hope the marinara sauce that had dripped from my slice would one day be purged from the front of my vintage City College of New York sweatshirt.

The last place I entered was a wine shop close to the corner of Castro and Jersey. The owner was from the Bronx and, in spite of the sauce stain, he admired my shirt. He was a fellow City College graduate, who still couldn't get over the 1951 basketball scandal.

He couldn't help with the matter at hand, but he was eager to reminisce and tried his best to sell me a bottle of

Cabernet. It was almost eight, so I had to drag myself away. In an attempt to be polite, I handed him one of my business cards.

I spotted Sonny and Darlene when I turned back onto 24th Street. Vinnie was crossing Noe from the east. We crowded together against the strong wind that had come up from the Bay. To passersby, we might have looked as if we were planning to knock off the wine store I had just come out of.

When all of the reports were in, we were huddled at the spot where we had begun with little to show for our efforts.

"What now?" I asked.

"C'mon, Jake, we need a quarterback," said Darlene, "we're running out of time."

"Okay," I said, winging it. "Vinnie take the Toyota; drop Darlene off at the Vallejo Street police station. Try to find Lieutenant Lopez, Darlene, try to convince her that we need help. If she can at least send a few squad cars to cruise the neighborhood, it might scare the guy off. Lopez likes you, maybe she'll bite."

"And if she's not there?" asked Darlene.

"Then look for Sergeant Johnson, but don't mention my name," I said. "Vinnie, you go back to the office and wait there. Maybe, by some miracle, this guy will call again by mistake. I'm going to stick around down here. Call me on my cell phone if either of you has any good news."

"What can I do, Jake?" Sonny asked.

"Call your mother-in-law, Sonny, and ask her to say a novena."

Sonny stayed behind with me. We covered the search area again, circling the blocks as we moved out from the center. We were hoping that we might spot student types arriving for some sort of class. We took opposite sides of each street, checking the doorways to every flat that sat above a market or delicatessen, reading the names on door buzzers for anything that might offer a clue.

Darlene rang my cell phone. She had spoken with Lopez and had sweet talked the Lieutenant into sending the troops out. Lopez said she could only spare two cruisers, but she would have them roll through the area until eleven. Darlene wanted to come back and join us in the search. I told her that I would rather she to go back to the office to check on Vinnie.

It was nearly 9:30. Sonny insisted we take a short break for coffee. He suggested that at 10:00 we could go out again, splitting up this time, to look for students letting out.

We sat at the counter of a coffee shop near where we had started. Sonny finally broke the silence.

"Is this your first contract hit?" he asked.

"Very first," I said, playing along.

"The first is always the toughest," Sonny said.

I gave Sonny a hard look.

"You're joking, right?"

"Yes, Jake, I'm joking. What's on your mind?"

"I'm thinking about the phone call. How I stood there listening to this motherfucker in awe. I heard him through without interrupting. Maybe if I'd opened my fucking mouth I could have done something."

The counterman came over to refill our cups.

Sonny took a five-dollar bill from his wallet and placed it on the counter.

"Look, Jake. There's a good chance that the guy never realized that he called the wrong number, in which case the woman should be safe tonight. If you had cut him short, he would probably have set it up with the real assassin. And you wouldn't have heard enough of the details to get us at least this close to the woman. There's still a chance we may find her, it's almost ten, let's go."

We both rose and moved toward the exit.

"It was strange. After I listened to the guy, I felt as if I had actually accepted the contract," I said.

"In a way you have," Sonny said.

We split up outside the coffee shop. The streets were Friday-night busy. Thirty minutes flew by. I saw a squad car moving slowly up Castro Street; it didn't make me feel much better. I pulled out my cell phone to report in with Darlene. I turned it on and it rang immediately.

"Hell, Jake, I've been calling for more than an hour."

"I must have turned the phone off without thinking, what's up?"

"Some guy from a wine store called, said he had some information about a dance class on Noe Street."

The wine store was less than a block away. I quickly thanked Darlene and ran back to the shop.

I skipped the formalities.

"Tell me about the dance class," I said.

"A very nice woman stopped in just before nine, for a bottle of Merlot. I'd never seen her before so I tried to make a little conversation. She was in a hurry. She said that she was a dance instructor, working out of a studio on Noe, and had to get to class. I thought she might be the woman you were looking for."

"Where on Noe?" I asked.

"Right around the corner, between Jersey and 25th."

I ran out.

I looked up and down the street for any sign. It was much quieter here than on Castro. It was 10:35. Finally I spotted it, a small shoe store in the middle of the block.

Above the door was a painted sign, displaying the name of the shop.

The Market.

I had no way of reaching Sonny. I debated whether I should simply walk over and try finding my way up into the studio when a woman came out. She was in her mid-twenties and very attractive. I watched as she moved toward Jersey Street. She stopped into the newsstand and came out with a newspaper under her arm. I followed a safe distance behind as she turned the corner at Jersey, going south.

I looked around to check if anyone else was following. I dug into my jacket pocket and I took hold of the butt of my .38. I had taken it from my desk when we were waiting for Vinnie and Sonny to show up at the office. The woman crossed to the opposite side of Jersey Street and reached into her purse.

Suddenly she was unlocking the door of an automobile parked on the street. The street was comparatively quiet, but it was fairly well lit and there were a good number of pedestrians. I rushed over to the car as she was climbing in. She quickly closed the door, locked it and started the engine. I stood looking at her through the car window. I must have appeared either harmless or pathetic, because she rolled down her window and spoke.

"Can I help you?" she asked.

"Do you teach a dance class over on Noe?"

"That would be Mrs. Landers; she probably came out of the building right after me. I'm one of her students. Is there something wrong?"

"Where does she park her car?" I asked.

"Over on 25th, behind the Middle School."

Then I was running back toward 25th and Castro Street, my hand deep inside my pocket, still clutching the grip of the .38.

I caught sight of a woman walking into the driveway

alongside the school building. I took off after her. I had unconsciously pulled my hand from my pocket. I held my arm at my side, weapon in hand. I came into the small parking area behind the school. It was unlit. The woman was moving to the solitary BMW parked there.

I heard a sound from the opposite side of the car and I raised my arm.

"Mrs. Landers," I called.

She stopped and turned. She looked at my extended arm and then into my eyes.

"Are you going to shoot me?" she asked.

"No," I said, moving quickly toward the car.

"Jake," a voice called from behind the BMW, "it's Sonny."

I saw Sonny's arms come up over the roof and then he stood.

"I called Darlene and spoke with the wine store guy," said Sonny, "followed this woman from the studio and came in from the back in case anyone was waiting."

"Would someone please tell me what's going on?" Mrs. Landers said.

Then we all turned toward the flashing lights and siren of the police cruiser coming up the driveway.

It was nearly midnight. We were sitting outside of Lopez's office at the Vallejo Street Police Station, waiting for the Lieutenant to finish with Sarah Landers.

Lopez had not seemed very happy about having to be there at that hour.

Lopez came out with Landers, asked the woman to take a seat in the hallway and then ushered me and Sonny into her office.

"Sit," she said.

"What do you know, Lieutenant?" I asked.

"Not much," Lopez said, "the woman is a bit eccentric. She's loaded with money; made a bundle dancing on Broadway and in movies. Retired, moved out here, and teaches dance for the love of it, and she can't imagine why anyone would want her killed."

"That kind of thing takes a lot of imagination," Sonny said, "does she have a husband?"

"It was my first thought. She's a widow," said Lopez. "I asked her who she supposed might benefit from her death, she wouldn't even consider it."

"So, what now?" I asked. "Whoever has it in for her is going to try again."

"Not much I can do, Diamond," Lopez said, "I can put a tail on her for a few days, tops. Maybe the guy will call you back, ask you how you fucked it up."

"Cute."

"I have an idea," Sonny said, "but I doubt that either of you will like it."

"Go ahead," said Lopez with little passion.

Sonny was right. We weren't crazy about his idea. For lack of better one, we decided to give it a shot.

Lopez led me and Sonny out of her office and then she escorted Sarah Landers back in.

The call from Lopez woke me before eight the next morning. So much for sleeping in late on a Saturday.

Lieutenant Lopez had come down hard on Sarah Landers the second go around. She learned that the woman had one child, a son who stood to inherit everything. Lopez told me that she scared the crap out of the woman with talk of obstruction of justice. Lopez warned Landers that if she tried reaching her son, who was now formally a suspect in a conspiracy to commit homicide, she risked imprisonment. Landers was told not to answer her home telephone.

It was a colossal bluff, Lopez figuring Sarah Landers could not reach a lawyer before 9:00 on a Saturday morning for consultation. The Lieutenant had a uniformed officer drive Landers to her home and stay outside the house; the BMW remained where it had been parked in the school lot.

Lopez then called the son, reporting that a late model BMW had been discovered abandoned behind a school building. There was no sign of its owner, who had been identified by the vehicle registration as Sarah Landers. The woman could not be reached at her home address. The car would be held at the city auto impound until someone came to claim it.

"Did he sound mildly concerned?' I asked.

"He gave it a good try, he asked if there was anything that he could do," said Lopez. "I asked him to phone me as soon as he heard from his mother, and I said we would phone him if we heard anything. Got a pencil?"

"Go ahead," I said.

I jotted down the son's number.

"I'm at my office, Diamond. I'll be hunched over my telephone waiting for your call."

"Don't hurt yourself, Lieutenant," I said, and ended the connection.

When the dial tone came back, I punched in the number that Lopez had given me. After three rings a man answered.

"Time to settle up," I said.

"What the fuck happened, they didn't find her body?"

"They will, eventually, I took her for a little ride. Do you have the cash?"

"Yes."

"Meet me in an hour. The Home Plate on Lombard, I'll be at the counter. Don't be fucking late."

"How will I know you?" he asked.

I was very glad to hear that he had to ask.

"I'll wear a fucking carnation," I said, "I'll know you. Don't make me fucking wait."

I hung up. I called Lopez.

I sat at the counter of the Home Plate Diner drinking coffee and glancing out the front window waiting for Daniel Landers to arrive.

Before long, a car pulled up and double-parked across the street. I watched as he climbed out from the passenger side, carrying a large brown envelope. A woman behind the wheel rolled down her window to say something to him as he started to cross. I recognized the driver; I had followed her from the dance studio to her car the night before.

Landers walked in and I waved him over. He sat at the stool beside me. He placed the envelope on the countertop without looking at my eyes. I asked if he needed a receipt and he shuddered. He was about to get up when Lopez walked in. It was the first time I had seen her out of a business suit. She looked good.

"Daniel Landers," she said, slapping handcuffs on him in the blink of an eye, "you are under arrest on suspicion of conspiracy in an attempt to commit murder. You have the right to remain silent, I hope you do. You have the right to an attorney; I would not recommend using your mother's attorney. If you cannot afford a lawyer, we'll see what we can do."

"Lopez," I said, as Landers stood frozen in disbelief, "there's a gal in the Pontiac across the street who you may want to talk with."

Lopez took out her two-way radio and called Sergeant Johnson. She told him to pick up the woman in the Pontiac before we came out. I saw Johnson's unmarked Ford pull up beside the other car less than a minute later.

Daniel Landers confessed the moment they got him over to Vallejo Street. He claimed that it was her idea, the girl in the Pontiac. He'd met her a few months earlier when he picked his mother up from the studio, one of Sarah Lander's dance students. They began to see a lot of each other and before too long she was filling Dan's head with visions of a rosy and financially secure future for the two of them.

Daniel Landers had no idea who the hired gun was. He had dropped word here and there that he was looking for one and someone contacted him. Landers had deposited the first twenty-five thousand at a drop the previous Sunday night, a trash barrel at the corner of California and Van Ness. The only phone number Landers had was the number for my office, Daniel had apparently written it down incorrectly. Without the contract killer it would be a tough case to prosecute, but the experience would certainly discourage Landers from trying anything like it again and perhaps give his mother reason to reconsider the provisions of her last will and testament.

And that was that.

Or so I thought.

Five days later, late Thursday night, I arrived at my apartment from a pinochle game at the Pacific Heights home of a fellow P.I. As I pushed the key into the door lock, I felt what could only be the barrel of a handgun pressed up against the back of my head.

"Don't fucking turn around," the voice said.

"Not a chance," I said.

"Word has it that you cost me twenty-five grand, Mr. Diamond, and that really fucking upsets me."

"It wasn't my intention," I said.

"Nevertheless."

"Look at it this way; you *made* twenty-five thousand without having to kill an innocent woman."

"In my business, Diamond," he said, "that is little consolation. If you ever try pulling something like that again, intended or not, you will find yourself at the top of my fucking list. Contract work is getting difficult to come by these days, and I won't have someone pinching any of the few jobs that still trickle my way."

"Don't worry, it was my first and last hit," I said.

I felt the gun barrel move away from my head.

I finally found the courage to turn around.

I found myself alone.

Freddie Swings In

David Terrenoire

Every morning I would lie in bed and listen to my neighbor dress for work. She was so close, and the walls were so thin, that I could hear laundered cotton against her skin and her voice humming to the radio. Her sad songs of Latino love drifted through my room on the aroma of warm corn tortillas and I closed my eyes and imagined she was my wife, and soon I would wake our children and walk them to school, nodding to the old women in the plaza as we passed. On my way home I would stop to talk about the weather with the old men in the caf and maybe play a game of dominos in the shade.

Then I would open my eyes to the cracked plaster ceiling of my apartment and I was back where I was, which was nowhere.

When he asked me, I thought it was Bob's little joke. So I laughed and said, "I'm not a killer, Bob."

"Yeah, I know," Bob said, "but you've hurt people."

"That's different. A fracture is more like incentive."

"For people to pay."

"Yeah, an incentive for people to pay what they owe. People can't pay what they owe when they're not breathing, Bob. That's just bad business." I paused, hoping logic would change the flow of this conversation.

Bob nodded, chewing it over. "OK, point taken." He sipped a red wine and touched his napkin to his lips. "So if it makes you feel better, think of this as an incentive for others to pay." He sat very still and stared at me, his hands in his lap with his napkin.

I grew up making collections and deliveries for Bob, so I knew that look. It meant negotiations were over. The subject was closed.

Resigned, I said, "When do you want this?"

"Sometime this week."

I nodded. "That gives me time."

"Time for what?"

"To pray I get hit by a truck," I said.

"You want some advice, don't think about it." He squeezed my forearm. "Just step in and do it quick."

"Thanks, Bob. For the advice."

Bob leaned back in his chair and watched me. "Aren't you curious about who?"

"Yeah, I guess so, Bob."

"Freddie. I need you to do Freddie Bolan."

I felt weightless, like it was just me and Bob in space, floating around that restaurant. I knew Freddie. We weren't friends, exactly, but we sometimes had a beer up near Lincoln Center and one thing I knew: Freddie was harmless.

Freddie usually rolled in around four, ahead of the crowd, and if I was there he'd have me read whatever he'd written that day. I didn't mind, although the plots were always the same: the hero swung in on a shoelace, dispatched the bad guys and rescued the blonde with the pouty lips. The women were always blonde, even the Asians, and as far as I could tell, none of them wore underwear, ever.

Freddie was older than me, in his forties, wore pancake to hide acne scars and he batted for the other team. I knew this, although he never hit on me, and I appreciated his sensitivity to my hetero persuasion. The closest he came to making a pass was when I told him his hero was too honest and strong to be believable. Freddie looked at me over his Chardonnay and said, "I based him on you, Jake. He's you. I hope that's OK."

So I knew that killing Freddie couldn't be anything but bad. Bad for Freddie and bad, karma-wise, for me.

It started the minute I stepped out. A cab stopped, I got in and, swear to God, I had to give the driver lessons on getting around Manhattan. I explained how Fifth divides the city, east and west, and how Sixth is the Avenue of the Americas and that big green thing, the thing with all the trees, that's called Central goddamn Park. Then he made a wrong turn on 26th, got stuck behind a schmatte cart and by the time I made my first appointment I was in a mood that could alter weather patterns in Brazil.

Bob had sent me out to collect from a piano player who bet heavy on college hoops and lost. Bob wanted me to break her finger, one of the little ones, as a reminder of her obligations.

The piano player lived in a fourth floor walkup on Ninth. I climbed the steps, heavy with the weight of Freddie on my mind, and knocked on her door. She let me in, all nervous, and started in on why she didn't have the money.

Her place was nice, the furniture and all, but the air was so thick you could have knitted it into a stink sweater. All because of an evil yellow tom with one good eye.

I was in negotiations with the piano player when the tom backed up against my Coach bag, looked me right in the eye and emptied his cat bladder on four hundred dollars worth of tanned leather.

The piano player, joy in her heart, said, "He's making water."

"I can see that."

"He had crystals in his urethra."

"Looks like he's over it."

"I took him in yesterday," she said, "to the vet's. They put in a catheter."

"Jesus," I said, conjuring up a mental image I did not wish to see.

"It cost three hundred dollars."

I blinked, more stunned by the amount than the ammonia. "You spent three hundred dollars so your cat could piss on my bag?"

"He was blocked," she said.

"Excuse me for saying this, but I'm about to break a finger here, one of the little ones, in lieu of currency, three hundred of which could postpone this unpleasantness for both of us another week. Seeing as how cats are, you know, disposable pets, I don't see the logic."

"But Mr. Chumley was uncomfortable," she said.

"No," I said. "This is uncomfortable." I scooped up the fat tom in one hand and tossed him out the window. I like to think he had a new look in his eye, possibly one of regret, but I know cats and I know he was giving me the evil eye all the way down to the hard landing on Ninth. I looked out and Mr. Chumley, too nasty to die, was staggering toward the curb. But a passing cab thumped him and that was that.

The piano player's hands flew to her face and she started to cry. I softened, I guess, and said, "I'll cover the vig this week with Bob, just to show you I'm sorry I had to do that." I put my hand in my pocket. "Now do yourself a favor and get some help. The way you gamble is not, you know, healthy long-term." I dropped a few bills onto her coffee table. "And get some air freshener, huh? My eyes are burning." I let myself out.

That night I sat in the dark in my apartment and listened to my neighbor cook dinner. She sang a sad song about broken hearts. Her voice rose above the traffic noise and took me to a warm place where I smelled beans and chilies and the evening rain as it stirred the dust of the plaza.

On Tuesday, Bob handed me the black valise that held the week's receipts. "Don't let a cat pee on this, huh? There's sixty-three large in there."

A shadow must have crossed my face because Bob leaned in and said, "You thinking about Freddie?"

I nodded.

"Today?"

"Yeah, today."

"That's good," Bob said. "Believe me, you'll sleep better once it's done."

I didn't think I'd ever close my eyes again. Freddie Bolan was a bad writer, sure, but if that was a capital crime you couldn't walk down the street without stepping on poets, playwrights, and dead ad guys.

Bob pushed a crumpled paper bag across the table. It held something heavy. "I got you something," Bob said.

I looked inside and saw a small caliber automatic, foreign made.

I nodded again, but not because I agreed with anything. After I'd dropped the money off with O'Connell, I caught a cab back to my apartment.

I took the little .32 out of the bag and broke it down. I cleaned it and wiped each piece, including the magazine and bullets, before putting it back together. I dropped it into my pocket and walked up to Freddie's place. I felt like I was walking through wet cement.

Freddie buzzed me in. "I was expecting you," he said.

"You know why I'm here?"

Freddie shrugged. "Things get around." Freddie took a seat on a sofa sagging under stacks of newspapers, magazines and manuscripts. He leaned forward, his fingers hanging between his knees like ripe plantains. "I'm sorry," he said. "I'm sorry you have to do this."

"You know why?"

Freddie sighed. "I owe some money."

"How much money."

Freddie shook his head. "Too much. Almost thirty grand to Jimmy Marbles."

"Jeez, Freddie."

"I know," Freddie said. "I know. And when Jimmy wanted his money," Freddie shrugged and looked out the window, "I kind of threatened him."

The hair on my neck stood up. "Threatened him? With what?"

"I know some stuff. I found out about a girl Jimmy killed over in Queens."

I couldn't believe this. No one could be dumb enough to threaten Jimmy Marbles. Not even Freddie.

Freddie looked back at me, a half smile on his face. "Not too smart, huh?"

I blew out a big sigh. "Freddie. You put me in a very awkward position." I took gloves from my pocket.

Freddie got up from the sofa. "No sense dragging this out." He turned around, his back to me, and hunched his shoulders up around his ears. "Go ahead," he said.

I pulled on the gloves and when the latex snapped Freddie said, "You going to shoot me or check my prostate?" I racked a round into the chamber and picked up a throw pillow to muffle the shot. I aimed at the small bald spot at the top of Freddie's head.

Freddie said, his voice in a whisper, "Aren't you worried

that somebody might hear?"

I thought about the thin walls at my place and said, "Maybe we should take a walk."

Freddie nodded and said, "I'll get my coat."

The next morning, Bob asked how it went.

"It went," I said.

"I haven't heard anything about the body."

"Give it a couple days. They'll find him."

"Good," Bob said, but he looked nervous, like maybe he was getting pressure from Jimmy Marbles. Bob gave me the bag again and made a joke about not running off to Mexico with all that money, but it wasn't funny and the joke died away like a bad smell.

Instead of catching a cab down to O'Connell's, I crossed the street and headed uptown, to Sixty-sixth, where I went down into the subway and crossed over to the southbound platform. There was a big crowd, drawn to a show at Lincoln Center, and I put myself between a man in a suit and a woman with a small boy. I looked across the platform and there, leaning against the wall, was Freddie. He smiled at me, and I nodded. I had Bob's black valise and Freddie had his suitcase. We waited for the train.

"You!"

Her voice rose above the racket of the Manhattan underground. Then I saw her face, bunched up, angry as scuffed knuckles.

"You bastard!"

The crowd began to part. The man in the suit backed off to the right. The woman with the boy slid off to the left. The piano player pointed at me with one hand. Her other hand was in her pocket. "You killed Mr. Chumley!"

I glanced around, like maybe she was talking to somebody else.

"I've been looking everywhere for you," she said. She took her hand from her pocket. In it was a gun. She fired a shot that zinged by my ear and scattered the crowd, the crack echoing off the tile.

From the tunnel came the building roar of a train, its wheels squealing with the same high-voltage intensity as the shrieks of the people around me. The piano player fired again and this one tore into the fabric of my jacket, creasing my shoulder.

A soft shape moved toward the shooter, against the rushing human tide. The piano player turned toward him, her gun hand trailing behind. Freddie, his head down, a few steps away, was moving fast and his arms were stretched out to gather her in.

The train blew from the tunnel. The piano player brought the pistol around and fired at Freddie. The roar drowned out the shot and the people's screams. The piano player fired again but Freddie's momentum carried him into her. I watched her fold over his shoulder. I watched the gun fall from her hand and bounce off the concrete. I felt the squeal and rumble shake every atom of the station. Then the piano player and Freddie were gone, lost over the platform's edge. The train slammed through, unable to stop. People screamed and surged toward the stairs. I let myself be carried up and outside into the sunlight of Sixty-sixth street.

I never sleep. I lie on my cot and listen, but the walls are too thick for me to hear my neighbors sing. I follow the pattern in the plaster above me and I imagine the workman who made those strokes and I wonder if he has a wife who brings him cool drinks in the evening.

Before the one o'clock rains I dress and walk to the

bodega. The women nod and call me Se–or. I take a small table in the shade. The waiter, one of the bravest men in the village, brings me a beer. I ask if there have been any strangers in town and he says no. I choose to believe him because he stands close by, waiting for my order.

I sit beneath hanging baskets of flowers. I ask the waiter what kind of flowers they are but it's either my Spanish that's insufficient or his knowledge. Either way, he does not know, and smiles an apology. Their petals fall, as red as blood, and land on the backs of my hands.

I touch the pistol beneath my shirt, its grip already slick with sweat, and I hum a sad song as if the music will somehow rewrite my life.

A warm breeze blows over the plaza, and as I wait for them to come I smell warm corn tortillas, and dust, and the one o'clock rains as they begin to dot the leaves of the surrounding trees.

Captiva

David Bart

Florida sunshine streamed though glass patio doors over his prone, naked body. The woman standing beside the bed hurriedly stuffed twenties into the breast pocket of her shiny red, white and blue, starred and striped blouse as —

— electronic card-lock chirped, the hotel room door hissed inward over plush aquamarine carpet, loudly crashing against the wall!

"You son of a bitch," Rachel said in an icily calm voice as she entered, aiming the little Beretta at a nude Scarboro who casually sat up on the bed, grinning.

He admired her classic Native American features: prominent cheekbones, thick mane of gleaming black hair — looked a little like a pre-surgery Cher.

"You get a line on 'em?" he asked, ignoring the movement to his right; the other woman was hopping toward the open hotel room door, pulling on a high-heel cowgirl boot, the flag-blouse hanging out of a white, faux-leather skirt the size of a postage stamp.

Rachel snorted. "Been busy with your patriotic little friend?"

She bent down, scooped the medium-blue cowgirl hat off the floor and sailed it out the door after the departing woman — moved to within six feet of Scarboro, still reclined on the bed.

They stared at one another in open confrontation . . . from their adversarial but relaxed demeanor an observer might conclude they were hardened criminals. Or mercenaries.

After a few beats Rachel lowered the gun a ways, holding at his crotch for a brief eternity.

Scarboro swung his legs off the bed, putting his bare feet on the blue-green carpet. "Anger-management not making it?" he asked — figured when she dropped the arm he could reach over and —

Crack!

Incredible stinging sensation.

They both looked down at his left foot, frowning as though neither could get what'd just happened — though no doubt about the pain, Scarboro on the edge of the bed clutching the sheet, gritting his teeth — *Christ, partners don't shoot one another in the goddamn foot!*

Glad she'd used her small purse-piece, though; a nine millimeter would've left a lump of hamburger at the end of his leg instead of a tiny hole leaking red. And it'd no doubt sounded like little more than a wet towel snapped playfully at somebody's butt — another occupant wouldn't call the cops.

Rachel pivoted, stormed past a wall-print depicting a bunch of flamingos — glanced hatefully back at him — and of course he's wondering what in hell you call a group of the big pink birds, watching her march from the room while stuffing the Beretta back in her purse.

Scarboro pressed a folded hand towel over the wound, pulled a sock over that to hold it in place — quickly slipped into gray running shorts and black T, hobbled out into the hall and commandeered a maid's cart to use as rolling support, the short little woman screaming at him in Spanish, following him to the elevator.

Had to wait till the car Rachel'd just used came back up.

— through the lobby to the cab-stand and a Senegalese driver gazing disinterestedly at his foot, the hand towel blossoming red — asked which hospital.

Under way, Scarboro said, "Whatta ya call a bunch of flamingos?"

The cabby sighed, maneuvered a toothpick deep into the corner of his mouth, his tongue making a clicking sound. "Give up, whatta ya call a bunch of flamingos?"

At the private clinic they removed the twenty-five caliber slug, the doc telling him: "no worse'n stepping on a big nail," Scarboro suggesting the doctor shut the fuck up, including any calls regarding bullet wounds. Unnecessary, of course, given the liberal orientation of the clinic, located upon his arrival in Southwest Florida.

The next morning . . .

They'd insisted on a wheelchair to the front door — antibiotics in hand, dressed for the street in ecru cotton slacks, black linen shirt, small white cast on one foot, a closed-toe leather sandal on the other — parked him near the discharge desk to wait for his ride. Course, Rachel had shot him, odds of her showing up might be long and lonely.

"Hey, Scarboro."

From behind him, rapid clicks on gleaming gray-tile floor — a sudden, *boisterous* splash of crimson filling his view, blood-red dress adhering to a curvy form like grim death.

Rachel smiled down at him. "Sorry about the foot," she said, leaning forward, gravity contesting the already questionable modesty of her very low-cut bodice — reached out toward his cheek but stopped before touching.

"You were angry," he said.

The only real flaw she had, *incredible* rage.

He nodded down toward the cast on his foot. "Told the doc I wanted to get around on it."

Shrugging, Rachel said, "I didn't know she was a working girl, thought she meant something to you."

But Scarboro was having a whimsical thought, tuning out, as often happened when someone made a superfluous gesture such as apologizing . . .

— he was thinking about how life was like a one-way mirror: look to the future, *at* the mirror, you see only your own reflection, grinning like an idiot, oblivious to what's coming . . . but after you've lived into that future you can look back *through* the mirror and see, blatant as a prom night pimple, a definite pattern.

Like the pattern of getting in trouble — bad kind you see in the movies. Life-threatening. Often involving women.

In a low voice he said, "So, where are they?"

"Holed up on an island just off the mainland — perfect for us."

"The client didn't make the drop, did he?" he asked, glancing toward the slender nurse who held out his new — according to the bill — *five-hundred-dollar* aluminum cane.

As he took it Rachel said, "Nope, he's waiting till you say."

He nodded. "They'll sell her to a broker if we screw this up — South America or the Middle East — it's what Dagen tried the last time he grabbed a kid."

Scarboro had come up with Charles "Chucky" Dagen as one of the perps behind this particular kidnapping after an NCIC scan of newly released cons, flagged for dipshits who'd done a kid-grab before. Oftentimes they try the same gig got them busted. Apparently trying to prove something — which was not a bad definition of "loser." Turned up a half-dozen guys who'd just been paroled and Chucky Dagen was in that six-pack. After eliminating most of the ex-cons, Scarboro chatted with Dagen's cell-mate — usual threats and promises — and got the Ray Poole/Chucky Dagen connection. Tight inside, tight outside — parole sheets gave the same address in Ft. Myers for both men. Cross-reference program at Corrections must've missed it — rules prohibit cons from fraternizing.

The address given was the obligatory fleabag motel — which the kidnappers had already vacated. But Rachel and another female P.I. found them again.

The hooker'd been a mistake, what with his partner's temper and all — though he didn't believe the theory about men past forty chasing skirts to reclaim their youth; hell, his youth wasn't worth resurrecting. Bipolar disorder had put him mostly on the outside, the only "friends" he'd had back then were teammates, because he was good at sports. But when he'd badly hurt one of them who'd been disrespectful to his sister he'd ended up with a choice. A tour in Southeast Asia or jail.

Scarboro heaved to his feet, surprised how difficult standing can be when initiated from a wheelchair, the wounded foot flaring brightly.

"You're supposed to flip up those feet-rests first," Rachel said — turned away into the foyer, automatic glass doors swooshing out of her way.

Hobbling behind her, his eyes dropped to a world-class derriere, shrink-wrapped in bright crimson, moving to some sensual primitive rhythm. He took a deep breath of gulf air as he gimped his way outside, the bright Florida sunshine *painfully* glinting off car windshields, the chrome on the ubiquitous SUVs, an upper row of hospital windows and as blue glare off Rachel's sunglasses as she raised them to her exquisite face.

Rachel Boltera. Jicarilla Apache father, French-Canadian mother — a disparate ethnicity that'd recombined genetically into a near perfect female form. He'd met her at the casino up on the Jicarilla rez in Northern New Mexico; she'd asked him to meet her there to talk about a kidnapped niece. He quickly located the kid and Rachel and some tribal people had gotten her out — left a mess behind. She was beholden in some ancient never-ending way and eventually had partnered with him in his agency back in Albuquerque — she got her ticket right away because she'd been on the tribal police at one time.

Man, that'd been eight years ago.

The white Mercedes convertible she'd rented was parked at the curb, top down, and of course unlocked — a circular Native American symbol representing nature, a snake eating its tail, dangled from the mirror on a strand of turquoise beads. Rachel opened the door for him.

He lowered himself onto the passenger seat, shaking his head and grinning at all the shit she got away with — put on his own shades, tossing the cane in the back seat.

"What?" she demanded, coming around the back.

After she'd gotten in he said, "You leave the car open, keys in the ignition . . . both of us are lucky, that's the edge we got."

Now, if he just believed that — 'cause *lucky* people don't get shot in the foot. He told her that.

"Well, you're lucky I didn't shoot you in the *cahones,*" starting the motor and putting the car in gear — thrust the Mercedes into the thick flow of traffic at an opening barely three car-lengths long — *screech* of brakes, guy behind pounding his horn button and shaking his fist.

"Whatcha thinking about?" she asked, ignoring the commotion behind.

"Tonight," Scarboro replied, adjusting his side mirror to keep an eye on the pissed driver — and it didn't hurt to scan for a tail either. No reason there'd be one, but watching for danger was part of his vigilant nature. The shrinks could call it what they would.

She took palm-lined McGregor Boulevard to the highway leading to the Sanibel Island causeway — low, bridgelike crossing with spaced signs recommending a slow speed.

A curious dolphin, homing on vibrations off submerged pilings, jumped up out of the bay beside them, poised just beyond the railing, peering out of a flat black eye. And as usual Scarboro felt uneasy, closely scrutinized by an intelligent life form.

On the island they turned right at Periwinkle Drive, headed north; a sign indicated that Captiva Island lay in that direction, the map showing it to be connected by another causeway or land bridge to the north end of Sanibel.

He watched the flow of yellowing pine, towering palms and condos on pilings perched above the pristine white sand — tourists in rainbow-colored swimwear held dripping ice cream cones away from their pink bodies, others were slathering on sun screen. Down on the sugary beach kids gleaned the green and white surf for newly deposited Gulf shells.

Traffic was glacial — tentative entries and hurried exits from side roads created a kind of pulse or rhythm, evoking thoughts of patterns again. But he kept his mind on the coming night.

"Right there," Rachel said after parking in a multi-condo parking lot across the street from some individual structures, set way back amongst spindly pine.

The sand seemed white as snow in the sunlight, a dingy-gray in the shade. Smell of the sea. He watched a wayward egret stiltedly make its way through sparse trees toward Pine Island Sound separating Captiva from the mainland, then glanced at the condo she'd indicated. "Little girl inside?"

Rachel gazed out her side window — light coral condo

perched on pilings, badly peeling white shutters, shingles missing from the high-pitched roof, the place almost qualifying as run-down. She nodded her head without looking at him.

Scarboro knew what she was thinking; unkempt condition of the place reminded her of reservations and pueblos back home. Before the wealth of the casinos.

"This'll probably get wet," he said, knowing the promise of violence had an odd effect on her — often cheered her.

Rachel sighed, sat up a little. "Well, they got it coming — hope they haven't hurt the kid."

"Course they've hurt her," he said, a dull sensation ratcheting upward along his spine — sudden urge to scan the shadows for enemies. Stepped hard on the impulse.

Rachel said, "Jane and I alternated round the clock and neither of us saw 'em carrying out anything big enough to have a little girl in."

Jane Torneau, the local P.I. they'd hired — at first just to run IDs of recent rentals in the area. Any that didn't register as authentic she and Rachel checked out in person till they found Dagen and Pool's location again. But then she'd helped on the stake-out, and quickly begged on for any coming action, little piece of their fee.

— *a sudden chill rippled over him.* "Can you trust this broad?" his eyes narrowing against that odd but familiar cold-fever feeling he experienced whenever finding himself in the darker territories of his psyche.

Rachel glanced at him, frowning — *appeared to be sneering, as if she was hatching something.*

In a serious tone he said, "You're not going to shoot me anymore."

Rachel studied his expression, let out an enduring sigh. "Jesus, Scarboro."

He gave her a minimal shrug. "Reasonable question."

She replied quickly, "Yeah, if you're borderline paranoid."

"So . . . answer the question."

A few beats went by and she turned toward him as much as possible in the bucket seat, red dress bunched high on her brown thighs — leaned forward, her low-cut bodice all but abandoning its duty — *suddenly centered in a tunnel-vision cameo, her beautiful face over swelled cleavage above perfect knees.*

And that face: full, peach-glossed lower lip, thin upper-lip, dark-brown sultry eyes communicating an intent that'd melt a monk's resolve — sweet breath wafted over his face as wintergreen possibility.

"We're a pair, eh?" she said softly.

He wasn't sure what she meant. Asked her.

"Well, you're bipolar and I've got rage issues."

He made a face. "Those quacks don't know shit — I'm vigilant, moody, and you're testy — shrinks have more labels than Campbell's Soup," he said, turning in his seat, peering out the back window, down the sandy lane into a shaded copse of stunted pine.

Did something move back there?

She cleared her throat, reached out a hand to his chin and gently brought his gaze back to her. "How bad's the foot?" Voice husky as she shifted on the seat, light penetrating down the inside of her thighs a ways.

He felt his throat tighten. *Jesus, right here in this tiny damn Mercedes?* Shifted in the seat, wondering what the hell he'd been thinking before his libido took charge. Something about . . . trees?

She managed to get over to him.

Six minutes later . . . breathing hard, they pushed away from each other, uncomfortable, humidity a palpable though invisible fog inside the small car.

Rachel started the motor, switched on the air and retrieved a hastily abandoned garment. "Brief, but nice," she said — frowned at Scarboro as he abruptly swiveled in his seat, stared behind them.

A rap on Rachel's side window.

Rachel shut off the engine and let the tall woman into the back seat of the small Mercedes — the female P.I. had to scrunch sideways to accommodate her gangly legs. Wore faded blue jeans and a white T-shirt with a trio of question marks — ??? — on the front.

"You guys should get a room," the woman said.

"Are you armed?" Rachel asked.

Jane Torneau nodded, put her fanny pack on the seat beside her. Light brown hair cut in a scalp-hugging helmet, no makeup. Lanky as a basketball player. Fairly pretty, in a Cajun backwater sort of way — Scarboro would bet a C-note she'd tasted raccoon and swamp possum. Maybe beaver, he thought, grinning to himself.

"That a Sig nine?" he asked, nodding down at her pack on the seat. Sharp outline of the automatic against thin canvas.

"He has a thing about guns," Rachel told her, grinning at the rearview mirror, adding, "and you know what that means."

The women cackled companionably.

Scarboro wondered: where in hell had he taken the turn in his life that'd led to this scrawny-pined island off the coast of Florida, cramped in a small car, two broads busting his balls? He was about to remind Rachel of the sounds she'd been making earlier but a door in the raised condo swung open, slamming hard into the side!

— aggressively unattractive man resembling an orangutan emerged, scratching his crotch . . . walked out to the edge of the cantilevered deck, leaned his puffy gut heavily against the railing, engulfing a three-foot section of the barrier. Thick but angular body, matted red hair over most of what was showing; wiry tufts sticking out from the black vest he wore, furry bowed legs below baggy green Bermuda shorts. A decidedly simian face — round and flat, mildly vacant.

Rachel said, "Be still my heart."

Scarboro nodded. "Meet Raymond Poole."

"My god, he's beyond disgusting," Jane said, nearly whispering, as if not to offend the man, though he was a good fifty yards away.

Scarboro shook his head at the thought of yet another odd pattern. Genetics.

After Ray went back inside, Scarboro and Rachel continued the stake-out while Jane walked to her Explorer and drove to a caf back on Sanibel Island, picked up some beer-batter gulf shrimp for her and Rachel, ground sirloin on sourdough for Scarboro.

— they sat, crowded in the Mercedes, eating.

With her mouth full Jane asked, "Why didn't your client pay?"

"I told him not to — Chucky's intent is to sell the kid even if he gets the ransom, they'd never give her up alive."

Wadding up the large, blue and white carry-out sack with the name "Pearl's Dive" on the side, Jane said, "Didn't put it together when you hired me — you're the guy found Pamela Alice Floyd, what was that, ten years ago?"

Scarboro nodded.

"Gimme," she said eagerly.

"You know the drill — you ask around, look around," he said over his shoulder.

"That thing they had on CNN told how the kidnappers weren't connected in any way to the family and nobody saw the abduction — there was no trail," Jane said.

Scarboro nodded. "Besides some things that didn't

work, I put Pamela's classmates and their parents out on a sweep of convenience stores and markets asking for someone buying her choice in goodies — got lucky — a sharp Vietnamese clerk remembered some weirdo buying chocolate sponge fingers with green icing called Wormies and a four-pack of lime Perrier — Pamela's favorite combo. Security camera picked up a slice of him through the front window, getting in a van — lab enhanced the plate number."

"You gave the bust to the Feds, huh?" Jane asked, taking a sip of her now cold coffee and grimacing.

"Had an underground bunker in his barn — Feds give good rescue — scope out where everybody is inside with heat-imaging and parabolic mikes — it's what they do best."

— explaining to her that Ray and Chucky were very different, though — too far off the straight and narrow, both wholly certifiable, they'd kill the kid and then themselves. The Feds told him if their tactical team went in they'd have to "shock captivity coordinates, probably damage the kid." Less than a full assault against stone killers was not in their play book.

So he'd have to take the kid without the feds — figured to scam into position before the shooting started, because if they lost the kid there'd be no fee.

"That when you started specializing in kidnappings?" Jane asked.

Scarboro nodded. He'd gone on from the famous Pamela Alice Floyd case to a fourteen out of nineteen retrieval record, his fee coming from the client in the amount of half the ransom. Payment due when he returned the abductee. He accepted nothing, even when offered, if it didn't work out.

Wasn't being a nice guy, he explained — matter of personal power — didn't want to feed anything within his psyche that excused failure.

Scarboro canted his head to one side at the lower left corner of the window, right where a sliver of an opening allowed view to the interior — he silently squished a mosquito siphoning blood from his bare shoulder, flicked the crumpled insect into darkness.

He, Rachel and Jane were hunkered down on the elevated deck, south side of the dwelling. It was just before midnight. There was no kid in view. Just that hairy shithead Ray, still wearing the black vest. He figured Chucky to be in the can or something, the kid probably sleeping in another room. The other windows had offered no view to within.

Reaching through darkness, Scarboro took hold of Rachel's bare arm. In fact, red bikini panties and a brief red bra were all that elevated her above a profoundly bare-ass condition. Jane was similarly clad, white panties and white bra dimly glowing in the dark, though producing a somewhat reduced effect. But not bad.

"Jane, you can change your mind," he whispered, reaching behind Rachel to check the Glock nine taped there.

Jane stiffly shook her head.

Scarboro motioned for her to duck-walk a half-circle so he could check the nine millimeter taped to the back of her waist — noted with amusement the effect this had on him; well-toned musculature moving sinuously beneath all that bare female skin. Shadowed hollows and pale swells.

The tape had loosened from the weight of her old Sig Sauer and he smoothed it down onto goose-bumped skin, trying to not get further aroused. After all, Rachel was still armed.

He nodded definitively and they all got to their feet, Scarboro favoring his cast as he sloshed some bourbon over the women's bare legs, taking a swig of the booze himself, letting it dribble down his chin and bare chest, all of this to provide the desired barroom effluvium. He wore blue jeans, a deck shoe on his good foot, his Browning nine in the waistband at the small of his back. "Listen," he whispered, repeating his earlier instructions, "we get inside before we make a move, try to clear the interior for the kid before we take them out."

The women just stared at him.

"If we try to take them alive the kid could die," he said.

Bourbon in one hand he reached out with the cane, poked the doorbell . . .

— loud thumping sound of someone lumbering across the suspended floor of the stilted condo, white curtain moving a bit at the window to the left of the door.

". . . hundred bottles of . . . on the ball, four hundred bottles of *beer*, and if those balls should . . ." Scarboro trailed off, guffawing into a coughing jag.

The girls were giggling, Jane making a show of pinching his butt and Rachel rubbing his bare stomach, biting playfully at his shoulder.

"Fuck ya want?" someone shouted through the door.

"Wanna par-*tee!*" Jane shrieked, pounding on the door, "C'mon, Tony, open up!"

The door swung open and Ray stood there scratching his crotch, wearing what looked to be a black flotation vest, watching the girls paw Scarboro. After a leering appraisal of the two women in their underwear he checked out the male intruder, noting the defined shoulders, pecs and abs, the six-foot height — glanced down at the white cast on his uninvited guest's foot, the cane in his hand, and visibly relaxed. "You got the wrong party, cripple," Ray said sneeringly, hand behind his back, pushing the door with the other.

No doubt a piece back there, Scarboro thought — but better in a waistband than already in his hand — thinking this as Rachel let go, reached out to stop the door . . . she sidled up to the orangutan, cooing something distractingly prurient.

Jane shrieked, "How 'bout some mu — *sik,"* weaving her way inside, glancing around through bleary-looking eyes. Scanning for the kid. "Where's that fink Tony?" she demanded.

Grinning and weaving drunkenly, Scarboro leaned heavily on the cane as he entered, eyes sweeping the interior — *door on the left was closed, a hallway through there and another doorway at the far —*

Ray shouted at Scarboro, "Hey, get outta here, asshole!"

Chucky Dagen appeared in a doorway to the right — Scarboro matching him to his mug shot — the con also in a black vest.

— not Kevlar, too bulky, could put a couple right through it — Scarboro's eyes narrowed as he then registered on the little girl being lifted up, held in front of the con.

"Who the hell are these people?" Dagen shouted at Ray.

— the little girl, Scarboro knew from his file, was six years old — wore a soiled school uniform: skirt and blouse, but bare feet, Chucky pressing a gun hard against her head. Dark bruise beneath her left eye, split lip, dried blood at the corners of her mouth. *Christ, they really smacked her around* — his mind suddenly jumping to Rachel and her quick temp —

Too late.

— all pretense gone, Rachel stared at the little girl, *roaring* something unintelligible, reaching behind with both hands, clawing for her gun, fully enraged — tearing it free in an upside down grip, fumbling . . .

— Jane lowering into a crouch, grabbing at her own weapon!

Ray put his gun on Jane as she brought the Sig around — he shot her twice in the chest, her gun discharging but the slug going wide and shattering a window behind and to one side.

Then Ray swung his arm toward Rachel — she was kneeling down, reaching under a heavy plate-glass coffee table for the gun she'd dropped —

Scarboro swung the cane in a flat arc like a bat, slamming Ray's forearm so hard the gun spun free of his grip — hit the floor and discharged, the slug slamming through a wall, Scarboro's weight on his wounded foot rekindling into a nine-alarm blaze!

— and now Chucky's screaming at him to back off or he'd kill the kid.

They all froze, staring at each other — the little girl whimpered softly as Chucky crushed her against his barrel chest, though oddly the gun not pressed to her temple, carrying her fast toward the door. Held the gun down to his side, almost casually.

— Ray sidled in close behind his partner — turned as he backed out the door, hand extended, gripping what appeared to be a video game control.

Sounds of their hurried footsteps descending wooden steps.

"Why didn't you shoot?" Rachel screamed, glaring up at him from a kneeling position next to the female P.I., a shiny red slick spreading out from under Jane's body and around Rachel's bare knee.

The Browning in his hand was cocked and ready to fire but he hadn't shot at either of the perps, even when Ray had aimed the gun at Rachel — he'd batted Ray's gun out of his beefy red hand without hesitation but he couldn't shoot either con.

Rachel looked up at him hatefully, daring him to answer.

He visualized the black vests both men wore; barely visible wires sticking out of what had to be packets of explosives beneath, wires no doubt leading to battery packs — fucking Middle East terrorists giving these low lifes ideas. "Vests were wired — I hit Ray, Chucky would've set his off

— shoot Chucky, Ray'd trigger his detonator."

No need to mention that Rachel's rage had once again precipitated violence. Hell, she'd just reacted to the little girl's badly abused condition — her play didn't have to go wrong, it just did.

He knelt beside the downed P.I., ignoring the fire in his foot and checked for a neck pulse, staring at the black cordite specks burnt into her white bra, the ugly wounds in the pale skin no longer bleeding.

Scarboro levered himself to his feet with the cane, trying to fight down the nausea caused by his smoldering foot. "She's dead, we gotta get after them."

They caught up with the trio at the entrance to South Seas Resort near the far tip of Captiva — Rachel called an ambulance on the way, just in case they could do something.

A brightly illuminated golf course bordered the west shore of the island, a lone player two hundred yards downrange. An insomniac, Scarboro figured, the figure hunched over a distant hole like a tiny wedding-cake figure on green icing. Night sky overhead a deep, tuxedo black.

Scarboro figured Ray had gone the wrong way, no way off the island at this end — map showed it to be three or four miles to the mainland so swimming was out and —

"Over there behind that building," Rachel shouted, pointing at the bronze Toyota Sienna parked in shadow behind the dry-dock. Ray stood beside the vehicle, not wearing the explosive vest, apparently taking a leak into the pristine Gulf beach sand.

Scarboro figured the girl was in the van — where the hell was Chucky?

He parked along the road in deep shadow, lowered his window.

Movement down near the dock — a black cigarette-speedboat grumbled in the night, churning up a white froth behind. Looked to be Chucky at the controls. Wearing a vest.

The cons had a backup plan; must've learned *something* in the slam.

But the little girl was nowhere to be seen — either she was in the van or they dumped her. If she was in the Toyota Ray would grab her, schlep her down to the boat, maybe the flesh-broker out there waiting in some rich dude's yacht to pick her up, take her to Columbia or Saudi Arabia.

"This is as good as it's gonna get," Scarboro said through clenched teeth, "stay here."

— outside and moving, hobbling across the road toward the van, silently dropping the cane on the sand . . . soft click of the car door behind him and bare feet swishing. Rachel obeying his commands in her usual way.

At the Sienna he peered through the rear window and saw a small figure in the fetal position, lying on the floor. "She inside?" Rachel whispered, a little too loud.

— Ray spun toward them, snapped off a quick shot — *finger of blue flame snaking out, the shot missing!*

— the con sprinted down the slope onto the floating walkway, running toward the rumbling speedboat and shouting as he jumped aboard — lost his balance, nearly tumbling overboard at the far side of the pitching craft.

Scarboro watched from above as Ray regained balance — grabbed a vest from the bottom of the boat, slipped it on.

"We got her," Rachel shouted thankfully, emerging from the van with the little girl in her arms.

Scarboro could hear her assuring the kid as he hurriedly limped down to the walkway, the ramp swaying — his foot felt like a lump of molten lava. He moved to the end of the dock, peering at where the boat must be . . . out there in the dark, only the white wake visible, dimly illuminated by shore lights, rapidly moving away.

He raised the Browning and aimed, put pressure on the trigg —

From behind and above he heard Rachel's voice: "Let's call the coast guard, let them get 'em!"

But something had happened to his thinking process — irrationally vengeful about his foot as if those guys had shot him — and a dead associate lay back there at the condo. He wanted some payback.

Under his breath Scarboro whispered, "Fourth of July's coming up, I like fireworks," pulling the trigger, absorbing the recoil, re-aiming — visualized a square-yard, white outline floating in the dark above the wake — putting shot after shot into it until he'd gone through the thirteen-cartridge clip . . . slide was back, chamber open and empty, little wisp of smoke curling into the night air.

The sound of the boat motor might've changed but there was no explosion — sounded about quarter-throttle now but still running.

He lowered the Browning, disappointed at the lightless black void — had expected to flinch a little at a horrific boom, bright orange glow, pieces of boat and chunks of kidnappers hurtling through the air . . . would've been something to see.

Turned and limped up the walkway, noticing the splotch on the top of his cast. It looked dark and colorless but he knew it was actually red; blood appeared black at night — suddenly Rachel shouting from the top of the stairs, "Look," pointing toward the Gulf.

Scarboro pivoted, his foot flaring, and saw the speedboat in a tight circling pattern, going round and round, lower-throttle even than before, the curved white wake glowing against the black water like a comet's tail across a night sky.

Must've hit one of them without igniting the explosive vest — whoever it was probably fell, knocked the throttle back on his way down.

Quickly as the foot allowed he was down to the boat-slips, fired up an outboard-powered skiff by jumping the ignition, sped out into the dark, wood hull thumping over the waves, Scarboro trying to judge where the circling speed-boat would pass by . . .

— damn thing nearly swamped him on the first go-round and he maneuvered to where it would come by again . . .

Jumped aboard, landing painfully on hands and knees and right beside both empty explosive vests and a dead Chucky Dagen, wearing an orange life vest. Apparently Ray Poole had gone overboard, the victim of a skillfully placed barrage of nine millimeter slugs.

He pulled back the throttle to near-idle, the speedboat settling to level on the surface . . . maneuvered to alongside the skiff, shut off the speedboat. Scarboro summarily dumped Dagen overboard, pulling the vest off the body as he did — quickly punched a hole through the hull with a steel gaff . . . transferred himself to the skiff and waited in the dark while the speedboat sank.

— noticed a water-darkened lump bobbing in the water.

He flashed a quick beam of light on it, idled over . . .

It was Ray, barely conscious, neat hole in the orange vest just off center. Scarboro unclasped the preserver and pulled . . . Ray weakly pawed at the water as he rolled over, groaning something as he slowly disappeared beneath dark waves.

"Shouldn't hurt kids," Scarboro mumbled.

— checked the vest for any possibility it harbored a traceable slug from his Browning, tossed it into darkness. Staring after it for a couple beats, the cold fever coming on . . .

The kidnapped little girl, Amy Brandt, was standing next to Rachel on the floating dock when he pulled up in the skiff, tied the bow line to an aluminum ring. The little girl was clutching and kneading a handful of her filthy uniform skirt, gazing at him with an expression of dull fear — he was, after all, a stranger, and it'd been two strange men who'd abducted her from her father's limo outside his building in Atlanta.

Scarboro shivered — *turned suddenly* — peered up into the black shadows beyond the boathouse. Couldn't see a thing. There had been no sound of course, just the same feeling he'd experienced hundreds of times before. He shuddered heavily, like a draft horse, breathing audibly in the night air — managed to climb up out of the boat, then purposefully put some of his weight on the injured foot in an attempt to get back to himself. Didn't work. He'd already moved into the dark territory — *something was coming for him* —

Wide-eyed he glared at Rachel. "Where's your gun?"

Rachel sighed, shook her head, looked away.

Scarboro stared for a moment, fighting the disorder, clenching his teeth. He shifted full weight onto the foot, the increased pain immediately sending waves of nausea through his gut . . .

After a few beats he glanced down at the kid, noting with surprise that Rachel was holding the child's hand.

Females. Trouble.

Far in the distance, out on the brightly-lit golf course, the lone figure was standing still, appeared to be facing them, his hand held to his ear.

Cell phone. Cops.

Scarboro shifted his weight off the bad foot, paused for a moment . . . hobbled on past them toward the parked Mercedes, scanning the darkened boat yard for where he'd flung the goddamn cane — ignored the sensation of being watched from the shadows.

The little girl immediately released Rachel's hand and without coaxing fell in behind her wounded rescuer, unconsciously mimicking his limp.

Kane's Mutiny

Bev Vincent

Life isn't fair. My car's AC went out in the middle of July and I couldn't afford to get it fixed. What made it worse was sitting out on the street in my toaster oven on wheels knowing Jimmy Webber was probably cool as a penguin, wherever he was hiding out.

Webber was a bail jumper. It was my job to find him and bring him back.

Greek Phil runs Bob's Bail Bonds ("Open 24 hrs") out of a storefront down by the county jail. There's never been a Bob; Phil picked the name for the alliterative effect. He also believed people who see the triple Bs might think the Better Business Bureau endorsed him.

The BBB probably wouldn't approve of a hole in the wall operation specializing in getting crooks out of jail while they wait for their trial date. Phil's customers sign away their humanity for ten percent of the bond — up to forty percent for risky cases.

Earlier, I'd checked in with Mallory, his receptionist, to see if Phil had anything for me. On any given day, Phil's got about five mil in active bonds. Hardly a week goes by without someone doing a runner. That puts Phil on the line for the entire amount unless I can drag the yahoo's habeas corpus back to jail. When I do, I get ten percent of the bond, plus expenses. It's like the skip is paying my wages for hunting him down. I appreciate the irony.

I'd read about Webber in the paper like everyone else, surprised that he got bail at all. Even more surprised that Phil was willing to risk a quarter million on a sleazebag like that. If he'd asked me, I would've told him to just hand me my ten percent rather than filtering it through the court system and save us all the trouble. Webber had "flight risk" written all over him. Now, four months after posting bail, he'd failed to show up for his preliminary hearing.

Phil doesn't ask my opinion; he just hires me to take care of his screw-ups. No skin off my nose. The twenty-five Gs would fit in my bank account nicely. Maybe I'd buy a new car. At least get the AC fixed.

"Bogie! Good timing," Mallory said when I called. "Come by the office. I've got a file for you."

"Webber."

"How'd you know?"

"Don't ask. Be there in fifteen."

Mallory will never appear in a dictionary next to the word pretty. You know how some guys hire a babe to spiff up the place, one who can't figure out how to alphabetize the files but sure can dot your eyes? That wasn't Phil's style. He hired someone who actually knows how to run an office, didn't matter what she looked like. She was the first one to make the laborious connection between my name and profession.

"A bounty hunter named Kane? That's priceless."

I shook my head and shrugged.

"You know. The *Caine Mutiny,* with Humphrey Bogart?"

"Yeah?"

"Mutiny? You know, like *Mutiny on the Bounty?*"

"Oh. Yeah. I see."

She smiled so wide it hurt my eyes. Since then she's called me Bogie. When she tries to explain it to someone else I cringe.

I think she wants me, but I assume that about a lot of dames. Doesn't mean it's true.

So, I got the Webber file. If you think a police report is detailed, you've never seen a bail bond form. Phil knows more about these lowlifes than most of their mothers do. The only thing missing is a place to leave a piece of skin for DNA matching, and I'm sure Phil's working on that. The report lists all known associates and frequent haunts, and the kicker is that these guys almost always tell the truth. It never occurs to them that the reason Phil asks for this info is so I'll know where to start looking when they go AWOL.

Anyhow, I'm sitting in my Focus without any AC and it's ninety-five outside in the shade — and I'm not parked in the shade. I've got both front windows down half way but there's not even a hint of a breeze. I've had way too much coffee and I'm starting to glance at the empty soda bottle that I keep in case of emergencies, not looking forward to using it one little bit.

To distract my mind from my bladder, I tweaked my bobble-head Boba Fett, the Star Wars bounty hunter, our patron saint. From my dashboard he nodded his agreement that yes, indeed, this was one ungodly hot day to be sitting in the car.

The local cops knew I was working the case — that's the first thing I make sure of. They stay out of my way most of the time. They don't have the manpower to go chasing after every skip, not 24/7 like I can. Even if it is a creepazoid like Jimmy Webber, certified grade-Z scum of the earth. The cops appreciate the help and somehow the news always makes them look like the heroes when I pull someone in.

Doesn't bother me. I'm in this strictly for the thrill of the hunt.

And the dough, of course. Some guys say they're in fugitive recovery, but I'm proud to be a bounty hunter. Ain't no shame in it.

Every bail skip's got a weak point, and it's almost always a family member. Sometimes it's a wife or girlfriend, but more often it's Mom. You'd be surprised at how many grown men go running back to Mama when the chips are down.

Webber had a trophy wife — a sexy young thing who seemed oblivious to the fact that her husband was financing her lifestyle with drug money. God only knows how she ended up with such a goon. She appeared often in the society pages handing out donations at fund-raisers or dressed to the nines at some gala. In the clippings Mallory had stuck in the file, the other people faded into the background. In some photographs of her handing over an oversized check, you could almost see the recipient's conflict. Ten thousand dollars in drug profits to support the local teenage safe house. Ironic, or what?

If I had a woman like that, I know where I'd head if I were in trouble.

Mexico.

But I was counting on Webber being unable to leave those creamy thighs that peeked out from long slits in designer gowns.

Their damned street had no trees, so I parked across from the mansion in the blazing heat and watched for signs of activity. I'd already papered the neighborhood with "Wanted" notices offering a reward to juice him up a little. Someone close to Webber might appreciate the opportunity to make a little cash by ratting him out. It was worth a shot; it makes the skip nervous. He doesn't know who he can trust. Mothers have been known to turn in their sons.

I don't know how she did it. One minute I'm staring

through the binoculars, checking my side and rearview mirrors regularly, when all of a sudden she's beside my car, rapping on the roof.

I reached for my stun gun — I never carry a revolver — before I realized who it was. She looked far better in person than in any of those newspaper glamour shots. If she had reached thirty like it said in the file, it wasn't more than a few days ago. She had on this long, purple dress covered with astrological symbols, and not much else. The sunlight went right through the wispy cotton and I was in a good position to appreciate the view.

Once my heart started beating again, that is.

Never again would I cheap out on my wheels, I promised myself, feeling like a yokel running the stiff crank around to get the window down the rest of the way to talk to her. Once I brought Webber in, I was getting something with electric windows, power locks, and an AC that worked after more than twelve months of Texas heat.

"I thought you might appreciate something cold to drink," she said. Her gentle drawl sounded more Georgia than Texas.

"Is Jimmy inside?"

"Why don't you come in out of this sun so we can talk like civilized folks?"

I briefly considered the Taser, but my arrival wasn't going to be a surprise. All I took with me was a file folder containing a copy of the warrant, a letter authorizing me to make an arrest, and Mallory's info on Webber.

Until a couple of years ago, bounty hunters could break and enter to arrest someone, but the law changed after a couple of numbskulls invaded the wrong house and accidentally killed two innocent people. Now, even if we can prove the skip is in the house, we can't enter without being invited in. Just like vampires. And here I was, being ushered into my target's cool abode by a southern peach with only a thin veil of cotton between her and indecency.

What's the catch? a voice asked deep, deep inside my head, but it was so soft and masked by so many other conflicting thoughts that I didn't pay attention.

Beads of sweat on my back and legs turned to ice the minute she closed the front door. We were in an enormous entry with vaulted ceilings and tall narrow windows that wouldn't have looked out of place in a church. More irony.

The house's interior had a Caribbean feel that would have cooled me off even if the climate control hadn't been set at something like seventy-four. Selma glanced back to make sure I was following. I was a dutiful three paces behind. Far enough not to crowd her and close enough to admire the action going on beneath her dress. The stars and the planets were in motion. Call me an amateur astronomer.

"So, is Jimmy here?" I asked again.

"How does iced tea beside the pool sound? Go out through the patio doors, make yourself comfortable, and I'll be with you in a few minutes."

She disappeared down a brightly lit hallway toward what must have been the kitchen. I quickly surveyed the ground floor rooms. By the time she reappeared with a pitcher of tea and two glasses, I was standing beside the pool staring into its crystal depths. Her pool boy did a good job — it looked brand spanking new.

My bladder reminded me that I'd already had my fill of fluids for the afternoon, but I accepted the glass of tea anyway. I would have done anything she asked at that moment. I wondered which tail wagged the dog in this household.

"Appreciate the cool drink, ma'am, but you must know why I'm here."

She sipped tea slowly. Her throat, long and smooth, worked as she swallowed, then she sat on a deck chair and motioned for me to do the same. If she'd waved at the pool,

I think I would have jumped in without hesitation.

"They call you Bogie."

I nodded, though it didn't sound like a question.

"Because of the movie."

"Not many people know that," I said. "Or get it."

She leaned back in the chair and stretched her long legs out in front of her, crossing them at the ankles. A thin gold chain circled her right ankle, the only jewelry she wore. I felt the temperature rising again and had some tea. It was strong and unsweetened, just the way I like it.

I wasn't used to feeling out of my depth with people. "Where's Jimmy, ma'am?"

"Call me Selma . . . or Sel, if you like. All my friends do." Her *like* sounded like a body of water.

"Begging your pardon, ma'am, but this isn't a social call."

She sat up abruptly and leaned toward me, as if what she was about to say was of paramount importance. The scooped neck of her dress ballooned open to reveal graceful curves and hints of more. It was probably a ploy, but I took my time affording myself of the view before returning my gaze to her eyes.

"You're a detective, right?"

If she knew about Mallory's nickname for me, she knew my credentials, too. Somewhere she probably had a file on me more detailed than the one I had on her and her husband.

"Yes, ma'am. Bounty hunters have to be licensed P.I.s in Texas."

She relaxed into her chair, closing up the window on her private world. "I'd like to hire you."

"I'm already working for someone, ma'am. Trying to find your husband."

"Please, call me Sel. If we're going to be working together, we shouldn't stand on ceremony, should we, Bogie?"

"I'm not for hire." The increasing pressure in my bladder made it hard for me to sound as forceful as I wanted.

"I want you to look for my husband."

Whatever I had been expecting, this wasn't it.

"I'm already doing that. For someone else."

"You only get paid when you find him, though, right? When you bring him in?"

"Uh huh."

"I'm offering to pay for your time while you look for him."

"You don't know where he is?"

She refilled her glass and held the pitcher out toward me. I shook my head. If I drank another drop I was going to injure some internal organs I was quite fond of having intact.

"Why would I hire you to look for him if I knew where he was?"

"Why, indeed?"

She had this way of looking at me that made me feel like she was running a background check while she decided what to say next. "I'll pay you well for your time." She suggested a number that made me think I was about to be asked to do something illegal.

"To look for your husband?"

"Plus expenses, of course. That's how you detectives operate, right? Two hundred a day, plus expenses, isn't that what Rockford always says?"

Her dress was an interesting piece of work. One moment it hung so loose that I thought something important would tumble out. The next instant it clung to those very same features exactly like I imagined myself clinging to them, should the opportunity ever present itself.

"What would you want me to do when I found your husband?"

"I don't expect you to find him."

I shook my head. Stimulus overload, that's what was happening to me. The combination of the baking hot sun, far too much liquid, and Selma Webber and her wonderful astrophysical dress was more than I could handle. For a moment I contemplated peeing into her pool just to see what reaction I'd get, but I opted for a little more decorum and had her point me to the bathroom.

When I returned a few minutes later, feeling like a new man — one whose bladder wasn't on the verge of exploding — Selma had relocated to a *chaise longue*. Yards of tanned legs protruded from the bottom of her dress, which was bunched up around her thighs. The bodice was doing something completely new, both clinging and exposing.

I needed a drink, and not just iced tea.

"Let me see if I've got this straight. You want me to look for your husband, but you don't expect me to find him."

Her smile made me want to sell all my belongings and take her off to a remote desert island for the rest of my life. "You won't find him."

"Why not?"

"Let's just say he's unlikely to surface any time soon."

"Then why pay me to look for him? I mean, I appreciate the offer, and the iced tea, and the lovely view and all." I nodded toward her. "It beats the hell out of sitting in my car for the rest of the day, but I was looking for him already. I either would have found him, or I wouldn't, or someone else would."

She shrugged minutely. I was beginning to think she had invented an entirely new set of laws of physics. "Maybe I took pity on you. This way, you can look — but not too hard. Go through the motions, put on a good show. The cops know you're on the job, so they won't strain themselves. Everyone's happy."

"You're happy Jimmy's gone?"

She tossed her head a few millimeters as if nothing I said really mattered.

"This could seriously affect my success rate," I told her.

I picked up the money-stuffed envelope from the dining room table on my way out. No point in counting it. What difference did it make if she was off a little?

While I watched Selma Webber through the patio window, her magic dress performed its last trick of the afternoon, disappearing into a pool at her feet. Facing away from me, she stepped out of the puddle of cotton, turned enough to give me a quick profile shot, then executed a clean dive and disappeared beneath the pool's surface.

I pocketed the envelope and returned to my sweltering Focus, feeling like I had just had a religious experience.

Selma hadn't told me not to do my job; she'd merely suggested that looking for her husband would be a waste of time. Never one to take someone else at their word, I spent a solid week following every lead I could think up.

A morning on the computer and the telephone got me the phone records for the Webber hacienda. I plugged every outgoing and incoming number into a reverse lookup database and noted each recipient's name and address. Selma had a weakness for vegetarian pizza. Where she put it, I don't know.

In some communities, neighbors and shopkeepers are my best resources. Tell them they've got a wanted criminal down the street and they become my eyes and ears, especially if there's a couple of hundred in it. Jimmy Webber's wealthy neighbors lived in insular estates and studiously minded their own business. Two hundred bucks wouldn't make a dent in their pockets. No one I spoke with had a clue where Webber was. No one seemed to care much, either. Good riddance was the unspoken response.

Being patient is the key to success in this business, but I was quickly tiring of chasing my tail, especially when I had reason to believe Jimmy Webber was wearing cement shoes or occupying the foundation of a new building somewhere. Maybe he and Hoffa were sharing war stories in whatever purgatory is reserved for missing hoods.

By the middle of the second week, I started easing up. When an envelope of money appeared on my apartment's dining room table one morning, I treated myself to a day off while I had the AC replaced on my car.

Selma's picture ran in the newspaper's society section the next day. The photo showed a group of similarly coiffed and bejeweled rich young wives, but the other women might as well have gone to the powder room because the only real person in the picture was Jimmy Webber's wife. She faced the camera lens with a smoldering intensity that made me feel like she was looking at me.

I stopped by Greek Phil's to see if he had anything new, but it had been a quiet week. Mallory teased me about not bringing Webber in and looked shocked when I told her to can the comedy. Phil had some suggestions about where I should look. I nodded dutifully. Eventually I'd follow up, but I wasn't in a hurry. Having a regular income — especially five figures a week, tax-free — drained a lot of my motivation.

Every successful recovery ends the same, with me dragging the skip off to jail, with or without the benefit of a 50,000-volt jolt from my Taser. For me, the thrill of bounty hunting has always been matching wits with someone who doesn't want to be caught. Occasionally you encounter an adversary with more than a handful of brains and they make the job a challenge.

I didn't think Jimmy Webber posed much of a challenge, but I was starting to realize that his wife qualified as more than a trophy. She had looks and brains — a lethal combination in someone devoid of scruples.

The third envelope materialized in my locked car, tucked under the sun visor. It smelled of cash that has been through a hundred hands . . . and something else. A faint floral aroma that brought to mind a purple cotton dress covered with astrological shapes.

I spent the evening parked down the street from her house, watching lights shift from room to room. A pizza delivery car arrived shortly before eight. Vegetarian, I knew. Extra olives.

My cell phone rang at 7:45 the next morning, rousing me from a mild doze. I hadn't been asleep for more than a few minutes. I rummaged among empty fast-food containers to find the phone.

"Thank you for the pizza," Selma said. "I would have asked you to join me, but you might have gotten the wrong idea."

"I don't know what ideas I have about you," I said, groggy enough to speak the unguarded truth.

"If I invited you in for coffee, would you promise to be a gentleman?"

"No."

"The front door's open."

I found her in what I guess knowledgeable people call a breakfast nook. She wore a short night jacket decorated with a Japanese motif. It ended about three feet above her knees and barely closed in the front. I don't know why she bothered — the gown didn't have enough material to keep more than one shoulder warm at a time.

"If you want me to be a gentleman, you need to wear something besides that," I said.

Her reaction told me she heard that sort of thing all the time.

"I'll behave a little better with some coffee in me," I said.

Of course it wasn't Maxwell House, but rather something she ground fresh in the kitchen and infused through a steam gadget that blended it with hot cream. I wanted to turn my nose up at it, but it both smelled and tasted fantastic.

She perched on a stool in front of a small oval island and crossed her legs while she sipped from a transparent mug.

Her gown didn't leave many safe places to look.

"How goes the hunt?"

I met her forthright gaze and shrugged. "Another day, another two thousand dollars."

"Are you a patient man?"

Never before have I been so conscious of breathing. And I'm not talking about my own. "I can stick with a case for as long as it takes."

She nodded and sipped more coffee. "Loitering outside my house is part of the job?"

"I got bored." Her coffee tasted so good I didn't know how I could go back to the stuff I made in the one-cup machine in my apartment. I surveyed the cozy room. Pictures of Selma, alone or with friends, lined several knick-knack shelves. "No pictures of Jimmy? Or have you already boxed him up?"

"Hadn't you heard? He took off on me. Skipped bail."

That made me think. Why had Jimmy needed a bail bondsman in the first place? He could easily have posted his own bond. I asked the question.

"Why spend all that money when you can get someone else to pay most of it for you?"

And suddenly I knew why Greek Phil had agreed to take a risk with Webber. He might not hire office staff based on good looks, but that didn't mean he was invulnerable to the pleas of a beautiful woman. It also explained how Selma knew Mallory's pet name for me.

Then the rest of the pieces fell into place. I don't know why I didn't see it all before.

"You bailed him out." It wasn't a question, and she didn't treat it like one. "But how did he get arrested in the first place? I'll bet there was an anonymous phone call involved."

Her shoulders raised and fell a few millimeters. She ran some more coffee through the steam engine and refilled our cups. "Do you like it?" she asked. "The beans were on a vine in South America less than a week ago."

I blew on the surface before taking my first taste. "He's arrested for the first time in his illustrious career and his lawyer gets him out on bail. The cops probably have enough evidence to put him away for a long time, thanks to whoever set him up. So he skips bail. Everyone expected that — even I knew he was going to disappear when I read about him in the paper."

"Would you like some strawberries and cream with your coffee?" she asked. The more I looked at her, the less Japanese gown I saw. The delicate cords holding the front closed seemed to have slipped slightly in the past few minutes, but maybe that was just my imagination.

"Sure. Why not? How could you be sure he'd get bail?"

She leaned into the crisper for the strawberries and I saw stars. Could a person really be so self-aware of their effect on someone else all the time? What must it be like to occupy that pretty head of hers?

"It didn't matter one way or the other," she said.

I nodded. "Inside, he was a goner. Same deal outside, though he didn't know that. Either way, you get it all. He disappears and everyone's sure he's just another bail jumper. One of the ten or fifteen percent who's never located. He doesn't have to be found or declared dead. All this is yours anyway."

"The cream is a couple of days old," she said. "I hope it's okay."

Her act was amazing. Most of the time she ignored what I said, but every now and then she dropped a mini-bomb that told me the whole story without really saying anything. She was smart enough to know how smart I was and how much skin to flash to keep me on the hook. Men think we're the stronger sex, but I'm here to tell you it ain't so.

"Could you bear to work for me for, oh, another month

or two?"

I did the math. I wasn't going to end up rich, couldn't retire off my ill-gotten gains, but I saw a new car in my future. I'm not greedy, but I've never managed to get ahead. I gave up a chunk of money to a couple of ex-wives, and had little to show for my life's work.

All I had were suspicions, so what I was doing wasn't technically illegal. Well, okay, there's the undeclared income part, but nothing seriously bad. The government gets enough of our money as it is, don't they?

"I think I could manage two months. I may have to do some other jobs at the same time."

"No problem, so long as you make it known you're still on the case. There'll be a bonus at the end."

She wanted me to ask what it was. I wouldn't give her that satisfaction. "The cream is fine, by the way."

She smiled, and if I had any doubts they vanished in that moment.

"Bring your swimsuit next time you're in the neighborhood. Try out my swimming pool. It's new."

A confession? Or a warning? "I thought swimsuits were optional. I wouldn't mind diving in right now."

She gave me one of those burning looks that seemed only half serious.

"I never promised I was going to be a gentleman," I reminded her.

Her eyes twinkled. I was going to have to be careful around this woman. Concrete buildings and swimming pools were constructed in this city all the time.

In a passable imitation she said, "I think this could be the start of a beautiful friendship."

I dipped another strawberry in the two-day-old cream and remembered the joke about how porcupines made love.

Very carefully.

The Right Man

James S. Dorr

Mary, Mary. Mary Contrary — she had just been dumped, but life had to go on. She resented her old fianc , naturally enough. In fact, she hated him for what he had done. Leading her on like that.

Taking advantage.

It was her curse, somehow, to end up with the wrong man every time, men like Arvin who *she* should have dumped if she'd had more courage. If she had had more belief in herself.

Men like Arvin, she knew, had no future. They had no careers, they just went from job to job. And, as she knew now — she'd known this before, too — from girlfriend to girlfriend.

She found them together. In bed together. "Arvin!" she screamed.

He had answered her, smooth as silk, "Mary, I told you never to let yourself in with your key like that, without knocking first."

Then he had dumped *her.*

"Mary," he had said, "we can't go on like this if you

won't trust me."

But she had read somewhere: Today is the first day of the rest of your life. So it would be, she vowed.

Make lemonade from lemons, that was her motto — but more to the point, she got a new boyfriend.

His name was Giuseppe. He was everything Arvin was not. Tall, clean-shaven, smooth. He lived in a nicer part of the city — but not *too* nice. Not in so high-toned a neighborhood that Mary felt out of place.

He wore suits and ties to work, not jeans like Arvin did. When Arvin *had* work.

But Mary realized, just like every cloud had a silver lining, the reverse was true too. Nothing was perfect.

"Giuseppe," she asked him once, "why are you out of town so many times? Sometimes on such short notice we have to break dates — dates I've looked forward to."

"Mary, Mary," he said. He kissed her. "Mary, you know I'm disappointed too. But it's the business. You know how it is, you start at the bottom, you work your way up. Right now, it's me that has to go out of town, go on the business trips. That's what the boss says. But one of these days, you'll see, I'll work myself up. I'll be a boss myself, then other guys'll have to go out of town."

Mary kissed him back. Giuseppe had such a romantic accent — the way he talked was like a movie she'd once seen on TV. Something on the Lifetime channel, movies they made just for women like her.

That was the first time she let Giuseppe get his hands in her bra. Giuseppe was like that, always a gentleman. Never trying to move too fast for her, never doing anything like that with her until he was sure he had her okay first.

Not like Arvin.

Giuseppe told her once, "It comes from being a Catholic. I mean from being raised as a Catholic, to have respect for women like you. For *ladies* like you."

That was the time she gave him her okay to do a lot more than just get his hands on her titties.

She had a job too, a dime-store sales job. Well, not a dime store literally anymore, but she worked behind a counter. Cosmetics and perfumes.

She got samples sometimes, new products the drummers would bring around to sell. She and the other salesgirls would try them on, then she'd go back to the apartment Giuseppe and she now shared when he was in town. It was a bigger place than she could afford alone, but she insisted on chipping in something, even though Giuseppe had told her he'd rather go the whole rent by himself. He was sweet that way.

By now the two of them practically were engaged, but not quite engaged yet. Giuseppe was sweet about things that way too. He admitted he wasn't sure he was ready to make that big a commitment yet, nor that, he suspected, she was either. Even though she *was.* He said he didn't want to hurt her, if things didn't work out.

Not like Arvin she thought, still seething. Still remembering — her humiliation when he had dumped *her.* This was after *he* had insisted they be engaged — even though he'd never bought her a ring — using it as an excuse to get them shacking up together, even though she had wanted to wait. She'd wanted to get to know him better.

And not like Arvin had been the first either.

But with Giuseppe, well, she knew he was a man of honor. She didn't know everything about him yet, but that was part of the fun of romance. She had met his mother —

his father was deceased, some kind of accident that the family didn't like to talk about, which she could understand. As for the mother, she was sort of shifty-eyed — some sort of tic that made it hard for her to look directly at Mary — but she was open and warm and friendly. Very "Old World," with an accent like her son's, but a lot stronger. Very religious, with crosses on the walls.

But to the point, at Mary's work they sometimes got cosmetic samples, which she'd try on and show to Giuseppe. Giuseppe had taste that way. He could tell her which lines would sell, which ones made her look ladylike, as opposed to those what weren't so good, that perhaps were too garish — that just made her look cheap. She used what he told her in her job sometimes, steering customers to products that would be the best selections for them. Telling them also what to avoid, but telling them why, too, and always showing them what would be better. Leaving them happy, and ready, the next time, to come back to her counter for their next purchases.

Her boss noticed this and gave her a raise — over and above her commissions. He also gave her a promotion, along with the afternoon off to celebrate.

Mary went home to share the good news, but Giuseppe wasn't there. Of course, she thought. He'd still be at work.

Then it occurred to her she didn't really know where it was he worked, where his office was those times he wasn't being sent out of town.

She rarely went through his drawers or his closet — in fact she never did. Unlike some that she'd had in the past, this was a relationship that *was* based on trust, and, when Giuseppe had asked her when she moved in to leave his personal things alone — "It's just man stuff, you know," he had said, "things that wouldn't interest a lady like you" — she'd been okay with that. But now she wondered, perhaps there was an address somewhere, or a phone number she could use to call him.

But then their own phone rang.

She had, of course, wondered at times if there might be some other woman that he was seeing, those times he was out of town. But he wasn't out of town all that often, and it was becoming less and less often now, as he had told her once or twice of advancements in *his* work, just like he had promised.

"I'll work myself up," he'd said, "then other guys'll have to go out of town."

Still her hand trembled, just a little, as she picked up the phone.

What if the call was from a woman?

But it was no woman. The voice was a man's, who called himself Angelo. "What is this," Angelo said, "has Giuseppe got some kind of answering service or something?"

"Uh — uh, sort of," Mary said. "This is Mary. If you'd like, I can take a message."

"Yeah? Well, okay, Mary. Normally I wouldn't just talk to anyone like this, but Giuseppe's mentioned a 'Mary' to me once, and anyway this is sort of an emergency. Like they could get someone local to do it, but usually we like it to be someone from out of town, like it's harder to trace it that way, you know?"

Mary didn't know quite what to say. "Uh — uh, yeah," she stammered.

"Well, good. So you tell Giuseppe this, that Angelo called and he should call back if there's any problems. He knows the number. I need him to get on a plane to Detroit — the first one he can get out of La Guardia. I got a job for him."

Mary wrote this down. "Uh, sure," she said.

"Good. You tell him that Angelo owes him a favor then — a *big* favor. If there's anything one of the guys from Detroit can do for him . . ."

Mary wrote that down too. "Sure, Angelo," she said. "I'll see that he knows."

She wasn't stupid. She had watched other movies on TV than just romances on the Lifetime channel those nights when Giuseppe was out of town. She went to their bedroom and to his closet, the one he had for himself, and got a chair to stand on when she looked on the shelf. She got a flashlight so she could see better as she moved some old coats or something out of the way to see what was behind them.

She knew better than to touch anything so she just gaped when her light caught the glint of blue gunmetal.

She forced the issue. She gave the message to Giuseppe when he came in a half hour later, and she knew that he knew she wasn't stupid. While he was in Detroit she went to the library and looked up newspapers, and books as well. She wasn't surprised when he got back home the evening after and greeted her with an armload of roses.

"Mary," he said, "put on your nice clothes. I'd like us to go out to eat tonight, anywhere you suggest."

She nodded. "Yes," she said. "There's a new place that's just opened up I've been thinking about. We might go there."

She paused and gulped. "Giuseppe, we've got to talk."

"I know," he said. "But not till we get there."

She nodded again. Then, over dinner, she told him about her past. About Arvin. About before Arvin. About her bad luck in romance before *then*. "Giuseppe," she said, "I've thought, with you, that lightning had finally struck. You know what I mean? Like in you I've found the right man for me, finally. But now, with this . . ."

Giuseppe winced. "Mary," he started, "it's not what you think . . ."

Mary shook her head. "It *is* what I think. But that's not

the point. Giuseppe, it's time that we stopped having secrets from each other, that we finally made a commitment — that's what *I* think. That we should start talking about getting married."

"You mean you want us to be engaged? In spite of . . ."

She nodded. "Yes."

Giuseppe leaned over the table and kissed her, then broke into a grin. "Mary," he said, "I've *wanted* to ask you. You don't know how much — except I was afraid. You know, my profession . . ."

"All I know is you're getting advancements, isn't that right? Just like you promised. That pretty soon you'll be a sub-boss or something and won't have to go out on the road so much?"

He nodded himself now. "Yes," he said. "But — do you mind that I don't have a ring to give you? That is, not on me. I mean, tomorrow we can pick one out. Maybe a ring for every finger if that's what you'd like. But do you mind, Mary, if I ask you to marry me right now?"

Mary had trouble holding back tears, she was so happy. "Of course I don't mind," she said. She took a deep breath. "And as for a ring, I don't need a ring.

"But there is something else . . ."

"Yes?" Giuseppe said.

"Well," she said, "it's about your friend Angelo. You know, from Detroit — that owes you a favor?" She rummaged in her purse. "I've still got a picture of Arvin here somewhere, and I was thinking. For his first contract . . ."

Killer Legs

Chelle Martin

"Killer."

The word snapped me out of deep thought. Not only because the term was frequently used in my line of work, but also because the only other occupant in the elevator was blatantly staring at my legs.

I shifted slightly as I gauged his appearance. Wedding ring — blatant cheater. Designer suit — wealthy or wanting to appear so. Shoes — sported the shine of a new pair. Bad hairpiece — well, what could really be said about that?

I longed to swipe the salacious grin from his face. Because if he thought the obvious bulge in his trousers was going to impress me, I would impress him more. I casually adjusted my jacket to reveal the .38 I carried. His grin disappeared like magic, while I smiled until our car arrived at the casino floor. Not surprisingly, he exited abruptly and walked ahead of me, never looking back.

Atlantic City may not possess the glitz of Las Vegas, but it nevertheless attracts millions of visitors a year. On occasion, I'm one of them. But on this particular night in June, I'm here on business.

I passed through the skywalk and took the short ride down the escalator to the front desk where I asked the clerk to ring Mrs. Gorton's room and announce my presence. Moments later, I arrived at a luxury suite reserved for exclusive use by casino whales, the aquatic nickname given to high rollers.

I knocked on the door, wondering what my client might look like. It wasn't long before a well-coifed, tastefully dressed woman in her sixties answered the door.

"I'm Ivy Parton," I said, handing her my card.

Mrs. Francine Gorton welcomed me inside and motioned for me to sit in the elegantly furnished living area.

Wasting no time, she said, "I've dismissed the help so we can talk in private. Would you care for something to drink?"

I opted for a blackberry brandy and let her talk while I sipped.

"I just know something isn't right about Conover's death. The police have ruled it a robbery resulting in homicide, but I think Conover knew his killer." At the mention of his name, she produced a photograph of her late husband. Also in his sixties, his photo projected a warm smile beneath pale blue eyes and a full head of white hair.

Mrs. Gorton wrung her hands as she spoke, but her voice held steady. "Something was on his mind of late, but he wouldn't talk about it. I think he may have gotten himself into something . . . illegal."

"What makes you think that, Mrs. Gorton?"

"Please, call me Francine."

I nodded.

"I went through Conover's personal belongings that were returned to me after they checked his room." She motioned about the place. "He stayed in this very suite.

"I noticed that he'd written several large checks, all made out to cash. Our accountant looked into it and found that Conover had cashed each one himself. All through the casino credit desk."

"That's not unusual, Francine. Not for the amounts that your husband dropped here." I considered her statement. "Just what kind of money are we talking about?"

"All totaled, close to two million dollars." She held up a hand before I could speak. "Yes, he could afford to lose it. But Conover never wrote personal checks to cover his gambling costs. He played here on credit, and Sheldon Bennett, our accountant, handled payments of any debts my husband accrued. I'd like to know where the money went, Miss Parton. I think it might be a clue to who killed him."

"So you believe the money wasn't spent here?"

Francine nodded. "Do you think you can help me?"

"There are no guarantees," I told her. "There may not be anything to contradict a B&E," I said, then explained, "breaking and entering. Your husband may have simply been surprised by an intruder who didn't want to leave a witness." I reminded her of my rates. I don't come cheap, but she could obviously afford me.

"Please," she said, "if anyone can uncover the truth, I know you can." She smiled. "You've come highly recommended."

"Mind if I have a look around?" I asked. Her husband died in this suite ten days ago, so I really didn't expect to find much in the way of evidence. Still, it was always best to begin at the scene of the alleged crime.

Francine took her leave while I poked through drawers and checked closets and under furniture. The rooms boasted of luxuries at their finest: an oversized sunken hot tub, large screen televisions in the master bedroom and living areas, a hidden television in a rich wood cabinet in the guest room that raised at the touch of a button, remote dimmer lights, a completely stocked bar, a sauna, an exercise room, a large mirror over the king size bed, several authentic oil paintings by well-known artists, and more gadgets than you'd see at The Wiz. Not to mention the penthouse view of the Atlantic City beach, boardwalk, and ocean. Indeed, Conover Gorton had lived the high life.

Satisfied that I hadn't overlooked anything, I decided it was time to check elsewhere. But just as I was about to close the door to the master suite, I noticed something lying near the bed skirt. I bent to retrieve the silky yellow strand. It looked as though it had been plucked from a graduation cap's tassel. As I fingered the object, I took a mental inventory of the rooms I'd passed through. It hadn't come from any of the draperies within the suite. I opened my purse and slipped the strand into an interior pocket for contemplating again later.

Returning to the lobby, I made my way to the casino credit area and settled into an empty chair while I waited for an attendant. Down the aisle from me, a machine was ringing loudly and drawing a crowd to the jackpot winner. Of course, this was the quarter machine area, not the high roller room where Conover Gorton would have been playing.

Momentarily, a woman named Monica Howard greeted me. From my purse I withdrew a picture of my client's husband and inquired as to whether she recognized him. "No," she replied, "But I've only worked here a week. Perhaps you'd like to speak to the Credit Services Manager."

Monica motioned to an older, well-dressed woman with frosted gray hair. After a brief exchange between the two, the woman took Monica's seat and extended a hand toward me. "I'm Anne Watts. Miss Howard tells me you're inquiring about someone whom you think may have used our services."

When I asked her about Gorton, she immediately recognized the name and the face. "Yes, he was here frequently. Why do you ask?"

I handed her my card. "I'm investigating his death," I said. "He was murdered in this hotel," I said, keeping my voice low. She didn't appear surprised, so perhaps she'd read about it in the papers or had been informed of his passing by the casino since he was both a regular and a whale.

"How can I help you?" she asked.

"Do you recall the last time he visited your department?"

"I can tell you in a moment," she said. Her fingers tapped away at the computer keyboard on the desk. "According to our records, he was here last on the 4th."

That was the day before he was killed. I jotted the information in my notebook.

"Did he cash a personal check on that day?"

Anne Watts hesitated as if to weigh how much information she was willing to give me. To encourage her cooperation, I added, "I have access to his personal accounting records, but you'd do me a favor by saving me the time."

"It was the largest check he cashed with us. Two hundred thousand dollars," she said.

Another note in my book. I extended my hand, thanked her, and decided to take a look around the casino floor. Francine had told me her husband favored the blackjack tables and the hundred dollar slot machines.

Neither gaming area was hard to find. There were only two high roller tables, and the high roller slot machines were in a secluded area partitioned from the main floor. I hit the machines first. There were numerous five dollar machines in that section, along with a generous amount of ten and twenty-five dollar ones. There were only two boasting $100 coin slots. I figured the best way to get attention was to sit at one of them.

I pulled several bills from my purse and fed them into the bill taker. The sign above said play one or two coins. If I were Conover Gorton, I suppose that would have been standard procedure, but I preferred to play slowly and make my money last. One pull. Nothing. Second pull. Nothing. Third pull. One cherry, which awarded me three hundred dollars. I was even again.

I sensed a presence over my shoulder. Normally, I would have been annoyed at being watched. But since I was on assignment, it gave me an opening. I turned, crossing one leg over the other in the process. The move caused a downward shift of his eyes, but only for a moment before he met my gaze.

"That machine usually pays," he said.

"Is that so?" I asked. "Does that mean it's a favorite of yours?"

"I switch between the two," he said, nodding toward the other hundred-dollar machine. "When one doesn't hit, the other usually does."

"So you're a regular here?" I asked.

"Regular enough," he said, and extended a hand. "Dan Potter."

He settled at the machine next to me, withdrew a large number of bills, and fed them in. Several pulls later, his machine started ringing, and the top light flashed a jackpot. It wasn't the top prize, but it was $7,500. Nice chunk of change.

"I guess you took the lucky machine," I said, as mine registered another cherry. So it would take me a little longer. At least I wasn't broke yet.

The attendants arrived within minutes to congratulate Dan, left briefly, and then returned with a large stack of bills.

As the one attendant counted off the last of them, Dan took two bills and gave each one a tip. Not bad work if you can get it.

They weren't gone long when my machine started ringing. I'd hit triple bars combined with a wild symbol. "Five grand," I said and smiled. Dan high-fived me.

"Looks like your luck is changing," he said.

The attendants returned to collect my identification and social security number as they had done with Dan. When they returned with my cash, I was ready with questions.

Slipping a bill into each of their hands, I said, "Before you go, can you tell me if you remember this man?" I flashed Conover Gorton's picture.

Both nodded simultaneously. "He's a regular," the taller of the two, nametag Jason Wilkins, said. "Likes these two machines in particular."

"When was the last time you saw him?"

They both looked at each other as if in consultation. "About three weeks ago?" the shorter one, nametag Drew Pearson, said to his friend, who nodded again. "He hasn't been here for awhile."

I guess news didn't travel down the ladder. "Did you wait on him frequently?"

"Oh, yes. Mr. Gorton was a hefty tipper. We would bring him whatever he wanted, whenever he wanted."

"Like?"

"Cigars, drinks, sometimes even caviar or whatever food he was craving that night. He even asked for my cell phone the last time he was here."

"You're allowed to carry personal phones on the job?"

"Well . . . no," Jason said, realizing he could get into hot water.

"I'm not here to cause trouble," I said. "I'm an investigator."

"Did Mr. Gorton do something wrong?"

"Not that I know of." Yet. I handed each of them my card. "If you remember anything odd about his last couple of visits, please give me a call." To encourage any such memories to resurface, I slipped each another fifty.

When I turned my attention back to my machine, Dan was still playing away. "I believe you dropped this from your purse," he said, handing me the tassel strand. "You frequent Legs often?"

"Legs?" I asked.

"You mean you didn't get it there?"

My puzzled expression led him to elaborate. "Legs is a bar on Pacific. Gentlemen's club, to put it a nice way." He grinned.

"I gather you've been there."

"A time or two. It's almost a requirement if you're a high roller, but some of us slip in there on occasion."

I gather he didn't consider himself a high roller, even though his profits were eagerly being gobbled up with each pull of the handle. Or, in these days, push of the button.

"What made you associate the strand with Legs?"

"Girls there have a tradition of snipping a tassel from their pasties as a souvenir for big tippers. But these dancers aren't in the front room. They're in the Gold Room. Makes it more exotic I guess, and major players want the best. Only those who can afford to get in, get in."

"How do they know who can afford to get in?"

"There's a five hundred dollar cover for the Gold Room."

"Where abouts on Pacific is the club?"

"Near the north end of the Boardwalk. You can't miss it. It's more or less a landmark. It's been here forever."

"Thanks," I said, printing out my remaining balance. After taking the receipt to the window for a cash exchange, I headed back to the parking garage. Perhaps I had my first lead.

The south end of Atlantic City always seemed a bit less sleazy than the north to where I was headed. As I drove up Pacific, I realized how long it had been since I'd been in that part of town. Once decrepit buildings had been torn down. In their place were new high rises, new businesses, a vacant lot or two, and a landscaped area, which served as somewhat of a park. Perhaps casino tax dollars were going to some good use after all.

I was almost to the end of the strip when a pair of pink kicking neon legs came into view. Glowing brightly below them was the club name, Legs. Dan had been right. Not hard to miss.

Street parking was hard to come by, so I swung my black H2 into self-park at the nearest casino and hiked across the street. Not many people lurking on the boulevard tonight. Even the hookers weren't on the block, or perhaps they'd changed locations when the wrecking ball swung by.

I pushed my way through the front door of the club and waited for my eyes to adjust to the darkness.

"You looking for someone, miss?" The man at the door was well dressed, with a greasy slicked-back do and gold jewelry on every body part visible. And probably on some not so visible, though I had no desire to know.

"You might say so," I said, pulling the gold tassel strand from my purse.

The guy almost salivated at the sight. Was it the cover charge, or did he think I was there to flirt with the babes? He just nodded. "You've been here before, then. Enjoy," he said, waving me through. The two men who entered after me were asked for ID and informed of the $30 cover charge, which had obviously been waived in my case.

Music blared, while several topless dancers were doing their thing on dance poles. No tassels here. Just G-strings in which to collect tips. I stood off to the side for a moment to analyze the crowd. Variety of ages, though mostly thirties to fifties. All male, which was no big surprise.

Slowly I made my way toward the opposite end of the bar where another doorman stood. A black curtain separated the renowned Gold Room from the rest of Legs. This time I had to delve into my slot profits and cough up the required $500 admission fee. No stamping of hands followed. I assumed if you came out, you would have to pay again to reenter.

Plush barrel seats surrounded private tables, giving patrons an up close look at whoever was dancing at their station. Each table could seat about five people comfortably. I was led to a table with two patrons and a dance already in progress. Pink tassels decorated her pasties. I needed to find the owner of the gold ones.

As my escort turned to go, I noticed another table, completely empty. "Do you mind?" I shouted over the music. He shrugged his shoulders, which I took to mean he couldn't care less, so I seated myself.

A waitress soon took my drink order, while I waited for the entertainment to show up. I'd been in worse joints, though I would much rather have avoided the place had I a choice. Unfortunately, the tassel was my only lead at the moment.

Five minutes later, my ginger ale arrived, and soon after a slender brunette with straight shoulder-length hair appeared on center stage, where she did a few pole gyrations before stepping onto my private table. Adorned with pasties and blue tassels, she moved well to a Bon Jovi tune, and it was nearly impossible to catch her eye as she danced. I pulled the gold tassel from my purse once more and tried to lure her to eye level. I imagine each dancer had their own ritual of bump and grind, followed by the pasties in your face to collect their tips. As the song finished and something slower began, she made her descent and spotted the sliver of gold.

I motioned for her to come closer so I could ask about the tassel. "A friend of mine got this. I'd like to find the owner."

"Nadine," she shouted. "Backstage."

"Could I meet her?" I asked. "Just for a minute?"

"What's it worth to you?" she asked.

I pulled a hundred dollar bill from my purse and laid it on the table. She discreetly took it and slid it into her G-string. "Outside, around back." She motioned to an exit door.

I slid from my seat and hastily walked toward the door, hoping nobody would stop me. If anything, I would tell them I needed a breath of fresh air.

Safely outside, I ventured down an alley to the back stage door, which the brunette held ajar. "In here," she said.

The contrast of the dressing area to the bar stage was startling. No d cor to speak of. Just several racks of clothing on wheels and a row of seats with makeup mirrors and accessories arranged at each station. Women paraded around in various stages of undress.

The brunette pointed Nadine out to me, and then went about her own business. I sat in the makeup chair next to her. "Got a minute?"

She was layering on heavy eye shadow, which covered more than her costume. "Do I know you?" she asked.

"No, but perhaps you know my friend," I said, producing a photo of Conover Gorton.

"Wink?" she asked.

"Excuse me?"

"The girls know him as Wink. On account of he winks a lot to get their attention. Good tipper."

"Did you give him this?" I asked, showing her the tassel strand. It matched the so-called outfit she wore at the moment.

"Wink's got a whole collection of those. Not just mine." She put down her eye shadow and started outlining her lips in pencil. "Who are you? His daughter or his mistress?"

"What makes you think he had either?"

She shrugged her shoulders.

"Nadine, Mr. Gorton . . . Wink, was murdered recently. I'm investigating his death."

"You a cop?" she asked, her eyes slanting suspiciously.

"Private investigator," I said, producing my card. "If you can think of anything he might have said to you that might help my investigation, please give me a call."

Nadine glared at me, but said nothing.

I slipped out the side door again, planning to take the alley to the street. I hadn't gotten far, when I heard footsteps behind me. Instinctively, my hand went to my gun, but before I could retrieve it, I was grabbed from behind and knocked against the building.

"Unless you're applying for a job here, I don't want to see you near the girls, got it?" In my peripheral vision, I could make out the face of the bouncer who had greeted me upon entering.

"You got something to hide?" I asked.

He tightened his grip on my arm, and I gritted my teeth against the pain. It didn't help that I was off balance with my cheek scraping the wall.

I figured my smart-ass question would produce a less than desirable answer, but I heard a moan, and then he crumpled onto the ground beside me. My gun now in hand, I turned to find the blue pasty girl holding a brick.

"C'mon," she said, grabbing my arm and pulling me back down the alley toward the stage door. "Give me a second," she said. And she'd meant it, for it only took her that long to grab a pair of sweat pants and a T-shirt from inside, which she hustled into in nothing flat. "Go, go, go," she said, swinging her purse onto her shoulder. Neither of us stopped until we navigated the back end of the bar and came out onto the strip again from the opposite direction. From there, she hurried me down a block and into a dingy all-night coffee shop.

We slunk into a corner booth in the back. She opted to watch the door, since she'd be able to spot whomever she expected to follow us.

Fumbling for a cigarette, she managed to light it. I gave her ample time to catch her breath before asking, "Bozo back there, what was his problem?"

"He's got it bad for Nadine."

"What's your name?" I asked.

"Amanda Wazinsky."

"Thanks, Amanda," I said. "Now you mind telling me what's going on with Nadine and Conover Gorton?" I asked, showing her his photo.

"Wink. I shoulda known that would set her off. She's pissed that he's gone."

"So she knows he was murdered?"

"Murdered? The paper said he died in a robbery."

"Don't always believe everything you read," I said. She was young, but she didn't strike me as ignorant. "So Gorton was a regular at Legs?"

"Oh, yeah," she said, nodding her head vigorously. "Only whatever Nadine did, he wound up asking only for her."

"Define 'did'?"

She raised her brows. "I think you legal types would call that speculation. Did she turn tricks? Probably. Wink was her Sugar Daddy, and she let it be known that he was hands off to anyone else at the club."

"She could do that?"

"With Manny Tantoli's help. He's the one that chased you down the alley. I think they rolled a lot of whales and split the profits."

"What's Nadine's last name?"

"Risenbach."

I wrote it in my notebook. "You aren't going back there?" I asked.

Amanda laughed. "Nope, I'm on the next bus back to Philly," she said. "I was never cut out for this. I'm a student on summer break. A friend of mine came up here with me, but she quit last week. We figured we could make some good money to help pay tuition, you know? For what we made in tips some nights, we'd have to wait tables for an entire summer."

I nodded, but offered no advice. It seemed she already learned that a strip joint didn't offer a future.

"You have to gather your things?" I asked. "Do you need someone to help you?"

"I'll be fine," Amanda said. "I only have one suitcase to pack. It's not like I needed a big wardrobe for work." She laughed, and I couldn't help joining in.

"Where did you get Nadine's tassel?" she asked.

"I found it in my client's hotel room."

"You think she killed him?"

"That's what I'm trying to find out. Anything else you can tell me?"

She shook her head. "Aren't you afraid?" she asked. "I mean your job is kinda dangerous."

"What can I say? The money's good, and I can't dance."

The whole time we were there, no one bothered to take our order. Amanda extinguished her cigarette, and we went our separate ways.

I could tie Nadine to Gorton, but I still needed a motive for murder. If he had indeed been her Sugar Daddy, then decided he wanted out, that could have, as Amanda put it, "pissed Nadine off" enough to want to kill him.

I surmised that the large checks Gorton had been cashing were to pay Nadine's expenses. Probably a luxury apartment, not to mention the requisite jewels, perhaps a car, and spending money to keep the girl looking good.

Something told me to return to the scene of the crime, so I drove back to the south end of the strip and again visited Gorton's suite. I gave Francine a brief rundown of the night's events, and then proceeded to the master suite a second time. I planted myself on the king size bed and glanced around the room. After scanning the ceiling and the walls, I got up to take a closer look at the big screen television. I ran a hand over the top and sides and inspected the rim. Nothing unusual. Then I noticed the large painting to the side of it. Upon careful inspection, a tiny hole, almost imperceptible to the naked eye, had been poked through the dark green paint that comprised flower stems. I tilted the frame away from the wall and discovered the surveillance wire that ran from the picture into the wall behind it. And upon further investigation, it didn't take long to find that the wall housed a closet on the other side. On the highest shelf, a recording device had been set up to capture the action in the room. Now I was getting somewhere. I doubted if Gorton had been taping his trysts with Nadine, but it seemed likely Nadine would stand to make a few extra bucks through blackmail.

My next step was to find Jason Wilkins, the slot attendant with the cell phone. Luckily his shift hadn't ended yet, and I found him writing up a win for a lady in the high roller slot room.

When he finished, I motioned for him, and he came over. I sat at my former machine, so as not to draw attention. "I need your cell phone number," I said. "Part of the investigation."

He looked nervous, but I assured him he would be assisting in providing justice. With that, he rattled off ten digits to me. I thanked him and headed back to the H2 where I had a special setup to aid in my investigations.

My fifteen-year-old cousin was a whiz kid when it came to hacking into things. Thanks to him, I had access to all sorts of goodies that saved me time and aggravation. One of them was a direct link to telephone records.

I punched in the numbers Wilkins gave me and searched the records to see who Gorton had called on the borrowed cell phone. Bingo. Nadine Risenbach's name and address appeared. She conveniently lived in a high rise directly on the beach next door to the casino.

I locked up the SUV and headed to the boardwalk. The crowd was thick with tourists, and the rickshaw guys were busy hauling fares up and down the strip. Several asked if I'd like transport, but I waved them away.

I entered the condo lobby from the boardwalk entrance, found the elevator, and took it to the ninth floor. The door to 905, Nadine's apartment, was slightly ajar. With nobody on the floor, I pulled my .38 and knocked softly. No reply.

Cautiously I entered the room, scanned the open area, and found the place had been trashed top to bottom. After checking the entire living quarters, I locked the apartment door, and began a search of my own.

Everything imaginable had been torn apart, so there weren't many viable hiding places left, and evidently, somebody had been looking for something in particular.

I sifted through clothes, shoes, papers, but found nothing of interest. The casino suite's closet had been lucky, so I righted a chair and dragged it into the bedroom to get a better look at the top shelf to see if anything was tucked away in a corner. Nothing. I turned to step off, when something caught my eye on a ceiling fan. I moved the chair and discovered a key taped to a blade. Looked like a safety deposit box key to me. I drew my wallet from my purse and slipped it into the zippered coin pocket. I knew the puzzle was coming together.

"Nadine?" a voice called from the outer room. Somebody apparently had a key to the place besides her.

Shit. Through the slit in the door I recognized Bozo the bouncer from Legs. I flattened myself behind the bedroom door, .38 in hand. A second later, the door pushed open, and he stepped inside.

"Hold it," I said, leveling the gun at him and stepping out to get a clear shot if need be.

"What the hell are you doing here?"

"You first," I said, giving the gun a slight wave.

"Looking for my wife," he said.

"Your wife?" My voice sounded incredulous even to myself.

"Nadine and I were married last weekend," he answered.

Right after Gorton was murdered. That was certainly convenient. "Well, Manny, looks like she isn't here," I said. "Maybe she skipped out on you with Gorton's money."

His eyes lit up, and I knew I hit a nerve. For his sake, I hoped he didn't play poker.

Time to cast a line. "Don't think I don't know about the tapes of Nadine and Gorton. Nice little setup you had at the hotel. Guess you didn't get time to dismantle it, or were you planning to make a career out of milking high rollers?"

"You ain't got a thing, bitch," he said.

A board creaked in the hallway, and a second later I caught a glimpse of Nadine in the dresser mirror, gun in hand. I swung to face her, backing out of Manny's reach at the same time.

"Don't be a fool, Nadine," I said. "I know about the tapes. I know Gorton was paying for this place. You just used him to set up a nice nest egg for you and your hubby here."

Her eyes darted to him. The *hubby* reference had done it. She had to wonder at what we'd been chatting about.

Manny sidled over to her, but she refused to give him the gun. "You shouldn't be poking your nose around. In fact, this looks like a B&E," she said. "And I shot you in self-defense."

I grinned slyly. "Like poor Conover. The paper said he died during a B&E, too. You could have tried being a bit more original."

Her face twisted angrily, and she fired in my direction. I'd already rehearsed in my mind the direction in which I'd dive, so I threw myself onto the bed and rolled off to take cover behind it. The first bullet had whizzed close to my ear, shattering the window behind me. The second two thudded into the thick mattress with the former exiting into the floor and the latter into the wall just over my head.

If I stayed put, I was dead for sure. Without hesitation, I crouched low, and then popped up like a duck in a shooting gallery and got off three shots of my own, which sent Nadine and Manny scurrying from the doorway. Keeping low, I heard Manny urging Nadine out of the apartment. When I was sure I could make it to the doorway, I jumped to my feet and braced myself inside the frame before turning to shoot at whatever awaited me inside the living room. Nothing. The door to the hall was open, and I heard voices and footsteps in the corridor.

Retrieving my purse from the floor, I shoved my gun inside it and headed for the stairwell, knowing my attackers had headed for the elevator. I arrived in the lobby in time to see them heading out the door to the adjacent parking lot.

By the time I caught up, Manny was at the wheel with Nadine riding shotgun. As their sedan backed up, nearly knocking me over, I was able to grab their bumper for a fraction of a second before pushing myself off safely to the side. Tires squealed, and I watched their tail lights disappear around the corner.

I'd turned my ankle in the parking lot, so I hobbled to

my Hummer as quickly as I could. Safely inside, I switched on my tracking system. A small map of the city appeared along with a flashing light pinpointing the sedan's location. Shifting into gear, I turned on my speakerphone, while heading down the avenue. Eight cylinders hummed noisily as I picked up speed, darting in and out of traffic.

I punched in 911 and stated my emergency and location. The operator quickly transferred the call.

"Sergeant Baylor, A. C. P. D."

I identified myself and gave a brief description of the earlier shootout at the high rise. The Sergeant radioed to his men in the area, and in the distance, I could hear sirens, while I pinpointed the sedan's location.

A few blocks later, I arrived to find Manny and Nadine surrounded by the city's finest. My job was over. For the most part.

I surrendered the safe deposit box key to Sergeant Baylor. He traced it to a local bank, where its contents revealed two videotapes, several hundred thousand dollars in cash, and a Rolex that was engraved with Conover Gorton's initials.

Baylor suggested it might have been Manny who ransacked Nadine's room looking for the tapes and money, though Manny wasn't talking. Perhaps my visit to Legs had put a scare into him, enough to make him want to take the cash and split, only Nadine was too clever to leave the money lying around. Or so she thought.

As further evidence, the police confiscated the camera and recording device from the suite at the casino hotel. The prints taken from it matched those on the tapes.

When the prosecutor was certain he had a case against Nadine and Manny, I met with Francine to give her the good news. This time she had checked into a deluxe room. Nice, but a far cry from the amenity-filled suite.

"Well, you were right," I said to Francine. She sat across from me, looking forlorn. "I'm sorry that certain things came up that you probably didn't suspect."

"He was a good man," she said, looking directly at me. "Whatever he may have done, he's not the first."

"No," I said simply, feeling her pain. Like many of my clients, Francine Gorton, had sought the truth to find justice, only to be hurt in the outcome.

"The money and the Rolex will be returned to you after the trial," I said.

She nodded.

I stood to leave, and she thanked me again. Moments later, I waited for the elevator.

When the door opened, I grinned. There stood the guy I'd met upon my arrival, bad hairpiece and all. For a moment, his eyes twinkled when he saw me.

"So we meet again," I said. He sobered up quickly and feigned checking his watch.

That's better, I thought. You don't mess with these legs.

A Flat, Dismal Whiteness

Dorothy Rellas

Sully stood in front of the desk, clasping his sweating hands behind him. The first time he'd been called to see Lippozi alone. Which probably meant he'd be told he was out.

"How you doin,' Sully?" Lippozi asked him.

"Pretty good."

Lippozi leaned back and studied him with narrowed eyes. It wouldn't be the end of the world to be booted out of the organization, of course. He was getting tired of sitting around Vicanzo's Bar, waiting for orders from Lippozi, watching the card games, listening to the wise-guys detail their latest conquest. The litanies were boring. Sully could give them all a few tips. And he'd know soon enough whether his rules for meeting women still worked. At not quite thirty, he'd be bar-hopping again now that Rosie had walked out on him.

Sully shifted, uncomfortable under Lippozi's appraisal. Rosie's last words floated through his mind.

"Time you got some smarts," she'd told him. "Stand up to people. Do something with your life."

The memory was tinged with a surge of regret because he really did miss her. And he'd been straight with her. Not a hundred percent. And no promises, of course. Not until he knew exactly where the hell he was going. His future was just as hazy in Los Angeles as in New York. And now, his last connection in the new area would end when Lippozi told him he'd washed out.

"You free for awhile?" Lippozi finally asked. "No other job I put you on or a particular broad you're hooked up with?"

"No one," Sully said.

Lippozi leaned forward, fingers steepled in front of him. "I need someone to watch one of the big boys they're sending from Vegas to check how we handle the money in our casinos. Name's Caruso — Mr. Caruso to you."

Sully kept his smile in place. As if he didn't know enough to call one of the big shots mister.

"Probably be here at least six months," Lippozi went on. "He don't know his way around town. Know what I mean?"

Sully tried to look as though he did, but he suspected that his confusion showed on his face, like always.

Lippozi sighed. "Just so you don't screw up, I'll spell it out. You run errands. Tell him the good places to eat, take him to bars where he can pick up broads."

Sully's heart thudded. Only not with fear for a change. Instead of being kicked out of the organization, he was being given a job with responsibility. A vacation from hijacking trucks or roughing up people late with their payments.

"Not too proud to be a gofer?"

"No, Mr. Lippozi. I'd be honored." He tried to sound cool.

"You ain't very smart, Sully, but you have something the other guys don't — class." Lippozi leaned forward in his red leather chair. "That's why I called you."

Sully tried to match the older man's smile. Hard to do

because Sully smiled with his whole face. Lippozi just smiled with his mouth.

"Here's the story. Donatel Caruso's six feet tall, good looking, great build. Women love him. The guy's loaded with charm and smarts, maybe too much smarts, if you know what I mean. And he's very cool. Ice water in his veins."

Lippozi rocked his swivel chair back and forth a couple of times. "We're gonna do the same thing the bosses in Vegas want Caruso to do — watch what's happening. He'll try to figure out how to get away from you when he wants to. But you don't let that happen. You'll be his shadow, stick like glue. Report back to me what he does, where he goes, who he sees. Know what I mean?"

Sully kept smiling. "Yeah, Mr. Lippozi." It sounded like Lippozi expected him to spy on the guy, not take care of him. His enthusiasm waned.

Lippozi pondered for a few seconds. "Don't try to think what's important to tell me, Sully, 'cause you're not smart enough. Just spill it all out — everything."

"A piece of cake, Mr. Lippozi."

"We leased a house in Beverly Hills. You live with him."

Lippozi swiveled around in his chair and was fiddling with something in a cabinet when Buzz walked in and stationed himself in front of Lippozi's desk, his beefy arms across his chest and his piggy face all crunched up in his phony smile. Sully shot out of his chair. No way would he look up at Buzz.

"Hey, Curly, you the one gonna baby-sit our Vegas big shot?" He snorted. "The question is, who'll baby-sit you?" He laughed as though he'd said something very funny.

Sully turned away so Buzz couldn't see the aggravation. The baby-sitting referred to the general opinion that because Sully didn't have an Italian name, he wasn't very smart. His sainted Italian mother hadn't done anyone any favors when she married an Irishman. Curly pointed out the fact Sully was losing his hair. Another legacy from his father. According to some old pictures, Michael Emmett Sullivan was bald at thirty.

"I hear Caruso shoots first and asks questions second. How you gonna handle that, Sul?"

Sully focused on Lippozi who'd taken something out of the safe. No way would he admit he'd never fired a gun let alone shot at anyone. Or that the sight of blood made him lightheaded. Had ever since a tetanus shot when he was a kid.

Lippozi turned and handed Sully a white envelope with hundreds inside. "Walkin' around money. Another envelope every week. There's a black Mercedes in the lot for you to drive." He nodded to Buzz who threw a ring of keys at Sully.

Lippozi looked him over again. "Caruso's a real classy dresser. You better get over to Mandella's and pick up some decent threads — on me," Lippozi added.

"Yeah, you dress like shit," Buzz said, scrunching up his face.

"Shut up, Buzz." Lippozi glared at the man, then turned to Sully. "You can leave your car here. Pick Caruso up tomorrow afternoon, LAX at two. Buzz'll give you the airline name. Shouldn't have any trouble finding him. He's in his forties, sharp dresser, looks like the guy in the movies — DeNiro. Kind of like you, come to think of it." His glance went to the black fringe around Sully's head. "Except, he has hair."

At the men's store, Sully let Mandella pick out a few things for him. Then he went to his apartment. After he packed, he poured a Jack Daniel's. With an assignment that didn't involve a muscle job nudging at his conscience and making his palms sweaty, his dreams might disappear.

The nightmares were always about snow — more snow than he'd endured during the winters in the small town near Buffalo where he'd grown up. A flat, dismal whiteness no matter what direction he looked, all the way to the horizon. Like something he'd seen on TV about the South Pole. In the scenario, he trudged across the expanse, lost, alone and cold.

When he woke up, trembling, heart pounding, he forced himself to picture the travel magazines at the barber shop and try to imagine sandy beaches, palm trees, blue skies, warm breezes. He'd expected Los Angeles would be his Garden of Eden when he'd headed west. Even though there hadn't been any snow in a year, it was still just another big city, congested and foggy. The nightmares came more often. Because no matter the name of the city, that's where he was — stuck at the South Pole, or in a booth at Vicanzo's Bar. Same thing. Worrying about drinking and smoking too much. Waiting for a job with Nick Lippozi. Listening to the bullshit around him. Now, finally, he was on his way like Uncle Sal promised.

Lippozi was right about Donatel Caruso. Tall, nice build. With his great tan and wearing a light gray tweed jacket, black pants and a silky patterned shirt, he looked classy and elegant. And he did resemble Robert DeNiro — and Sully, too. The same height and weight but with more black hair than Sully had ever had. And he carried himself like he owned the world.

"Name's Sully, Mr. Caruso. Mr. Lippozi wants me to get you settled."

"Glad to meet you, Sully, and drop the 'mister'." Caruso put out his hand like they were going to be buddies.

On the way to Beverly Hills, Sully told Caruso how he'd be living with him and showing him around. After he'd pulled up to the house off Sunset and taken the bags out of the trunk, he glanced up the street. Sully wondered which of the half-dozen cars parked in the adjacent driveways or on the street held Lippozi's wise-guys.

The two-story, sprawling Spanish-style house had twice as much space as the two of them needed. The living room was spacious with a big-screen TV, massive sofas and chairs and two large windows at either end. The window in front featured a view of the street. But the back window faced a garden, a pool and towering oak trees. Sully had never seen anything as grand.

They stowed their gear in two bedrooms upstairs, and Caruso poked around. Back home after dinner at a ritzy restaurant on LaCienega, Caruso suggested a few hands of blackjack.

"Help pass the time," he said.

They played cards until midnight, and over a couple of drinks, Caruso explained how he got things working smoothly at the poker clubs and gambling casinos he visited. Sully told Caruso about his mother who had died just before he'd moved to Los Angeles, and his Uncle Sal who was connected and lived in Brooklyn. About Brooklyn College where he'd gone to night school to study the Viet Nam war that his father had fought in.

"You're lucky to have your Uncle Sal," Caruso told him. "I don't have any family, but I want one some day, a wife and a couple of kids. It's just hard to settle down, being in the line of work we're in." As though their jobs were the same.

By two in the morning when they rinsed out their glasses, Sully decided he already knew Caruso just about as well as he'd ever known anyone.

"Let's go out to the patio and see if the stars look the same as in Vegas," Caruso said.

The reflection of pool lights danced on the water, and Sully thought he smelled orange blossoms somewhere in the back yard. He could see a lot of stars in the sky. He wasn't sure there were as many as in Las Vegas, but it was still a glorious, magical sight. If he lived in a house like this, maybe Los Angeles would be the kind of paradise he was looking for.

"It might not seem like it," Caruso said, looking up at the sky, "but when I started out, I was just like you, a dreamer, kinda na•ve, not always sure what was going on. I knew being stupid wouldn't get me far, so I decided I'd better figure out fast who I could trust."

He looked at Sully. "I don't have a big education, didn't even take classes in night school, but I have a talent for reading people. I think I can trust you."

Sully had developed a few talents, too. He met Caruso's gaze and kept his mouth shut.

Caruso took hold of Sully's arm and pulled him out to the center of the yard. "I understand why you've been hired, Sully, so I want you to think about what I'm gonna say. I like to keep my personal life separate from my job. That means you don't tell Lippozi everything — keep some things just between us. And we don't talk much inside the house or in the car."

He clapped Sully on the shoulder and turned to walk inside. "You can let me know what you think in the morning."

The question nagged Sully all night. After breakfast Caruso led him through the house and to a side door that creaked from lack of use.

"Let's walk outside before the housekeeper shows up."

Sully followed him behind some dense bushes and to an alley behind the houses.

"So, what do you think about what I said?" Caruso asked.

"I think it's okay," Sully said, hoping he was making the right decision.

A short time later they'd walked to a car rental agency a few blocks away, leased a Ford Taurus and driven to a garage at an apartment building near the house. "You don't need to tell Lippozi about the car," Caruso said when they reached the alley.

Sully met with Lippozi for the first time a week later. "We've been going to the poker clubs," Sully told him, feeling the sweat in his arm pits. "Caruso walks around, gets people's names, asks who does what."

"How about with the money? He help count it?"

Sully shook his head. "He doesn't count it, but he watches pretty close."

"You go in the room with him?"

"I stand inside, next to the door."

Lippozi stared at him for a few seconds. "How about the first few days? Any broads? Out to eat? What?"

Sully's heart beat thundered in his ears. "He told the housekeeper what he likes to eat, puttered around in the garden, watched TV. Now, we go to one of the casinos about noon, get home after midnight. When we're home, we rent movies and play cards."

"What do you talk about in the car?"

"Mostly I concentrate on my driving."

"Yeah, I forgot. It takes smarts to do more than one thing at once." He laughed. "Remember, Sully, keep your eyes open."

On the way back to the house, Sully's nervous system finally quieted down. Lippozi was wrong. Sully could do more than two things at a time. He focused on his driving while he thought about what he'd just reported. Lippozi was his boss, and he was paying him to do a job. On the other hand, Sully didn't trust Lippozi — in spite of the glowing testimonial from Uncle Sal. In only a week, his gut instinct told him he could trust Caruso — as much as you could trust anyone in the business.

He decided renting the car was unimportant. A rationalization, of course, a try at convincing himself it was merely an indication of Caruso's paranoia. Among other things. Like putting a lock on his bedroom door and insisting Sully get hold of his birth certificate and carry it with him. It was more difficult explaining Caruso's reaction when Sully had asked how money could be stolen in such a closely guarded operation as in the poker casinos' back rooms.

"If someone wants to steal, he'll find a way," Caruso had said. "One of these days, I'll show you how it's done."

A shiver shot through Sully. He wondered if he knew Caruso as well as he thought he did.

Caruso was teaching him the finer points of playing blackjack. One night, after they'd put the cards away, Sully told him about Rosie who walked out on him.

"You know, Sully," Caruso said, "with your looks and personality, you should have women lined up."

"Not many women around like Rosie. She didn't mind that I'm not very smart and practically bald."

Caruso frowned and stood up. "Never put yourself down, Sully. You have more brains than most people. What you don't have is confidence — and hair. Let's go upstairs."

Caruso unlocked the door to his bedroom, then to his closet. Hair pieces sat on plastic heads on two shelves under a mirror. More than two dozen, most of them with black hair, but a few in other colors and styles, some paired with matching beards and mustaches.

"The secret is, buy good ones. I wear these all the time, all expensive. Great for business." He waved his hand at the non-black ones. "And for play."

He picked up a black hair piece and put it on Sully's head, shifted it around, fluffed it up a little, patted one side. He pointed to the mirror. Sully stared at his smooth, polished reflection.

After Sully took it off, Caruso said, "Let's go out and

look at the stars."

Caruso stood on the patio and stared up at the sky. "We're going to Las Vegas Saturday night."

Sully frowned. "Lippozi'll know, so I'll have to tell him."

Caruso shook his head. "He's not gonna know."

The housekeeper was off on weekends, and with the help of a half-dozen timers, the alley in back of the house and the rental car, getting out of the house and disappearing for a few days was a slam dunk.

Saturday morning, Sully stood in the lobby of the MGM Grand while Caruso registered. He felt like a college kid in his dark blonde hair-piece, tan shirt and chinos. Caruso, with long brown hair, jeans, a jean jacket and carrying his usual beat-up briefcase, looked like an A&R rep from a Hollywood record company.

"New name, room number, key card," Caruso said when he came back. He stuffed money inside Sully's jacket pocket.

"See how far you can run it up. Mike'll get you anything you want." He nodded to one of the men behind the tables. "I'll see you later."

Unlike the other wise-guys, Sully didn't gamble, mostly because the reason for his father's disappearance had been a weakness for poker. But Caruso's blackjack instructions paid off. By Sunday when they settled on the plane again, Sully had won more than five thousand dollars.

"In the morning we'll find a place to stash our winnings." Caruso cradled the attache case on his lap. "Bring your birth certificate."

Monday before the housekeeper arrived, they picked up the Ford and drove to San Pedro. In a small, nondescript bank, Caruso rented two safe-deposit boxes, one for himself and one for Sully. Caruso insisted they sign each other's identification cards, and they exchanged duplicate box keys. Then Caruso called a friend who owned a photo shop. An hour later, Caruso tucked a passport inside Sully's jacket pocket.

"In case we want to hop over to London or Paris some weekend," Caruso explained.

On the drive back to the house in the Taurus, Caruso said, "you're about the first person I've met who's completely ingenuous. Know what the word means?"

"Sure." Before his father disappeared, he had told Sully that the Irish were lyrical with words. Sully took a couple of English classes after the ones on history and learned a whole new vocabulary. He thought the word meant trustworthy or gullible. He wasn't sure which one Caruso had in mind for him.

The next week Sully's doubts about Caruso reared up. They left the Royal Flush Casino and decided to stop at a place in Hollywood with a great jazz combo. Sully immediately lost Lippozi's wise-guys who tailed them wherever they went. At least he thought he'd lost them.

He parked on a side street around the corner. By one o'clock when they left the bar, they were both wired from the terrific music and the drinks. They'd almost reached the car when Sully heard something behind him. An arm snaked around his neck, and he spewed out a lungful of air. He twisted around until he finally put some space between the two of them and rammed his elbow into the man's stomach. When he felt the arm loosen, he broke away, whirled around and sent a sharp uppercut to the guy's face. Sully heard the glass jaw crack, and the man fell against the wall. He leaned over him. This was no gang-banger or neighborhood tough.

The small grizzled man who had Caruso on the ground wasn't either. Professionals. Sully recognized the type.

He lifted the man off Caruso and tossed him back toward the other one.

"Come on," he shouted to Caruso, the car opener in his hand. He rushed to the driver's side of the car.

The sound of shots shattered the silence behind him, echoing against the empty shops along the street. Sully turned, his hand frozen on the door handle. Caruso ran toward the car, stuffing a gun inside his jacket. Sully saw two dark heaps lying against the building's wall.

"Let's go," Caruso yelled, opened the door and slid into the car.

Sully sped away, keeping his hands tight on the steering wheel. He knew if he loosened his grip, his arms would shake right out of their sockets. He waited for Caruso to tell him exactly what had happened. Caruso didn't say anything then or when they were home. In bed Sully finally allowed himself to wonder who had fired first.

The following Friday, Sully pulled into the lot next to Lippozi's Restaurant and parked, his heart pounding and sweat beading his forehead. Sully knew he wasn't as smart as practically everyone else. He also knew he'd already done exactly what Lippozi had warned him against — made the decision about what he should report. Lippozi's attitude had already gone from contempt to irritation to outright suspicion.

On the news there'd been nothing about anyone being shot to death in Hollywood. Maybe the bodies of the two men were spirited away or they'd merely been wounded. Either way, Lippozi would know.

"That's all?" Lippozi asked after listening to Sully's usual ramblings about his and Caruso's visits to the casinos.

"Very unexciting life," Sully said, and swallowed. "Oh, yeah. We were mugged the other night."

Lippozi shot forward in his chair. "You were what?"

"Mugged." Sully told him just the bare bones of the story. He left out the part about the gunshots.

Lippozi's eyes opened wide. Obviously he didn't know anything about the incident. Which meant that someone else was after Caruso. Maybe a big boss from Las Vegas.

That night Lippozi called Caruso directly and suggested he and Sully have dinner at his place the next night. The first time he'd been in contact with Caruso as far as Sully knew.

All through dinner, Sully waited for Lippozi to show up. He never did. The two were almost ready to leave when a woman walked past the booth with a drink in her hand. Buzz lumbered by at the same time and bumped into her. Her drink spilled on Caruso, nothing much, but she made a big fuss, as though a dam had spilled over and threatened to flood the place.

Caruso hadn't socialized with any of the women they'd met on their nights out. Sully knew about a married woman in Las Vegas, and he figured Caruso'd made some kind of promise to her. That's why it was a surprise when he flipped over Glenda.

Glenda was a knock-out with a body all T-and-A, blonde hair, nice skin, big blue eyes. After only a week, Caruso couldn't go a day without calling her. When he and Sully left a casino early, Glenda showed up at the house.

Sully didn't trust her. A smart woman knew how to make you think you were the most important man in her life. When Sully mentioned it, Caruso laughed.

"You don't have to worry about me, Sully. I'm always a dozen steps ahead of everyone else."

Having Glenda around didn't stop their next trip to Las Vegas. Caruso made up a story. As he said, he hadn't climbed the ladder by being stupid. Sully won six thousand dollars, and they made their usual trip to the bank.

The next Friday afternoon, Sully sat in Lippozi's office. If, as Sully suspected, Lippozi had set up the meeting between Caruso and Glenda, he was hoping Lippozi would trust him more. He rattled off his report.

"So you ever see him with any big wads of money?" Lippozi asked. "When you're in the back rooms at the casino, he ever make any fast moves?"

"No," Sully said. But he had watched Caruso walk around to the different counting tables. The attention of the men working in the room wandered, not always glued to the money. Several times he'd thought he'd seen some kind of signal pass between a specific guy and Caruso. He'd dismissed it as his own brand of paranoia. He didn't mention his suspicions to Lippozi.

"Ever fall into shit, Sully?" Lippozi asked him after a few seconds.

Sully shook his head.

"It ain't pleasant. That's why you learn who to trust."

Sully was thinking about Lippozi's comment on his way to the car when someone yelled, "Hey, Sully."

He turned. One of the wise-guys from Vicanzo's Bar ambled toward him.

"You ain't paid me that C-note you borrowed. Being in with the big guys now, figure you'll stiff me?"

"What're you talking about?" Sully said. "I don't owe you —"

The punch landed in the middle of his gut, and he doubled up. A second later, he sensed someone else's presence, and felt a jab to his head. He fell down on all fours.

"Dangerous to forget who your friends are, Curly," the voice said, and Sully recognized Buzz.

He curled up in a ball, trying to protect his head. By the time they stopped and he figured they'd left, his chest was on fire, every breath an effort.

He finally managed to crawl to the car and drag himself inside. He didn't even look in the rearview mirror. The sight might make him throw up.

Caruso was lying on a chaise next to the pool in his swimming trunks, sound asleep when Sully walked in. A soak in the jaccuzi would make him feel better — couldn't make him feel worse. In the back downstairs bedroom, Caruso's trousers lay across a bed next to his shirt.

Sully glanced through the window at the sleeping Caruso. He reached into the trousers' pocket and found Caruso's bedroom door keys in a plastic card holder along with the safety deposit box keys.

Caruso often chided him about being na•ve, and he'd just been warned by Lippozi. Like Caruso said, what he needed was confidence. He slowly and painfully made his way upstairs.

He unlocked Caruso's door. Sully didn't know what to look for. He just knew his search had to be fast. He'd never noticed anything in the bedroom, so he rushed to the closet that seemed to hold Caruso's secret life.

Sully looked at his reflection in the big mirror. Except for his swollen right eye, he looked the same. After he'd gone through the jackets, he grabbed a couple of hairpieces and began turning them over. He took hold of the good-looking salt-and- pepper toupee that Caruso favored, and an envelope fell out. Inside Sully found a one-way airline ticket to Rio de Janeiro in a name he'd never heard of before. Departure date? Two days away.

Sully had been the witness to a shooting and he'd been beaten up. And now, Caruso was leaving. Did the man plan to say goodbye? Or would he just put on one of his rugs, slip into an old suit and disappear, leaving Sully to bob around in a vat of shit?

When Sully went downstairs, Caruso was getting up off the chaise. Sully put the key back in Caruso's trousers and slipped into the kitchen.

Caruso gaped when he saw Sully's face. "What the hell happened to you?"

"Would you believe I walked into a door?"

Caruso glared, picked up his clothes and went upstairs.

When he came down he mixed both of them a drink.

"How about I go to Lum's for take-out?" Sully asked him.

"You, me and Glenda are going out," Caruso said.

Sully took a sip of his drink. Something else he needed to dredge up — some smarts, decide what was best for him. "I'll pass," he said. "That door gave me one hell of a bump. I don't feel much like socializing."

Caruso nodded to the deck and they went outside.

"What happened with Lippozi?"

"Not him who sent the two goons the other night."

Caruso didn't seem to be surprised. "What else?"

"He thinks I'm holding out and you're stealing from him."

"He the one with the door?"

"His goons."

"What'd you tell him — about me stealing?"

"The truth. I've never seen you steal anything."

Caruso looked up at the early evening sky. "You know, Sully, sometimes the things we have to do can put people we like in the crapper."

"What the hell does that mean?" Sully asked him, pretending to not already know.

"If anything happens to me," Caruso went on, "you dress so no one recognizes you and get out of the house fast. Pick up the Taurus, go to the bank, get the money and leave town."

"That why you want me along tonight? You think something's gonna happen to you?"

Caruso flashed a smile. "I like your company. So come along as a favor to me."

With Caruso's departure, Sully would be holding the bag. He didn't much relish taking a bullet for him, too.

"Some other time," Sully said. Caruso eyed him for a few seconds and then shrugged.

A little later, Caruso settled on the big leather sofa to wait for Glenda.

Glenda was always late, and it was close to eight o'clock when Caruso told Sully to look out the front window to see if she was coming.

It was dark now, and the street was deserted except for the dark sedan just pulling up.

"Car stopping in front," Sully said. "Two getting out and looking at the house." A feeling of menace skittered down his spine.

Caruso abruptly reached over and turned off the light next to the couch. "Get outta here," he yelled, jumped up, ran into the hall and switched the foyer light off, too. Only a dim glow from the kitchen filtered in.

Sully saw Caruso standing at the foot of the stairs, his gun drawn. Before Sully could get to him, he heard footsteps outside. The front door crashed open. Three, four shots followed, and Sully felt a sting in his right arm.

At the deafening sound of gunfire, he crouched down. A sudden wave of nausea rose up in his throat, and he swallowed. Not the time to act like a kid, na•ve and indecisive. When Caruso's gun slid across the foyer's tile floor toward him, he forced himself to pick it up.

Footsteps sounded on the front walk, and a figure loomed up in the doorway. Sully fired and heard a thud. He waited long seconds before he switched on the hall light. There were two bodies on the tile floor and one in the doorway. Caruso staring up, unseeing.

Sully fell to his hands and knees, crawled to Caruso and pushed the body over. Fumbling through Caruso's pants' pocket, he found the plastic card that held the keys. Caruso's head twisted to the side and his hair piece fell off. He was completely bald.

Sully pulled into a convenience store parking lot. He began changing his clothes in the car. That's when he saw the crease in his arm. It ached, but the bullet hadn't zipped close enough to draw more than a thin trail of blood.

He put on jeans, a shirt and jacket he'd grabbed from Caruso's closet, transferred the airline ticket to Caruso's beat-up briefcase and threw his clothes in a Dumpster. With the gray-black hair-piece on his head he looked almost like a professor, except for his eye. In the store, he bought band-aids, some cream to bleach out the black eye marks and enough food to fill a large paper bag. He parked the car on a quiet street and switched license plates with the car in front of him. Just in case someone had spotted the Taurus in the last few months and jotted down the license number. When the San Pedro bank opened the next morning, Sully was the first customer inside.

He opened Caruso's box and stared at the money inside. More than he'd ever seen in his life. Underneath it all he found a passport in the name on the plane ticket to Rio and a small notebook. He riffled through the notebook pages that held neat lists of bank accounts in the Cayman islands, complete with account numbers and codes to empower either Donatel Caruso or him, Aloysius Sullivan, to withdraw the money. He stuffed everything, passport, money and the notebook into the shopping bag and briefcase.

By now, the police were probably at the big house in Beverly Hills. Glenda would have told Lippozi everything she knew. Someone would have looked around Sully's haunts and figured out that he'd run out. He left the Ford at a long-term parking lot near LAX and took a shuttle to Santa Monica.

In his hotel room, Sully counted the money in the bags and looked over the list of bank accounts again. He was a rich man. Caruso, a couple of steps ahead of everyone — until the end. The question, could Sully keep ahead of Lippozi and the bosses in Las Vegas? He obviously couldn't stay in Los Angeles. And he couldn't be sure Caruso's trip to Rio was such a big secret. He'd have to gather up his smarts again and think of the last place anyone would expect him to be.

He went to the Third Street Promenade and bought a cheap suitcase and some clothes. Then he took a dozen different bus rides to get back to San Pedro. At five o'clock the next morning he lay in a berth on a freighter, the suitcase wedged in next to him and the attache case clutched to his chest.

He could hear the wise-guys talking to Lippozi. "Sully? He's on his way to South America. Or maybe Hawaii or the Caribbean."

"He used to talk about Tahiti," his ex-girlfriend Rose would tell them when they found her. "Always looking for someplace warm where he could spend the day on a beach, get a tan, do a little swimming."

Maybe someday, Sully thought. But right now, he figured he'd be having the nightmares for awhile, the ones featuring snow where the land was white — and cold. He just hoped he could find a good plastic surgeon in Alaska.

Her Game

Ann Aptaker

The ringing of the telephone shook the talcum powder in the round tin at the edge of Lily Vera's dressing table, shook it enough to raise a puff of white powder, like a small explosion, into the golden glow of the shaded lamp beside the tin. In the quiet between rings, the powder settled in the tin as lightly as the silk robe of exotic floral pattern that settled along Lily's skin.

Lily let the phone ring. She knew who was calling, knew that the caller wouldn't hang up.

She opened a bottom drawer of the dressing table, lifted a checkered ebony and ivory box from the drawer, and placed it in front of her on the dressing table. When she raised the lid, lamp light shimmered along her nails and fingers as they moved with the delicacy of a spider among the rows of lipsticks, rouges, eyeliners, mascara and eye shadow of every color.

The phone kept ringing.

Lily looked at herself in the mirror. She thought about her game, about the phone calls she'd made earlier, about the call coming in now. When she was good and ready, she answered the phone with a quiet, "Yes?"

Tess Coll had to force her voice through the noise of clanging metal and shouted conversations that banged against the stone walls around her: "I bet you're as gorgeous as you were the first time I laid eyes on you, when you were a rookie in red high heels walking the streets." Then Coll listened for Lily, listened for the voice she remembered as something delicate and enticing as pink tissue paper around a fancy gift. She listened for the trace of an accent inside the voice, an accent she could never quite place. Coll waited. She gripped the phone so tight that her big, beefy hand hurt.

Lily's fingers were rubbing a light film of iridescent violet cream into the pale skin below her high cheekbones when she said, "What makes you think I no longer walk the streets?"

Coll swallowed what felt like a stone in her throat. It hurt all the way down. "You're as comforting as a relentless rain, Lily."

"You're not buying comfort."

"You don't think so? It's costing me enough. Look, I walk out in an hour."

"Then I'll see you in an hour."

"The money — the transfer into your account go all right?"

"I wouldn't be talking to you if it didn't."

No response came through the phone, just the noisy clanging and shouting behind Coll. Lily started to hang up, then:

"Lily, promise me you'll wear something red. I always liked you in red."

Lily hung up.

One of the ways Lily stayed alive in the life she led was never to reveal her intentions to a killer.

An hour later, at midnight, Lily drove up to the door of the women's state penitentiary. The place was barely twenty miles from the city, but the immense gray box jutting from the barren landscape could just as well have been the most miserable spot on the dark side of the moon. Then a slice of yellow light hit the ground when the big metal door opened. Walking out from the light was someone Lily once knew as a brute force of nature but who was now only a shadow growing larger as Tess Coll neared Lily's black Jaguar.

Coll opened the passenger door. The interior light went on. The light was cruel to Coll, Lily thought; it dug hollows into her broad face, clawed at the remnants of Coll's feral vigor. Lily had a tough time seeing the once natty Tess Coll in a dusty, five-year-old overcoat and a lousy prison haircut, a hash job that made her look like a chewed up, back-alley dog.

Coll slid into the front seat. She left the car door open so the light would stay on, let herself have a good long look at Lily's face. Coll didn't entirely trust her eyes after five years of drab walls and bad light, but she thought she saw a faint, violet iridescence above the high collar of Lily's black leather coat. Perfect. Iridescence, a shimmer, a magical illusion, that's how she remembered Lily every day during those caged years. Coll's eyes, heavy and hooded as a prizefighter's, widened like an awed child's when she saw Lily's hair — "Still more like mist than hair," came barely whispered from Coll's scarred lips. Points of a smile, gleeful and hungry, worked their way into the corners of her mouth. Then Coll's eyes narrowed again. She took a deep breath, let it out with slowly building greed. She said, "I hope the lipstick's not the only red you're wearing."

Lily's heart beat hard. Painfully hard. She let it beat twice before she raised her black-gloved hands to the collar of her coat, opened the single silver button that held the coat together. With a movement as smooth as a snake slithering from its skin, Lily slid the coat down her bare shoulders. There was red, just enough of it: a red spandex halter held Lily's breasts like cream-filled cups spilling over.

The sound of Coll's breathing filled the car.

"These are my work clothes," Lily said. She slid her coat back over her shoulders. "Close the door, Coll. Let's go." Lily started the engine, Coll closed the door. It was dark again in the car.

Coll said, "I didn't hire you for that kind of work."

"You think you're my only job tonight? I told you I still work the streets. What do you think I'll be doing after we finish this little business of yours?"

"*Little* business, Lily?" Even in the dark, the shadow of life that Tess Coll had become still wielded a power and a presence that could cause other living things to wilt: "Five years. Five years of having my shyster collect every favor ever owed me from every pol, every player, pay off every rotten judge to get my conviction overturned. Five years waiting to run down the piece of crap that framed me for a hit I had no part in. This night is not *little* business, Lily." Coll's words hit the air with a sharp snap, like ice cracking. It wasn't the first time Lily heard her sound cold like that. The first time was when Coll dragged Lily from the street, when Coll swore she'd kill anyone who tried to touch Lily again. Someone did try.

Coll said, "The word around the yard is that you're a fuckin' good P.I. Well, you'd better be."

"I found Bix Duveck for you, Coll. That should be good enough."

"We'll see."

"Maybe I should have just told you where to find him."

"That's cute. You know damn well how information from outside runs through a prison faster than lice. Some of

Duveck's girls are in the joint, some of 'em lifers, nothin' to lose. You can bet one of 'em would've gotten the word to Bix. All he'd have to do is promise a lifetime supply of free cigarettes, and I could've wound up with a shiv between my ribs while I stood in the chow line. And that would be on *your* head, Lily."

"True. You wouldn't have been able to arrange for ten thousand dollars to move into my bank account."

"Don't bitch me, damn it. Money. That's all I ever meant to you. Never mind what it took for me to knuckle my way to the top of the action, what it took to stay there. Maybe you liked that, too, maybe you liked the power and the ride . . . no, it was just money. It still is. My ten grand." Coll ran a calloused finger along the white leather casing on the bulb of the stick shift. The smooth hide felt like the first classy piece of skin she'd touched since the day she was locked up. "This P.I. gig — funny profession for you, y'know? Well, maybe not so funny. This shiny new Jaguar tells me the P.I. game brings you an armload of cash."

"Yes, quite a bit."

"So why sell yourself on the sidewalk if you don't have to?"

"I suppose it depends how you define 'have to'."

There wasn't a sound in the car now except the purr of the engine, no movement except for Coll's head turning toward Lily.

Lily said, "Buckle your seat belt, Coll. The road from the prison is rough."

The flashing colored lights in the honky-tonk part of town glare so bright they blind the suckers to the grubby hands that pick their pockets. Lily drove into an alleyway off the crowded, noisy strip. She parked the Jaguar in front of an old crusty building.

Coll knew the building. She pictured the rooms that were for rent by the hour, rooms where guns were hidden under the floor boards, where drugs were stashed in the walls, rooms where money was pried from broken fingers, rooms where no one who went in came out. Coll used to own the place.

Coll got out of the car, stood in front of the three-story building, looked up and stared at it, one mass of stone confronting another.

Lily stood behind Coll. She saw the bristly ends of Coll's prison haircut twitch in the night breeze. She heard Coll snicker, heard her say, "My shyster got me a good price for the place three years ago. Said it was sold to an entertainment concern. Duveck?"

"Yes. But now he goes by the name Barney Bravo." Lily saw Coll's head tilt back, but she couldn't see Coll's mouth open with a soundless laugh. Lily said, "Duveck left town right after your trial, Coll. He came back a year later with a new name and a new face. A surgeon had to build him a new one because a guy upstate smashed the old one to splinters."

"Yeah? You find out who?"

"A small-timer, so far down the bottom of the heap it made him tough to trace. But for ten grand, I thought you're entitled to top-drawer service."

"You never gave me anything less."

Lily steered away from that. She stayed on business. "Remember the check kiter you almost threw into the river?"

"Yeah."

"Him."

At the end of a long, descending whistle blown between her teeth, Coll said, "You really are a fucking good P.I., Lily."

"Yes. Now listen: Bravo — or rather Duveck — he owns the action in this part of town now, Coll. He takes a cut of every dollar spent on liquor, drugs, flesh, even parking meters, everything. But his favorite racket is the high stakes card game he runs on the top floor. He soaks the silk-thread types who come down here to play naughty behind the wife's back. Or the husband's."

"What's the action on the other floors?"

"Whatever profits. Same as you."

"No, not the same as me, Lily."

"No, Coll, not the same as you."

Coll walked up the three granite steps to the steel reinforced door she had installed when she'd bought the place. Her walk was stiff, not as quick as it once was, but even a slowed Tess Coll was stealthier than a human being had a right to be. She took Lily's breath away.

Lily followed up the steps.

Coll said, "Get out of here, Lily."

"Don't be ridiculous. I dealt you this hand."

"Go on. Go enjoy my ten grand. Maybe I'll help you spend it later. You brought me to Bix Duveck, you've earned your dough. Now I'm dealing you out."

"No, you're not." Lily slid a key into the palm of Coll's right hand.

Holding the small thing, the simple key, made big Tess Coll shudder. Every night in prison, when the cells were locked down, she'd hear the tantalizing jangle of the unreachable keys that swayed on the belts of swaggering bitches whose power came from badges and nightsticks and withholding those keys. But tonight, Lily slipped one of the precious things right into her fingers.

Coll steadied, unlocked the door, walked into the dim, silent hallway. "I thought you said Duveck supplies action down here."

"Not on nights when he runs the card game. He doesn't want anything to distract the suckers."

"The little shit always did have a good head for business." Coll moved to the stairs. She smiled a little when her foot touched the first carpeted step. The feel of it under her shoe brought back a memory of the night she dragged a rival down these stairs. The thick, expensive carpet had muffled the thump of the dead body.

The second floor was just as dark and quiet as the first, so quiet Lily could hear the clatter of poker chips and the low chatter of players raising bets one floor overhead. She could even smell the game, its sharp odors of whiskey, smoke, stale chicken sandwiches, sweat.

Coll stopped at the third-floor landing. This floor, too, was dark except for a line of light creeping under the door at the far end of the short hall. Coll said, "How many players we talkin' about?"

"He never goes less than four, but he can handle a dozen hands or so."

"What's it sound like to you?"

Lily didn't like the question. She never liked being tested by Coll. She said nothing.

Coll said, "For chrissakes, Lily, I had to put up with endless noise day and night for five years. My ears can't tell the difference now between a barking dog and a tweeting bird. Damn it, how many hands does it sound like to *you?*"

Lily had never heard Tess Coll beg. It surprised her how much she liked the sound of it. She took a moment of pleasure, then said, "Four hands. Maybe five, counting Duveck."

Coll nodded, said, "Okay," her head lowered like she was considering something, then she walked to the door. She could hear the action now, hear Bix Duveck, always the smooth talker, say, " . . . and a Jack of Diamonds to the lady."

Coll whispered over her shoulder, "Stay behind me, Lily."

Lily's "Yes," was barely a breath against Coll's back.

Coll cupped her right hand around the brass doorknob.

Her fingertips itched, her hand was hot and anxious, but she turned the doorknob real slow. She didn't let the doorknob make the slightest noise, didn't want to give Duveck even a split second's notice that someone uninvited was about to take over the game. The latch gave.

Coll flung the door open, looked around fast, then locked eyes on the guy at the far side of the gaming table. Coll paid no attention to the prim brunette and three guys in boardroom suits whose faces snapped to the doorway where they saw a big, dangerous boulder poised to run everybody down. Coll's icy stare stayed on the guy at the far edge of the table because after he'd managed not to choke on his chicken sandwich, he grinned.

Two memories had kept Coll sane whenever those bitches with keys locked her in the hole, the windowless stone box with a 40-watt bulb that burned day and night until there was no day or night, just Coll's two memories: Lily's face and Bix Duveck's grin, the thin, slitlike thing he kept on his smooth mouth while he sat in the courtroom every day of Coll's trial. His face and his mouth weren't smooth anymore. His nose was lumpy, his cheeks hollow, his eyes deep in their broken sockets. But the grin hadn't changed a bit. No surgeon could cut away the deceit that seeped through that grin.

Coll grinned back, a wide, bare-toothed expanse of vengeance. She said, "Barney Bravo. It's just like you to come up with a flashy name. It's a stupid name, Bix. Hey, you look like you're cringing. Doesn't Bix look like he's cringing, Lily? The creep is sinking in his chair. Why would you want to do a thing like that, Bix?"

Duveck's grin lost some of its wattage, but it was still there, like a broken shield. He said, "Welcome home, Tess. Care to play a few hands? I hear your money's still good."

Her eyes still on Duveck, Coll said, "Lily, you have a gun?"

"Yes."

"Unregistered? Untraceable?"

"I can't do that any more, Coll."

"Oh yeah, you're a licensed P.I. now. Is the gun out?"

"Yes."

"Who are you aiming at?"

"No one in particular."

"Aim it over there, at Miss Starley. Hello, Vivian. Nice to see an old friend here. Still enjoy losing lots of money, I see. I used to take it from you in better company, don't you think?"

Vivian Starley's bones shook inside her sleek gray suit and shapely flesh. "Tess, I . . . I didn't know you were getting out. Please, no trouble. I didn't know who he was. Really. Lily, tell her I'm just here for the cards. Tell her you called me today, that you set it up so that I could sit in on a high money game, my kind of game. Just let me get out of here. Please, I can't have a scandal. My husband's business affairs —"

Coll cut her off. "Well, well. It seems luck really is a lady. And Lily is quite the lady, isn't she. What are you carrying in your handbag these days, Vivian? Still the same Walther twenty-five auto I recall you always carried in your handbag when you dallied in rough neighborhoods? Well, they don't get much rougher than this one. Hand it over."

A pink-faced guy next to Duveck, a guy Lily figured a product of a stiff-jawed prep school, raised his hands like a scared tenderfoot in a cowboy movie. "Look, I have a wife . . . a — I'm not part of . . . whatever line you people are in!"

Lily said, "Shut up."

Coll said, "You boys get lost." The tenderfoot ran out the door like his shoes were on fire. The other two pinstripes didn't dawdle, either. Nobody even bothered to grab their money from the stacks on the table.

Even Vivian Starley didn't try. She just made for the

door.

Coll's hands were fast and brutal when she grabbed Vivian's arm, snatched her handbag, pulled a Walther twenty-five from inside and aimed it at Duveck.

Vivian tugged at Coll's arm. She was crying, close to hysterical. "No, not with my gun! Lily, please? Screw you, Lily! You did this. You used me like you always do! You set me up! They'll trace the killing to my gun!"

Lily saw Duveck in the corner of her eye. He slumped a little less in his chair, a big nine millimeter came up from under the gaming table. Lily pushed Vivian out the door, pushed her toward the stairs. "Get going! Call me tomorrow! Hire me, and I can clear you of this!" Lily heard Vivian's panicked steps all the way down to the first floor.

Lily walked calmly back to the game room.

She heard the shots before she got there, a high crack and a thundering roar with almost no space between. Then a muffled thud against the felt-covered table, then a thump like a sack of cement dropped to the floor.

When all the noise was done, Lily walked into the game room.

Bix Duveck's head poured blood onto the gaming table.

Coll was in a puddle of blood on the floor. Coll's eyes, wild as the day she first saw Lily, stared up at Lily now. Lily closed them with her black-gloved hand.

She took Vivian's gun from Coll's grip. Then she took the key from Coll's coat pocket. The shabbiness of the dust encrusted wool nearly broke her heart.

Lily walked down the stairs, walked out into the alley. She slid into the Jaguar, drove it out of sight into a rented garage she used when she worked the neighborhood. Then Lily walked back out to the bright, noisy, gaudy strip. Her black leather coat was open. Her breasts spilling over the red halter, her long elegant legs under her black thigh-high skirt, even her red high-heeled shoes, advertised the night's goods for sale. But she wasn't going to sell to just any customer, no matter how big the money. Her goods would go only to those who could give Lily street-smart information about any dirty dealings around town that might be useful to Vivian Starley's case, or any other client's case. Lily was a fucking good P.I.

Let Sleeping Dogs Lie

Nick Andreychuk

A beautiful brunette, a cheating husband, and a sleeping dog. All common sights at Ritchie's Diner. The bullet in the cheating husband's chest was, however, quite uncommon.

The guy's wife had hired me to find out if he'd been unfaithful. Did it even matter anymore?

Ritchie's was a dump, but a homey kinda dump. The kinda place where you can discuss business while the coffee's served, and not worry that the waitress is going to call the cops. The kinda place where they don't kick you out for smacking the waitress' ass. My kinda place.

I'd been there three nights in a row. Mr. Cheater always came for a late dinner, then left with Sherry Cuckle. She waited on his table, then he waited for her. I had proof from the first two nights, but I told my client I needed more time.

Why? Not because I wanted to bilk the broad. Because of Sherry. I'd become smitten with the cheater's lover. And not just because of her beauty, her short skirt, or her plunging neckline. There was something about the way she moved — like she had a soulful jazz band playing in her head. When I watched her, I heard the music in my heart. I loved her. Simple as that. So I lied to my client to stay close to Sherry.

Ritchie kept his dog, a black lab named Newt, with him in the eatery. Probably against a dozen health regulations, but what did I care? Ritchie's kitchen was still cleaner than mine. The night the cheater died, I had indigestion (probably a delayed reaction from the previous nights' meals), so I fed my entire chili dog to the pleading pooch.

Stuffed and content, Newt curled up next to my low-backed booth, and blocked half the aisle. Debbie, a plump waitress who could barely see her feet, tripped over the lying dog. She went down hard, and so did the tray of dirty dishes she'd been carrying. The shooter must have been waiting for the right moment, saw the opportunity and took it.

I didn't hear the shot over Debbie's startled scream and the shattering dishes. With all eyes on the accident, no one saw the shooter, much less noticed someone'd been shot.

A good five minutes went by while we helped Debbie to her feet and cleared away the scattered debris. Newt didn't stir through it all. Then Sherry screamed.

The blood on Mr. Cheater's chest made it look like someone had tried to rip out his heart in a literal representation of the figurative damage he'd caused to his wife's heart.

Other screams followed, and the handful of patrons disappeared out the door. Amongst the inadvertent dine-and-dashers were potential witnesses and suspects, but I didn't try to stop them. I'm just a P.I., not P.D. I walked over and confirmed that the man lacked a pulse.

Ritchie rushed out of the kitchen. "Where the hell did everyone go?" he asked. Then he realized that Mr. Cheater wasn't a messy eater. His face turned the color of his greasy fries, and he grabbed onto the table for support. He glared at Sherry. "Call the police!"

The police came and did their thing. They even managed to corral and question all the diners, since they'd all stuck around outside out of morbid curiosity. Maybe they thought the gun show wasn't over.

Lieutenant Parker of homicide came over to where I stood with the diner's staff. He looked lean and mean like a former high-school football star who hadn't let himself become the beer-bellied, clich d failure.

"Anyone know the victim?" When no one answered, he looked hard at everyone in turn, lingering the longest on me and Sherry. Did he suspect one of us? Think he recognized us from previous records? I didn't blink. I'd tell him what I knew when and if it became advantageous to me.

"Has he been in here before?"

"Sure," Debbie said, casting an apologetic glance at Sherry. "He comes in here almost every night, but I've never really talked to him." She failed to mention that he never sat in her section.

Parker looked me up and down. "You don't work here. You a regular or what?"

"Been here a few times now."

"You seen that guy before?"

"He's been here every time I've been. He eats alone." I should've told Parker that I was tailing Mr. Cheater, but then I would've had to tell him that I'd seen the guy leave with Sherry Cuckle the last two nights. If she didn't see the need to mention it, why should I?

Parker directed his next question at everyone. "Anything else?" Several shoulders shrugged. The lieutenant gave us a look that said, "some help you are," then sighed. "Well, if you think of anything else, you know where to find me." He turned and left.

Ritchie, Debbie, and the prep cook wandered off, but

I caught Sherry's arm. "I know you lied," I said. "Why?"

Her pretty eyes caught mine and I saw that the jazz band in her head was playing a somber melody.

"I didn't —"

"I know you took him home with you last night. And because his wife hired me to follow him, I have pictures of what you would have been doing right now if he hadn't been murdered."

"You, you were following him?"

"Don't worry, I'm not going to tell the cops, I just want to know why *you* didn't tell them."

"It was just a fling. I didn't want to get involved with a murder case."

"Come on. From just three days of small talk, I know you well enough to know you want something more from life than just a fling."

A small smile crossed her face. "I throw out my hopes and dreams like other people do weather and politics because I think it'll get me sympathy tips . . . not because I expect anyone to ever really *listen.* Brad never listened. It was just a fling."

"Parker seemed smart enough — he'll find out about it."

"Of course he will — right after you tell Brad's wife. Isn't that what you were hired to do?"

"Yeah, but maybe I can convince her to reassign me to finding Brad's killer."

"Don't you think Parker's smart enough?"

"Sure, but I want to solve this case before Parker discovers your connection and gets it into his head that you're the prime suspect."

Her eyes danced with mine. "Why do you care what happens to me?"

I'm not the kinda guy to wear my heart on my sleeve, and I'm not one to get all philosophical either, but between the two choices I chose profound over profoundly sappy. "Because *you* care," I said.

She started to respond, maybe to tell me that she could fall in love with a guy like me, but Ritchie called over for her to get her sweet ass back to work. The cops and the body were long gone, and the booth cleaned as well as possible — back to business as usual. I hadn't even noticed the new customers arrive. I chuckled with d j^ vu as one of them stumbled over the black lab.

Sherry hesitated, but then hurried off when her boss repeated his command. I didn't try to stop her. Something in my mind had clicked and I believed I knew why Mr. Cheater had been murdered.

I left the diner and went to the police station. I found Lieutenant Parker inside his office. He wasn't alone. Mr. Cheater's wife — my client — sat in front of Parker's desk, crying. "Mr. Stack," she said, "what has Brad been up to? Who could have wanted him dead?"

"You two know each other?" Parker asked.

"Yes, this is the private investigator I told you about."

Parker looked ready to put my balls in a vice. "I could have your license for withholding evidence," he said.

"Look," I said, "I came down here to tell you about the dog."

"I saw it already — it's not a police problem."

"Did you notice that it was dead?"

"I thought it was just sleeping."

"Me too, until I saw someone else trip over it. That dog didn't even flinch. It's *dead.*"

"I still don't see what this has to do with my murder investigation."

"I fed the dog my dinner. Someone at Ritchie's wanted me dead." Parker raised an eyebrow. He didn't look convinced. "It makes perfect sense," I said. I avoided eye contact with my client as I spoke. "Brad was having an affair with

Sherry, and anyone who paid me any notice would've seen the way I looked at her. Figure out who else is in love with Sherry, and you'll have your killer."

"Sherry Cuckle? The waitress?"

"Yeah."

Parker turned his computer screen towards me. It displayed a file from a murder case in San Diego. "Look what I just found. A couple years ago, Ms. Cuckle was the prime suspect when her then-boyfriend took a bullet to the head. The SDPD had a witness, but the witness disappeared and they had to drop the charges. The case remains unsolved." Parker smiled condescendingly. "Your dog story is cute, but I'd say we have ourselves a black widow on our hands."

I felt the blood rush to my face. "But she never married either of them," I said, trying to keep from shouting. "What could she have to gain?"

"You're in love with her after, what, three days? Maybe guys get so damn obsessed with her that the only kind of break-ups that stick are the messy kind."

He made a good point. But that didn't mean I had to like it. I told my client that under the circumstances there'd be no charge, and I hightailed it out of there before Parker reconsidered his threat to revoke my license.

Sherry lived in a small apartment over someone's garage. I'd seen her receive her mail at the diner, so I figured that the cops might not have quick access to her address. I took a short cut over there for good measure.

She opened her door on my first knock. She looked relieved to see me. Of course, she could have just been relieved that I was anyone other than Parker.

She let me in, and I saw the packed suitcases by the door.

"They're coming for you," I said.

"Because of San Diego?"

"Yeah. I want to be on your side, but even I think it's too much of a coincidence. I need to know though, why'd you try to kill me too?"

Her eyes welled up with tears. "You've always listened to me — I know that from what you said before — so please listen to me now. I didn't kill my old boyfriend, I didn't kill Brad, and I didn't try to kill you." She wiped her eyes. "I was home alone watching TV the night of the San Diego murder. I managed to convince the eyewitness that he was mistaken by relaying to him every last detail of the shows I'd been watching. They weren't repeats, but the witness worried that the police would think I seduced him. So he took off. He contacted me later and offered me a job. I couldn't stay in San Diego after what'd happened, so I followed him here to Buffalo."

Someone pounded on the door.

"Police!" I mouthed.

Sherry looked at her bags, then at me. Her shoulders slumped. "There's only one way out," she said as she reached for the door.

It was Ritchie. He pushed his way in. "We have to get out of here," he said. Then he saw me. "I should have known you'd be here, you sick stalker."

"So you're the witness from San Diego," I said.

"She told you our history, huh? You figure if you talk to her lots, you can get into her pants? It doesn't work that way. I've been talking to her everyday for two years, and —"

"Were you a witness tonight too, Ritchie? Of course you were. You witnessed both murders because you pulled the trigger both times. You're the sick stalker, Ritchie."

Sherry gasped.

Ritchie pulled out a gun, undoubtedly the same gun that'd fired the bullets found inside Mr. Cheater's chest and

San Diego boyfriend's head. I didn't let it bother me.

"Yeah, I killed them," Ritchie said, his voice a snarl. They didn't appreciate what they had. You couldn't possibly either. I should have just shot you too, instead of poisoning your food. Well, I can fix that right now."

He raised the gun to within inches of my face.

The shot nearly deafened me. The blood tasted hot and foul. But I was otherwise okay.

Lucky for me, Ritchie hadn't closed the door, and Parker hadn't used his flashers or siren on his approach.

The lieutenant's shot didn't kill Ritchie on impact. He lived long enough for Sherry to give him hell.

She knelt down beside him, careful not to step in his blood or touch his shaking face. "You just didn't understand," she said. "Talking with me everyday for two years doesn't mean anything if you don't listen to what I have to say. That's all a girl wants, is for her someone to *really listen* to her."

Sherry stood and hugged me. She whispered in my ear what she planned to do to thank me for clearing her name. I *listened* very carefully to every word she said.

Hollywood To Hollywood

Michael Hemmingson

I had bad credit and this made me a target. The money in my checking account was disappearing like morning fog on a hot beach. I hadn't worked in three months because of a back injury I got while shooting a stunt. I'm a tinsel town stunt man, or I was, and I had an accident. My lawyer and I agreed on a settlement with the insurance company, but it was taking a while for the money to process.

"Unfortunately," my lawyer said on the phone, "the proverbial wheels move slow in this business."

"Can you grease the proverbials?" I asked.

"Wish I could," he said. "Look," he said, "the money will be here any day, eh."

With rent for my apartment in North Hollywood, food, the monthly minimum on my two maxed-out cards and other necessary bills, I figured in three months I'd be out on the street. I couldn't work because my back really did hurt and no film director in town would hire me until I was in the clear.

"Go on unemployment," my ex-girlfriend suggested one night.

"I can't," I told her, "I owe the state money."

"How's that?"

"Seven years ago I was getting unemployment, then I did a few jobs I didn't report. *They* eventually found out; twice a year I get a bill asking for the $1,225.56 I cheated the state out of."

My ex-girlfriend gave me this look, and she sighed. "Vern," she said, "you have to stop doing shit like that."

"Not now, okay?"

"And you wonder why I broke up with you," she said.

Usually, when telemarketers call, I say no thanks and hang up, or just hang up. But not this time; the woman on the other end of the phone had a very nice voice, and at that moment — it was 10:30 in the morning — I needed to hear such a voice.

"Mr. Maddox? Mr. Vernon Maddox?"

"Yes?"

"May I call you Vern?"

I said, "Most people do."

She said, "Vern, I bet you could use some money right now. Vern, I bet a credit card would come in handy just about now. Am I right, or am I right?"

I said, "You're right."

"Well, then, I'm in a position to help you; the company I work for can help you. Yes, indeed, Vern, National Benefits Corp. is the ticket for your ride."

"So," I said, "what's the scam?"

"Hey, this is no scam," she said. "We *can* help you."

"How?"

"We can give you a MasterCard."

"Look," I said.

"Vern," she said. "Please, hear me out. Won't you hear

me out?"

"You'd be wasting your time."

"Give me two minutes, Vern. Can you give me two minutes?"

"Sure," I said.

"Your credit isn't so hot right now — that's why we have your number. Everyone working here at National Benefits Corp. has been there; we know how it goes. So here's the offer: we can give you a MasterCard with a $1500 credit limit. We have a one-time processing fee of $59.95 and an annual membership fee of $99.95. The one-time processing fee will be billed to your card the first month; the membership fee can also be billed that first month, or spread out over ten payments. Your choice. That's the key, Vern: it's all your choice. It's your life, your money, *you choose.*"

"That's almost $160," I said, "for $1500 of credit?"

"I think it's a good deal, Vern. I mean, you can't sit there and tell me that you *don't* need $1500 — right now or anytime soon. Plus, every six months, you're eligible for a $500 credit increase."

"What's the finance charge?"

"19.5%," she said. "Waived if you pay your full month's balance each month before the due date."

All I could think of was my impending dire financial situation and how another card might be nice in case of an emergency. "What the hell," I said, "give it to me."

Her voice brightened even more: "A *good* choice, Vern. Now, I have to tell you, there's this big package I *have* to send you — some paperwork you need to fill out, some literature about everything we offer. To defray the printing and postage costs, there's a one-time charge of $9.95. We can take care of this via Check-By-Phone, and I'll have that package out to you this afternoon."

I gave her my checking account information — router number, account number, check number — which she quickly processed.

"On behalf on National Benefits Corp.," she said, "I welcome you aboard."

"Hey, wait," I said.

"Yes?"

"What's your name?"

"Have a good day, sir."

The package arrived two weeks later. I didn't bother to read all the promotional materials — like the specials I could get on airline tickets, hotels, restaurants and theater seats if I signed up — and they seemed to want just way too much personal information on the "paperwork." It was a waste of ten bucks; so I called the 888 number to cancel my possible membership.

"Why do you want to cancel?" the operator for National Benefits Corp. asked me. Her voice was coarse and tired.

"I've decided that I'm not interested," I said.

"Why?"

"I'm just not."

"But why?"

"I don't have to tell you why."

"No you don't," she said, "but why don't you tell me anyway?"

"I don't want your damn card," I said.

"Why?"

"Would you stop asking me that!"

"Don't you *need* a credit card?"

"Actually, no."

"You were interested before."

"I wasn't thinking straight."

"Oh, *now,* Mr. Maddox, I *know* you can use this card."

"I don't want it."

"You don't sound sincere about that, Mr. Maddox."

"Look," I said, "are you going to cancel me or what? I don't want you to send me any more mail, and I don't want you to sell my address or phone number."

"Maybe you should sleep on this, Mr. Maddox," the operator said. "I'm sure you'll think differently in the morning."

I said, "Put me through to a supervisor."

"A supervisor? Why?"

"Just do it."

"Why would you want to talk to a supervisor, Mr. Maddox?"

"Because you're not being cooperative."

"Of *course* I am."

"You're not doing what I'm asking."

"What *are* you asking?"

"For you to cancel me from your system."

"Mr. Maddox, did you read about all the wonderful benefits you'd receive when you become a member?"

"Are you going to do what I say, or do I have to lodge some kind of complaint?"

"Why would you want to do that?"

"Listen, what's your name? What's your operator number?"

"Why do you want to know that, Mr. Maddox? You're being irrational."

I took a deep breath and told myself not to scream. "Look, you annoying bitch, cancel me out of your goddamn system."

"Very well, I will," she said, and hung up.

But that wasn't the end of it. A week later, looking at my bank statement, I noticed three withdrawals attributed to "NBC" for $9.95, $59.95, and $99.95. I called my bank and told them I only authorized the first payment, not the other two.

"They're ACH payments," the bank person on the phone said. She kept sneezing as I talked to her.

"What's that?"

"Did you do a Check-By-Phone with this organization?"

"Yeah," I said softly.

"Unfortunately, these transactions are more than forty-eight hours old. We can get the money back if we're notified within two days; after that, you have to go to them."

"I see."

"This happens a lot," I was told. "You have to be careful about who you give your account information to. If you'd like, we can notify you if this happens again."

"Please," I said. Then I called National Benefits Corp. The operator was a male with a southern accent. I explained the situation to him. "I canceled," I said.

"I see that you did cancel, it's here on your account. But there's no record of these payments, other than the $9.95 for the membership package."

"I have a record right here, on my bank statement."

"It's not here."

"What's going on? Are you people trying to rip me off?"

"There must be some kind of mistake, sir."

"You bet there is."

"I can give you the corporate number if you'd like. You can talk to someone there."

"Please."

I called the corporate number and got voice mail. I left a message. For three days I left messages and no one returned my calls.

Then the bank called, informing me that NBC was attempting to make two ACH withdrawals: $59.95 and $99.95.

"Don't let them do it," I said.

"We can make a stop payment on these requests," I was told. "The fee will be $10."

I sighed.

"If you'd like," I was told, "we can put a permanent block on any future ACH requests from this company."

"What will it cost?"

"$15."

"Do it."

This is when things got *really* interesting.

The first call from NBC came four days later, early in the morning. The man on the other end had a deep and serious voice. "Mr. Maddox," he said, "we have a bit of a problem."

"It's about time you people called. What's with stealing money from my bank account?"

"Yes, your bank account," he said. "You need to fix your bank account, Mr. Maddox."

"What?"

"You placed a block on your account. We have payments coming back, rejected. This isn't going to help your existing shabby credit history."

"You people took $160 out of my account, which I did *not* authorize."

"Of course you authorized it. You gave us the go ahead to enroll you in our program."

"All I wanted was to read your literature, and for that you got ten bucks out of me. I did *not* enroll, I did *not* want to be a member. You took two fees out, and I didn't even *get* a card."

"No, *our* attempts to collect the fees were met with rejection by *your* bank account."

"And not only did you take $160, you tried to take it *again*. Now tell me," I asked, "are you people thieves, or is there something wrong with your computers?"

"You entered a verbal deal with us over the phone," the man said, talking slowly, emphasizing each word, "and we expect you to honor it. And The Computer," he said with emphasis, "never makes mistakes."

"The fuck," I said. "You already got the money out of me. And what did I get? I don't want your card, I don't want your program. What I want, dude, is my goddamn money back."

"What we want," he said, "is the money you owe us."

"What do I have to do? Go to the authorities?"

He laughed.

"You find that funny," I said.

"No wonder you have bad credit," he said. "You obviously have a problem with honoring debts."

"I'm going to ask you one more time," I said, "and I'm even going to ask you nicely. Would you please return the money you unlawfully removed from my bank account?"

"Mr. Maddox," he said, "I believe you fail to comprehend the gravity of this situation."

"What's your name?"

"You don't need to know my name."

"Yes I do. Who are you?"

"Someone you don't want to know too well, believe me."

"Is that a threat?"

"Mr. Maddox, I'm going to ask — no, I'm going to *tell* you something *once* and *only* once, and it is this: take the blockage of National Benefits Corp. *off* your bank account."

I laughed, called him an ass, and hung up.

He phoned several hours later. He said, "Mr. Maddox, I hope you have come to your senses and have done what I asked."

"You didn't *ask*, you told me. Remember?"

He said, "Is the block off the account?"

I said, "Just who in the hell are you?"

"A nightmare for you," he said, and hung up.

I found the literature they sent me. The return address for NBC was a P.O. box in Hollywood, Florida. I shook my head and said to myself, "Florida." So when he called me again, early the next morning, I was ready for him. "Tell me," I asked, "how's the weather down there in Hollywood, Florida?"

He paused before responding. "What makes you think I'm in Florida?"

"That's where NBC is."

"That doesn't mean I'm there. Look, Mr. Maddox, if your intent is to intimidate me, it's not working."

"Oh, I forgot. *You're* the one who has the job to intimidate."

"Yes, you can look at it that way —"

"Is that your title?" I asked. "The Intimidator?"

"Listen, Mr. Maddox," he said, "you need to remove the block from your account."

"So you can steal more money from me?"

"You're viewing this whole matter in the wrong light."

"You listen to me, Mr. Whateveryournameis. I am going to the authorities. The cops there in Hollywood, the cops here in Hollywood; the FBI or the Florida attorney's general office — whoever it is I have to go to and file a criminal complaint, I will."

"You don't want to do that."

"No, I don't. So why don't you return my money, and I won't have to?"

"We don't owe you money," he said. "You know it's the other way around."

"What is it with you?" I said. "Do you want to go to jail?"

He chuckled — there was an echo. I pictured him in a big empty room, sitting at a desk with a phone or a head-set, wearing a cheap suit.

"I look forward to the day they bust you."

"Bust?" he said. "*I'm* going to bust your nose, Mr. Maddox. That's the only busting that's going to occur. I'm going to bust your nose open and show you a world of pain," and then the line went dead.

He called at midnight. He spoke in a whisper: "You go to the authorities, you'll regret it."

"Maybe I already filed a complaint," I said, half-asleep.

"I don't think you did," he said, "but if you did, you are going to be very sorry."

"Do you know it's illegal to make these kind of threats?"

"You should be afraid; yes, yes you should. I could be there in L.A., you know. I *could* be watching you."

"But you're not."

"How do you know? We have people in L.A. We have people everywhere. We have people to *take care* of our business."

"I'm not afraid," I said.

"You should be," he said.

"Then come get me," I said.

"If I have to come to you," he said, "I will punch you in the brain."

The next call:

"Yes, as I said before, I will punch you in the brain, Mr. Maddox."

"Listen," I said, "I don't even know what to call you.

Here we are, we're speaking on such a regular basis, you know my name but what's yours? What kind of relationship is this?"

"You're not funny."

"I've always fancied myself a comedian."

"This is not a funny situation," he said. "This is fucking serious."

"Yes, it is serious," I said. "If you don't stop harassing me, I'll call the police."

"And then what? Will you get a restraining order on me? You don't know my name, Mr. Maddox, and you have no idea where I'm calling from."

"I know who you work for."

"They'll categorically deny it. Look, Mr. Maddox, *look:* there is a very simple way out of this predicament you have found yourself in. Remove the block from your bank account. Then we'll all be happy."

"So you people can steal $160 from me once a month?"

"A small price."

"What kind of strong-arming is this? What are you, some kind of phone Mafia?"

"Ah, the Mafia," he said. "What do the Mafia do, Mr. Maddox? They break legs, they break arms. They break faces. These are things that can happen to you."

"Like I said before, come get me."

"Do you know what I can do to your life, Mr. Maddox?"

"Tell me."

"I could find your girlfriend and rape her."

"I don't have a girlfriend."

"Your boyfriend."

"Funny."

"You know what I mean."

"I don't. Tell me."

"People close to you — mom, dad, ex-girlfriend, best buddy. We have our ways; we can find someone, and we'll hurt this person."

"Maybe there isn't anyone I'm close to."

"If this is true, you are a sad *sad* man."

"You must be getting tired of my phone calls, Mr. Maddox."

"Actually, I've started to look forward to them."

"I'm getting tired of calling you. It seems to me we have to pay you a visit."

"I'll be here."

"We have guns."

"I'm shaking in my boots."

"Mr. Maddox, you will do as I tell you!"

"Testy."

"You are a dead man!"

The next call, he sounded drunk. "You fucker," he slurred. "You motherfucker. I hate you. I fucking hate you. Do you know much I stinking fucking *hate* you!"

I changed my phone number and the calls stopped. I rang my lawyer to tell him about the change. My lawyer said, "Speak of the devil! I happen to have a check here for you; a very nice big check."

"You're kidding."

"It came this morning."

"I'll be right there."

I drove fast to his office.

I thought about asking him for advice on the National Benefits Corp. problem, but I didn't feel he'd have any. Or he'd bill me an hour. I had a better idea anyway; it came to me in the car.

My lawyer asked, "So, now that you have your settlement, what will you do?"

"I'm going to take a vacation."

"Vacations are good."

"I'm going to Florida."

"Oh, I *love* Florida."

The weather in Hollywood, Florida, wasn't that different from Hollywood, California — there was less smog, of course, and the air was a little more moist and thick.

I got a rental car and checked into a motel in North Beach; my window revealed a nice view of the ocean and surfers catching waves.

I had a Plan A and a Plan B. Plan A was to apply for a job at National Benefits Corp.; I figured that a telemarketing operation like that had high turnover and was always hiring desperate people in a need of a quick job. I'd done the telemarketing routine when I was younger. Plan B was to just go straight to the Post Office and hang out near their box, wait for someone to pick up the mail.

Plan A it was; I found an ad for the company in the help wanted section of the local newspaper. I called the number listed, talked to a tired-sounding fellow for a minute, and was given an appointment time the next morning.

The address was in a complex of business buildings — drab concrete gray structures. I was prompt for the appointment, and so were a dozen other people. It was a group thing, and the group consisted of men and women young and old — American, Cuban, and Haitian.

We were all "hired" within a half an hour — all we had to do was sign some paperwork; we'd be independent subcontractors being paid on commission. We'd receive minimum wage for a day's worth of training, which would be the next morning, and after that, we were on our own.

The next day was half a day, three hours at most. We were given a five-page script that we'd use when talking to people on the phone; there was the initial pitch and the answers to just about any question a potential victim might have.

I say "victim" because that's what the people on the other end of the line — all across America — were. I was one, had been one. Everything about this operation was bullshit, I quickly spotted all the lies that I fell for and wondered how they got me in the first place.

Money.

The object, of course, was to get the bank account information from the people we'd call.

Did this organization actually issue credit cards? Supposedly. But it was not a phone operator's place to ponder such things. A phone operator sat at his or her station as The Computer dialed numbers.

During the break, I sat outside on the hot concrete, eating an apple and drinking from a small carton of milk I purchased in the break room. Cost: $2.

A young lady with soft white skin sat next to me. She was very skinny and had crooked teeth. I liked her eyes. Her hair was long, dark and straight. She chewed on baby carrots.

She asked, "So, holmes, what do you think?"

I said, "I think I'd rather be at the beach."

"I hear you," she said. "Man, it sucks needing a job."

I nodded.

She said, "You think the Feds might raid this place?"

"What do you mean?"

"You *know* what's going on here. All these places are alike."

I shrugged, trying to look dumb. I was undercover, after all.

She said, "Two months ago I was working a telemarketing gig across town. Buy three roll of films, you might win a vacation to Los Angeles. You know, go there and maybe you'll see the movie stars. Take pictures of them with your three rolls of film. I was there for *two* days and I go out for lunch, I go across the street to the Burger King, and I'm sitting in the B.K. eating a Whopper and I see all these black cars and vans swoop in and surround the place where I work. And I see all my supervisors and these people I work for being taken away in handcuffs. And that night I see on the news how the FBI cracked down on a telemarketing scam. Man, I was lucky I had that Whopper, or I would be in lock-up."

"It would make a great commercial for Burger King," I said. "'Aren't you happy you had a Whopper?'"

She smiled, exposing a lot of teeth pointing in various directions. "Yeah? Think so? Yeah. Cool."

I started work the next day. I was given a head-set and a computer screen. Before I began, I was told that if I had a difficult potential customer, I would transfer the call to Super A, a woman with dreadlocks. If The Computer sent me a call from an existing customer with a complaint that I wasn't equipped to handle (I could only deal with certain questions, which my script had the answers to), I would transfer my call to Super B, a handsome fellow with long black hair in a pony tail.

The guy sitting at the computer screen next to me said, "Super B knows how to deal with the jerks. He's been here the longest."

The job wasn't in me, but I did my best. I talked to men and women and lied to them. I was on a mission, I played the part. I signed up two unsuspecting people in my first hour. $45 a person, I made $90 commission. I decided this was a good time to request a bathroom break. I really did have to go. I passed by Super B's office. His door was closed. He was talking to someone via his headset. I couldn't hear him. He was a tall, slender guy with dark skin, wearing a white shirt, a blue tie, and black slacks. I went to the restroom and took a piss. Coming back, Super B's door was cracked open. I could hear him when I walked by:

"Listen, Mrs. Dalrymple, we can ruin your credit. More than it's been ruined. It'll be destroyed for the rest of your life. Do you want that? *Do you?* Mrs. Dalrymple? *Stop* crying. Stop crying like a goddamn baby. *I hate that.* Now, you listen to me. You do what I say. Okay? *Okay?* Okay, *now* we're talking. *Now* we're being reasonable, Mrs. Dalrymple."

It was him.

It was his voice.

I sat at my post, wondering how I'd do this.

I'd just do it. I didn't want to be here a minute longer. I was here for one reason only.

I got up, headed straight for Super B's office, closed and locked his door, and said, "Hey."

He was talking into his headset, then stopped.

I said, "Hang up."

He just looked at me.

I reached over and pulled the headset out of the phone-jack.

"What the —"

I smiled.

"What the fuck," he said. "What the *fuck* is your malfunction, buddy boy?"

I socked him in the nose. There was blood. He tried to make it for the door. I grabbed him by the pony tail and slammed his face into his desk.

"So we meet at last," I said.

"What the hell do you think you're doing?" he said.

"Don't you recognize my voice?" I asked.

"What?"

"I'm going to let you up," I said. "If you try anything funny, I will punch you in the brain. Oh yes, you *know* that phrase well. *I will punch your brain, asshole."*

I released him, taking a step back.

He touched his nose and looked at the blood on his fingers. "You can't do this to me," he said. "I'm a Seminole Indian."

"My name is Vern," I said, "Vernon Maddox."

It took him a moment. The color went out of his face. I liked how white he suddenly became, a true pale face.

He said, "No shit."

I said, "Oh yeah."

He said, "You want payback."

I said, "And I'm about to get it."

I was ready for a fight. He seemed fit. Instead, he screamed. His scream was quite up there in the decibels. His scream hurt my ears. He jumped up on his desk and cried for help. I tried to grab his legs. He leapt for the door. He ran out the door, shireking. I went after him. It was like an old Keystone Cops flick as I chased him around the many confused and bemused phone operators. I chased him out the building. He got into his car — a Honda Civic — and sped away from the parking lot. I got into my rental and contemplated a pursuit. He was long gone, and it was now time for me to go home.

The next day I called the administrative line to National Benefits Corp. A computerized voice said: "If you know your party's three-digit extension, you may dial at any time."

I knew his extension all right, *Mr. Super B*.

He was there.

He said, "Hello."

I said, "How's the nose, buddy?"

Silence.

"Hello?" I said.

"What?" he said.

"It's your favorite dude — me: Mr. Maddox. What do you have to say now?"

"You're in big trouble," he said softly, "you don't know who you just messed with. You're in a world of pain, a universe of double trouble, pal. *I'm* a Seminole Indian."

"And I'm a professional stuntman," I said. "The guy who's in the shit is you, my friend. Because I know *where you work*. And I know *where you live*. Yes, I know where your crib is, homeboy. I followed you when you high-tailed it out in your piece of shit Honda like some scared little bitch. You *hear* me, *bitch*? You're the one who's about to get punched in the brain."

He hung up.

When I returned to Los Angeles, I dialed Florida from an airport payphone. Super B didn't answer his extension. I was routed to an operator: "How may I direct your call?"

I *still* didn't know the guy's name. "I'm trying to reach Super B."

"Oh," I was told, "he doesn't work here anymore."

Empty Houses

Graham Powell

It's tough to follow someone who doesn't know where he's going. Two full days of false starts, sudden stops, and U-turns left me wishing I had something stronger than coffee in my thermos. On the plus side, this driver wouldn't have noticed if I'd worn a Santa suit and driven a sleigh.

I'd trailed the blocky beige Volvo up and down nearly every road, lane, and boulevard in the Broadmoor district, some of them three or four times. Low-slung ranch style homes lined street after street. The occasional ugly Art Deco house was a relief.

After two days with an unobstructed view of the back of the driver's head I felt like we were old friends, but I still had no idea what he was up to. I'd waited in line behind him as he bought a pack of smokes at a convenience store, sat beside him in a fast food joint, stood at the next urinal in a gas station restroom, and I knew no more about him than I could see from his photograph. The eight-by-ten picture clipped to my notebook showed a man in his early thirties, one hundred and ninety pounds, brown hair and eyes, and a small scar just below his chin. He wore his dress blues, the silver wings on his chest and bars on his collar shining. Across the bottom I had printed *Capt. Frederick Chapel.*

Just over 24 hours earlier, his wife had handed me the picture and said, “Please, Mr. Ross, you’ve got to help me.”

We had agreed to meet at a small restaurant just down the street from the west gate of Barksdale AFB. It was a diner, really, a lunch counter and a few tables topped with chipped formica. I liked the place. The coffee was hot and the waitresses always had a kind word.

I studied the photograph. “Your husband?” I asked. “He’s the reason you called?”

Patricia Chapel was tall, nearly six feet in her platform sandals, and a few years younger than her husband — late twenties, say. She wore a black knit top under a tan linen jacket, with a matching linen skirt. She was as trim and fit as the man in the picture. Aerobics, maybe. Or tennis.

“That’s right,” she said. “Fred’s been acting funny for a week or so. Quiet, moody. I thought it might be something from work — he flies B-52s — but now he’s started, well, disappearing.”

“Disappearing?” I said. “No longer visible?”

She smiled in spite of herself. “No longer *around.* He’s been up and out the door before eight every day this week. I thought he was down at the flight line, but I ran into Colonel Fleiss and his wife yesterday, and he said Fred’s taken a week of leave. No explanation. I was so embarrassed. I wanted to ask Fred about it last night, but God, I just couldn’t. What could I say?”

“You want me to find out where he’s going.”

“I guess I’m afraid,” she said. “I couldn’t bear to face Fred, to hear him say there’s someone else. But I can’t bear not knowing, either.”

I reached across the table and patted her hand. “Mrs. Chapel, I think I can help you.”

And here I was, still trying.

On the morning of the third day, Chapel found what he was looking for.

We'd been cruising the 900 block of Grover, a residential street much like all the others. Suddenly the Volvo swerved left into a driveway. As I drove past the taillights went dark and Chapel got out. I parked up the block and watched him in the rearview mirror.

The house was L-shaped. The long leg ran parallel to the street and ended in a garage at the far end. The other leg was short, broad, and jutted into the yard. An abbreviated porch ran from the garage to the front door.

Chapel walked slowly up the driveway to the porch. He peered inside a window, cupping his hands against the glass, then straightened up and walked to the door. He stood there for a moment, tense as a spring, then pushed the door open and went inside.

He was in there for maybe ten minutes. When he came out he marched straight to his car and drove away without looking back. I waited until he'd made the corner before I got out and headed for the house.

Inside there was nothing. Not a stick of furniture, no clothing, nothing. The kitchen cabinets held neither pots nor pans. The bedrooms were empty, not even marks on the carpets to show where the furniture had stood. Blank patches lined the walls where pictures used to hang. The house was vacant and had been for a while.

It didn't take me much longer to go through it than it had taken Chapel. There was simply nothing to see. I was getting ready to leave when I noticed the sliding glass doors to the back yard and decided to take a look.

The yard held the usual shrubs and flowers, dominated by a large weeping willow. I poked around for a while, then went and stood beneath the thick canopy of its branches.

It was cool under there, and pleasant. I shook a cigarette out of the pack and lit it, and stood there staring at the house, smoking and thinking. After a few minutes I took one last drag from the cigarette and flipped it away.

It came down on a patch of newly-turned earth, six feet by three.

I picked up Chapel again just before noon. He came out the west gate and sped across the Shreveport-Barksdale bridge. I had to hurry my car into gear to keep him in sight. No hesitation this time; he went over the bridge and down the road on the other side without slowing. When we arrived at Centenary College he turned into a small storefront shopping center.

The parking lot behind it was perfect for people who ride the bus. A line of cars snaked its way around, looking for a space. The Volvo was three feet ahead of me. Behind me a Range Rover rode my bumper.

Suddenly the Volvo stopped short. I had to jump on the brakes to avoid a collision. The Rover loomed up in my rearview mirror but somehow came to a shuddering stop just shy of my car. The soccer mom driver leaned out her window and yelled something obscene.

I replied in kind and turned around to see Chapel striding towards me. He yanked open the driver's side door and grabbed me by the lapel. "Who are you?" he shouted. "Why are you following me?"

I was made. "Calm down, Fred," I said. I pushed him away from the door and clambered out. "Listen to me for a minute . . ."

He drew back a fist and I stepped inside it, wrapping my arms around his chest. "Hold it!" I said. "I'm working for your wife! Your wife, Chapel!"

He struggled and pounded his fists against my back, but I had him wrapped up tight and I didn't let go. We wrestled like that for a few minutes before he gave it up. His breathing was ragged and his face blotchy and red.

"What about my wife?" he said.

Upstairs there was a diner not much different than the one I'd met his wife in. We'd beaten the lunch rush and didn't have any trouble getting a table. The waitress brought us some coffee, and after she'd left I said, "I'm a private detective, Fred. Your wife found out you'd taken a week of leave. She wanted to know how you were spending it."

He laughed quietly. "Oh, Jesus, that's too much. So all this is going to come out because she was afraid I'd miss a promotion. If she only knew."

"I expect she will."

"Yeah," he said. "Yeah, I guess she will after all." He sipped from his cup and stared down at the table.

"Last weekend," he said without preamble. "Me and Tim Oslansky and a couple of girls he knew went out barhopping. We hit three or four places, got pretty tanked. One of the girls, I think her name was Jenny, she worked at a real estate office. She said she had the keys to this house. She said we should have a party. We picked up a case of beer and drove over there. I don't even remember the trip. Christ knows how I found the place again.

"The house was empty. We sat around on the living room floor for a while, drinking and talking. Jenny and Tim started pawing each other like a couple of teenagers and headed off to the back bedroom. The other girl just sat there giggling. I was bored. I wanted to go, but of course I had to wait on Tim.

"About that time he came stumbling up the hall, trying

to run and pull up his pants at the same time. 'She's dead, oh God she's dead,' he said. 'Drugs, an overdose. She snorted something.' I let them talk me out of calling the cops. We were drunk, we weren't supposed to be there. They'd arrest us all for sure. Even if I didn't go to jail, my career would be over."

"Why did you go back?"

He shrugged and shook his head. "I don't know. We shouldn't have left her like that. It wasn't right."

I fired up a cigarette. "You know there's a grave there."

"Oh, God," he said. He pressed his hands to his face.

"Who is Tim Oslansky?"

"Just a guy I know. He's a navigator in my squadron."

"This girl Jenny. Do you know her last name?"

"I don't know. Tim would know."

"The other girl," I said. "What was her name?"

Fred thought for a minute. "Britney, Brandi, something like that. I don't remember."

I stubbed out my cigarette. "Now we're going to talk to your wife. Then we're going to talk to the police. After that, we'll see."

He didn't try to stop me when I picked up the check. I tucked away the receipt and noted it down in my expense book. Chapel was buying whether he knew it or not.

It was two o'clock by the time we returned to the base. His house was a small Spanish-style cottage just off the main boulevard, stucco and tile like all the older buildings at Barksdale. On the stoop he hesitated, steeling himself the way he had at the Grover Street house. Then he unlocked the door and we went in.

"Patti?" he said. "Patti, honey, it's me." He walked towards the back of the house, still calling her name.

This house had more furniture than the other, but it felt stuffy as though it had been shut up for a while. As though no one lived there.

There was a small den off the foyer, barely more than a couple of chairs and a bookshelf. I wandered in there and was looking around when he came back wearing a puzzled frown. "She's not here," he said. "Where could she have gone?"

"Sorry, it's not my day to keep up with her," I said. *"You're* the one I'm after. Probably nothing to worry about."

The phone rang. Fred hurried over and glanced at the caller ID. "My wife's cell phone," he said. "Thank God."

He picked it up and said, "Hi, honey. Where . . ." Blood drained from his face as his fingers tightened around the phone. I felt my own hands clenching.

Fred lowered the phone into the cradle and turned to me slowly. "He's got Patti," he whispered.

We sat at the kitchen table. I had my notepad out, going over what we knew. "No police," said Fred. "He said he'll kill her if we go to the police."

"That's all?" I said. "He didn't say who he was or what he wanted?"

"He said he wanted me to think about Jenny." Fred swallowed hard. "He wanted me to think about what I did to Jenny."

"All right," I said. "Here's what we're going to do. You stay by the phone. I'm going to find out what I can about Jenny. Maybe I can figure out who this guy is, get to him before he's ready." I pulled a business card out of my wallet and scribbled my cell number on the back. "When he calls, you let me know."

Fred's hand trembled as he took my card. He saw me

watching him. "I'll be okay," he said.

I looked up the address of the house on Grover in my city directory. A few phone calls later I found it was listed with The Winchell-Miller Company, a local real estate firm. Ten minutes after that I walked through their front door.

The lady at the reception desk was in her early fifties at a guess. I gave her my best smile. She didn't return the favor. "How may I help you, sir?" she said, her voice raspy. Automatically I glanced down at the ashtray on her desk. It was filled to overflowing.

"Hi," I said. "I'm here to see Jenny."

"Really?" she said. "When you see her, tell her she's fired."

"Excuse me? What for?"

"She hasn't been in all week, and it's her turn on the phones. I should be out selling right now, instead of sitting here on my duff."

I rubbed my chin. "Maybe you could help me get hold of her . . ."

"Already tried," she said, shaking her head. "Called her, paged her, sent her an email. Drew a big blank. Sorry, mister."

I was trying to think of something more to ask when she said, "And tell her friend Brenda she's fired, too."

"Brenda?" I said.

"Yes, Brenda. You must know Brenda."

My smile broadened. "Of course. Jenny's best friend. Say, maybe she could help me find Jenny?"

"I doubt it," she grumbled, but she found Brenda's number for me.

Brenda Tuggle lived in an apartment complex near the university. The place was a maze, but I finally sorted out the building numbers and found the right apartment. There was no answer to my knock. I glanced around and bent down for a closer look. She'd left the deadbolt off. I pulled out a shim and quickly worked the knob open.

The apartment was still and musty. There were only three rooms, a kitchen/living room combo separated by a bar, the bedroom, and a tiny bathroom. Brenda herself was in her late twenties, dark haired, and getting a little pudgy, a fact that her tight blue jeans did little to conceal. I never saw a shirt clash with jeans, but hers managed the trick. It was a garish floral print, sunflowers or something, that looked like it belonged on wallpaper. Ugly, without a doubt.

But no so ugly as the bruises that ringed her neck.

She lay on her back in the tub, bulging eyes staring up at the ceiling. The shower curtain had come loose and partially covered her. I stood in the doorway to the bathroom and turned to look at the front door. A straight shot. Someone forced his way in, shoved her back into the bathroom, and choked the life out of her. Yesterday, maybe the day before.

When my phone rang I nearly fell in with her. I managed to activate it and said, "Hello? Hello?"

It was Fred. "He called. He wants to meet."

I met Fred just outside the base and he followed me out to Dixie Gardens. Two or three blocks from our destination I stopped and popped the trunk. Inside was a lockbox I kept chained to the spare tire. I unlocked it and took out the .38 Colt Detective Special and its holster. Fred pulled in behind me as I clipped the gun to my belt.

He rolled down the window, his face tight. "What's the plan?" he said.

"This guy — what did he say his name was?"

"Williamson," said Chapel. "Earl Williamson."

"He's not expecting two of us. Give me ten minutes, then go on over to his house. Walk right up to the door and ring the bell. I'm going to go around back. I'll get your wife loose, then we'll jump on Earl and call the cavalry. Got it?"

My voice was hoarse, but Fred didn't notice. "Do you think she's alive?" he said.

The odds were even. "It's you he wants," I said. I clapped him on the shoulder. "She's fine. Hang in there, buddy."

I climbed back in my car and drove slowly down the street. The map said Dixie Gardens was within the city limits, but one look around and you knew you were out in the country. The streets had shoulders instead of curbs; the houses were older, the plots bigger. Many of the yards were fenced in, with dogs or even horses running around inside.

The address Williamson gave us was on the left near the end of the block, an old-fashioned frame house painted a crisp white. Three short steps led up to a little entry porch. An old Ford pickup squatted in the driveway.

I made a left turn and then another, then drifted to the curb. The house that backed up to Earl's was a dun-colored bungalow of concrete block. Twenty yards and a short chain link fence was all that separated them. I got out and walked casually up the gravel drive. No cars, nobody home. Once past the house I dropped to a crouch and ran. As I vaulted the fence my pants cuff snagged and ripped away cleanly. I didn't break stride and in a few seconds I had my back pressed against Williamson's house.

I shuffled over to the windows on the right and peered inside. Kitchen. A sink full of dirty dishes. No woman's touch here. Not anymore.

I moved to the left. Bedroom. Patricia Chapel lay on the bed, trussed up with duct tape. Another strip covered her mouth. I went to work on the window latch with my Swiss Army knife and had it open in less than a minute. The window squeaked as I raised it, but no noises answered it, and I clambered over the sill.

Patti was staring at me wide-eyed. I sliced the tape from her ankles and wrists and leaned close to her ear. "Go out the window and keep going past the other house," I whispered. "My car's at the curb." I pressed my cell phone into her hand and closed her fingers around it. "Call 911 and wait. Don't come back for any reason. Understand?"

She nodded. I helped her out the window and watched her run across the yard.

The doorbell rang.

Floorboards creaked and I heard footsteps from the front of the house. I eased the bedroom door open. Through a doorway opposite I could see another bedroom. Down the hall to the right, an archway opened towards the front. Slowly, slowly, slowly, I tiptoed towards it.

A living room filled the front of the house. On the right sat an overstuffed easy chair with an ottoman. A battered old sofa lined the left wall. Beyond was a small open area that served as a vestibule. Two men stood just inside the door, Chapel and a tall, heavyset man. Williamson wore a flannel shirt and sagging blue jeans, and held a Colt Python .357. It looked like it was a foot long.

I pointed my gun at him and started slowly forward.

"I ain't done nothin' to your wife, mister," said Earl. "I don't hurt women."

I was twenty feet away.

"It was an accident," Fred said. "I'm sorry."

"You accidentally raped her? Accidentally strangled her?" Earl chuckled. "I don't think so. You killed my Jenny.

Now it's your turn."

Fifteen feet.

"You don't know," said Fred, his voice even. "You weren't there."

"I know enough to send you to hell. Any last words? A message for your wife?" He thumbed back the hammer on the Python.

Ten feet. As close as I was going to get. "Hands up, Earl," I said.

He stiffened. "Who the hell are you?"

"Drop the gun. Now."

Earl spoke over his shoulder. "You'd better get out of here, mister, unless you want to end up dead like this one."

"Drop the gun and put your hands on your head!"

Williamson turned towards me, chuckling mirthlessly. The magnum rose in his hand.

"Drop it!" I yelled. I brought up my free hand to steady the .38 and spread my legs in a shooter's crouch.

And tumbled over the ottoman.

The .38 bounded out of reach. I looked up at Earl. He laughed again, his eyes full of tears. The Python's muzzle was wide and dark as a tunnel.

Chapel grabbed his arm as he fired. The bullet tore a softball-sized hole through the chair beside me. Earl smacked him open-handed, swatted him aside as though he were a fly. Fred clawed at him again, and Williamson's gun roared.

He turned towards me, but I rammed a shoulder into his ribs, sending us both sprawling to the floor. A bolt of pain shot down my back and my left arm went numb. Earl was on his hands and knees, groping for the gun. I jumped on him and drove my fist into the back of his neck over and over until he stopped trying to get up.

I wobbled over to Fred. He was barely conscious. Blood oozed from his abdomen. His shirt was already soaked through. I put both hands over the wound and said a desperate prayer.

The next day I stood on the porch of another stucco-and-tile villa. A woman answered my knock, a petite brunette, good looking in a Betty Crocker way. "May I help you?" she said.

"May I speak to Tim Oslansky, please?"

She turned and called, "Tim, dear! Someone to see you!"

"Send 'em back!" came the faint reply.

Oslansky was about thirty, stocky, and prematurely bald. He was grilling a couple of steaks on a small patio behind the house. "Tim Oslansky?" I said.

"Yeah."

"My name is Thomas Ross. I'm a friend of Fred Chapel."

"Oh, hell," he said, holding out a greasy hand. "You're that private detective. How's he doing?"

We shook. "I just came from the hospital. Looks like he's going to make it. I suspect his career won't survive, though."

Olsansky laughed. "Yeah, the brass frowns on that sort of thing. How's Patti taking it?"

"Better than I expected. They're probably closer than they've been in years."

"Great, great," he said. He eyed the sling on my left arm. "What about you?"

"Fractured collarbone. Not even a scar to brag about."

He laughed again and poked at the steaks. "Can I get you a beer? Maybe throw on a steak for you?"

"I came to speak to you about Jenny Williamson," I said. "You didn't mean to kill her, did you?"

Oslansky's face grew as red as the coals. "I don't know

what you mean," he said.

"You were playing rough, things got out of hand. An accident. But you tried to cover it up. You went back to the house the next day and buried her body in the back yard. Her husband, Earl Williamson, showed up just as you were leaving. You told him Fred killed her. That took them both out of the picture. Two birds with one stone, eh? Then only Brenda was left. You took care of her yourself."

"I have no idea what you're talking about," he said.

"Tim, do you think I'm making this up? *Williamson is still alive.* And he doesn't have anyone left to protect."

Oslansky turned towards me. The turning fork jutted out of his fist like a stiletto.

"She'll never believe it," I said.

His eyes narrowed. "Who?"

"Betty Crocker," I said. "Your wife. She loves you. She'll never believe you did it. Even if you plead guilty. Even if you go to jail. She won't believe you're a killer. Not unless you show her the kind of man you really are. So go ahead."

His shoulders slumped forward, his head sagged. The fork clattered to the ground. "Honey," he called. "I have to go out for a while. Keep an eye on the steaks."

I stood aside to let him pass. He walked ahead of me like a condemned man on his way to the gallows.

Dangerous Curves

Michael Bracken

Charlie Fischer watched my eyes as I watched the blonde cross the Pink Flamingo to an empty booth.

"Don't go there," he said. "She has dangerous curves."

My gaze traveled up the length of the blonde's legs, over the swell of her hips to her slender waist, then further upward, lingering for a moment on her ample breasts, then up her neck to her face, her full, moist lips and her seductive emerald eyes, and then flowed down the cascading waterfall of blonde tresses to her softly rounded shoulders and finally returned to her breasts where they strained against her tight-fitting red sweater.

"She ain't worth it," he continued.

Without looking at Charlie, I asked, "Is any woman?"

Charlie shrugged. Then he removed my empty beer mug from the bar and carried it to the sink.

I dropped a five on the counter, pushed myself off the barstool, and crossed the room to where the blonde had slipped into a darkened booth. I asked, "This seat taken?"

She looked up at me, then moistened her glossy red lips with the tip of her tongue. "Who's asking?"

I told her my name as I slipped into the booth. She didn't recognize it. I said, "Silverman said to expect you at nine."

She recognized Silverman's name. "I'm only a few minutes late."

"You often make men wait?"

A smile tugged at the corners of her mouth but never materialized. "You like it that way, don't you?"

I didn't respond.

"Silverman said you were the perfect man for the job." Hiram Silverman operated an alcoholic rehab center in west county. While I'd barely spoken to Silverman prior to his phone call that morning, I'd known his brother-in-law for years.

I motioned for Charlie, ordered another beer for myself and a Gimlet twist for the blonde.

After our drinks arrived, she said, "Mr. Rose, I —"

I interrupted. "My friends call me Nate."

"Am I your friend, Mr. Rose?" The tip of her tongue darted out to wet her lips.

She'd slipped off one shoe and I felt her toes press against my crotch. Without breaking eye contact, I reached into my lap and grabbed her foot. I twisted her silk-stockinged toes backward until her eyes widened in pain. "Until I learn otherwise."

"Okay, Nate," she said. I released my grip on the blonde's toes and she removed her foot from my crotch. She sipped from her drink and I waited. She inhaled deeply, straining her sweater, then inhaled again. "My husband," she said, "is Silverman's patient."

"And?"

"He's a mean drunk, abusive when he has a load on."

If she'd been bruised, she'd covered it well.

"I'd divorce him, but there's a prenup. I wouldn't get a penny."

"What's it to me?"

She leaned forward, her heavy breasts resting on the tabletop. "I want out. Silverman says you can make it happen."

The next morning, O'Shannon spent a few minutes networking with his former police associates and learned that my new client, Dianne Corbeil, had never filed any complaints with the police.

O'Shannon had joined Agnes and me after his ballooning weight had forced his retirement from the police department. He hadn't changed any since then and he squeezed his bulk into one of the guest chairs in my office. "You think she's serious?"

I slid Corbeil's retainer check across the desk for O'Shannon to examine.

He whistled softly. "That's a whole lot of serious."

I glanced at the photo of Lydie I kept on the corner of my desk. I'd met her when she'd hired me to scare away her ex-boyfriend, a dim-witted bruiser with a fondness for beating on women. Our marriage had lasted only a short time before cancer had stolen her from me and over the years since then I'd been employed by many other abused women. My new client didn't fit my expectations of a woman in fear.

"I'll run down the husband," I finally told my partner. "You follow up with the Mrs."

"Anything in particular you want me to look for?"

I shook my head. Until we knew something, I didn't even know what questions to ask. We talked for a few minutes more, then O'Shannon returned to his office.

I closed the file folder I'd begun for my new client, then grabbed my jacket. On my way out, I dropped Corbeil's retainer check on Agnes' desk. She looked at the amount, then looked up at me. "Money like this covers a whole lot of sins," she said. "Best be careful."

I stopped first at Silverman's west county rehab center. Years had passed since I'd last visited the place and it had grown considerably in the interim.

"Doing well," I said when Silverman met me in the lobby and ushered me into his office.

"Well enough," he said. "I have three kids in college and a wife who's trying to buy out Prada one pair of shoes at a time. Imelda Marcos would be proud."

With the door closed behind us and Silverman comfortable behind his desk, I asked, "Why send Dianne Corbeil to me?"

"Mannie says you're the best."

"She needs a good divorce lawyer," I said. "Not a P.I."

Silverman rested his elbows on the top of his desk and leaned forward. "He hits her, Nate. I've seen the bruises."

"He hit her when he's sober, or only when he's drinking?"

"When he's drinking," Silverman said. "Always when he's drinking."

"So how you long you been taking care of him?"

Silverman opened Pierre Corbeil's file. "During the past six years, he's been in and out of here four times," Silverman said. "He drys out, goes home, then does it all over again."

"Thought you cured these people."

"Once a drunk, always a drunk," Silverman said. "The best we can do is help them realize what it is that makes them want to drink. Sometimes we help them change the things in their life that drive them to the bottle."

"And what drives this guy?"

Silverman closed the file, discolored knuckles quickly

hidden as one hand covered the other. "Sometimes we never know."

O'Shannon finished a Milky Way before speaking. "She's so clean she squeaks."

I said nothing and O'Shannon quickly filled the void. "Not even a traffic violation," he said. "If you believe what everybody says about her, she's the kind of girl my mother always wanted me to bring home."

O'Shannon crumpled the Milky Way wrapper and tossed it into my wastebasket.

I told O'Shannon what I'd learned about our client's husband — family money, spoiled child, problems at school, attendance at three different colleges before receiving his degree and entering his daddy's business. He had no police record, but rumor was that daddy's money had lifted him off the hook more than once.

"Problems with women before this?"

"Not that anyone would admit to," I said. "But a couple of his ex-girlfriends seemed reluctant to talk about him."

"Let me follow her for a few days," O'Shannon suggested. "See what she does with her time."

The next evening, Corbeil called me to her home in Clayton. When I arrived, she opened her blouse. The recently-inflicted bruises on her breasts and stomach had just begun to discolor.

"See," she said.

"Call the police."

"I called you."

"Where is he?"

She named a bar downtown, hear the river. "He always drinks there."

I took a deep breath, then returned to my car. As I drove away, I looked for O'Shannon.

I waited in the parking lot on Laclede's Landing until Pierre stumbled out of one of the nightclubs. As he slipped the key into his car door, I stepped up behind him.

"Perry?"

"Yeah?" He turned and found my face in his. He leaned backward, bracing against the car door.

"Heard you like to hit women." I buried one fist in his gut, doubling him over. He dropped to his knees and retched, his vomit sour with vodka. "I don't like guys who hit women."

He protested. "But, I don't —"

I kicked him once, in the stomach, rolling him onto his back and half-under his car. Then I walked away as quietly as I'd arrived.

As I rounded the corner, I passed a vaguely familiar Mercedes with M.D. licenses plates. Out of habit, I noted the license number on a scrap of paper.

"You wouldn't talk on the phone," I said. "So I thought I'd drop in."

Sara Wilson stared at me for a long time before pulling her door open and ushering me into her living room. She had dated Pierre Corbeil for nearly a year before his engagement to Dianne.

As she settled onto the couch, Sara said, "There's nothing I can tell you."

So I asked about Pierre's drinking, and his temper, and the real reason they'd stopped seeing one another.

"Perry liked to drink," she finally said. She pushed long, dark hair away from her face, tucking it behind her ear. "So did I."

"What did you do when you drank?"

"Do?" she asked. "Not a hell of a lot. Perry was a fun drunk, the life of the party."

"And after the party?"

"There was no after," Sara said. She had her hands clasped in her lap and she stared at them.

"He ever hit you?"

She looked up. "Perry?"

I waited.

"Once," she admitted. "See, when Perry was drinking he —" She hesitated, looked away, then took a deep breath. "When Perry was drinking, he couldn't get it up. And Perry was always drinking."

"So he hit you?"

"It wasn't like that," she said. "He wasn't angry or anything. We'd been drinking that night and we went back to my place and Perry wanted to have sex but nothing was happening. He slapped my butt. I thought he was playing and I went along with it, but he kept slapping me and slapping me and slapping me and then we had sex."

She looked away again and I waited for her to continue.

"The next morning, I woke up alone," she said. "I had a hangover and I ached everywhere. I was so bruised my backside looked like twin plums."

"Did you tell anyone?"

"Who could I tell?" she asked. Moisture had gathered at the corners of her eyes. "I didn't try to stop him. I let him do it to me. But I never let him do it again."

"What happened?"

"I phoned him, told him I never wanted to see him

again."

"How did he react?"

"He didn't seem to care," she said. "I learned later that he'd been seeing someone else behind my back. I'm certain she's the one who taught him the Viagra of abuse. He married her a couple of months after we broke up."

Two days later, Pierre Corbeil's body washed up in Cape Girardeau, down river from St. Louis. A single bullet had lodged in his chest. He still had his wallet and the local police identified the body before the day ended.

As soon as I heard that Corbeil had identified her husband's body and had finished talking with the police, I drove to her Clayton home.

She answered the door wearing only a thigh-length silk robe, the loose sash barely holding it closed.

I pushed my way inside and my client stepped back involuntarily.

"You did it, didn't you?"

Corbeil swung her open palm at my face. I caught her wrist before she could strike me. Then I grabbed her other wrist and pinned both arms to the foyer wall above her head. The robe's sash fell loose and her robe gaped open. She wore nothing underneath and fresh bruises purpled her ivory skin.

"You like it rough, don't you?"

A smile played with the corners of her mouth as she thrust her hips forward and pressed her groin against mine. I felt her heat and my body responded to it.

"He never did anything you didn't want him to do."

My client wet her lips with the tip of her tongue.

"He never hit a woman before he met you."

"Fuck me, Nate," she whispered, her voice low and husky. "Fuck me now."

I released my grip on her wrists and stepped away.

She dropped her robe to the floor and stood naked before me.

I let myself out.

Agnes had already gone for the day when O'Shannon broke the seal on a new bottle of bourbon. He splashed two fingers worth into a shot glass while I told him about my evening, then pushed it across his desk to me. He poured his into a coffee mug, took a healthy swallow, then splashed more into the mug.

"How'd Silverman see her bruises?" O'Shannon asked.

"He's a doctor."

"Yeah," O'Shannon said, "but he ain't *her* doctor."

I thought about it for awhile, then said, "We need to find Mannie."

Mannie Goldstein — a short man with a ring of nappy black hair surrounding the crown of his head — had a thin, high-pitched voice that sounded like he'd never left puberty. He had connections all over town and if he wasn't in on something, he knew who was. I finally found him holding court at The Drinking Fountain, a strip club where all the dancers used drink names as their stage names.

"We need to talk," I said.

Mannie stuffed a twenty into the cleavage of each of the blondes at his table and the women disappeared faster than tax refunds.

I remembered something Mannie had once said. "Got to keep my brother-in-law in business or he'll send my sister back." After I settled into the booth, I told him about Dianne

Corbeil. He listened carefully.

"Silverman's doing her," I concluded.

"He's been warned about poking his finger in places it don't belong," Mannie said. "Family'll take care of it."

Corbeil stopped at my office after her husband's funeral. She wore a curve-hugging black dress and a black veil masked her eyes.

As soon as Agnes had her settled into the guest chair across from me and had stepped out of my office, Corbeil said, "Police report says someone roughed up my husband the night he disappeared."

I didn't respond.

"Two witnesses saw a big guy knock my husband to the ground and kick him."

"Why didn't they phone the police?"

"They're married," she said, "but not to each other. Thought it was just a mugging and didn't want to get involved."

"People are like that."

She placed a check on my desk. "Thanks."

"Wasn't me," I said. Without looking at it, I pushed the check toward my former client.

We stared at each other for a full minute, the black veil masking anything I might have read in her eyes. Then Corbeil retrieved the check and stood.

"I'll be leaving in the morning," she said.

I stood, stepped around my desk, and opened the office door. My former client stepped past me, the swell of one breast brushing against my arm. I watched as she passed Agnes' desk and let herself out. Her perfume lingered behind and I drew in a deep breath.

Agnes turned and looked a hard question at me.

"She tried to give me another check."

"I hope you didn't take it."

"Not this time."

"She plan to make good on the last one?"

"I don't think she can," I said. "But I don't think she realizes it yet."

I met Silverman in his office a month later. He favored his heavily-bandaged right hand and said he'd lost his index finger in an accident with a faulty table saw. He used his good hand to slide a check across the desk. "Mannie suggested I make good on your loss."

I picked up the check, folded it in half without looking at it, and slid it into my shirt pocket.

"Sorry I sent her to you," Silverman said. "Sorry I ever met her. Sorry I ever showed her the gun."

My eyes narrowed as I stared at him.

"Mannie gave it to me ten years ago. I kept it in my glove box and it disappeared the same night her husband died."

A few months later, local police located the .38 used in Pierre Corbeil's murder. Thrown in the Mississippi at the same time Pierre's body had been thrown in, it had lodged against a bridge abutment and didn't surface until the river level dropped.

I sat with Mannie and O'Shannon at the Pink Flamingo and told them about the gun.

"No fingerprints at all?" O'Shannon asked.

I shook my head.

"Too bad," Mannie said.

We both looked at the fat little man.

"My sister complains all the time about Hiram's hand," he said. "Maybe we could have saved the finger."

Charlie Fischer stopped at our table with a fresh round of beer. The Pink Flamingo had been closed for nearly an hour and he'd been listening to our conversation while he cleaned up. "So who killed the guy?"

"After Nate left the house that night," O'Shannon said. "Silverman's Mercedes drifted out of the driveway. He must have arrived before I rolled up because I didn't realize he was there. I didn't see the driver, but didn't figure it was our client. The car returned two hours later."

"I saw Silverman's car downtown," I said. "Didn't realize it was his until later."

Charlie pulled an empty chair to our table and settled into it.

"My brother-in-law says he was at her house that night," Mannie said. "They had drinks, they had sex, and he says he fell asleep."

Silverman had put the fresh bruises on Dianne Corbeil that night and he'd been asleep somewhere in the house while she was telling me about her husband.

O'Shannon picked up the story. "The Mercedes left the house again around four. By then, Silverman's .38 had disappeared from the glove box."

"Mrs. Corbeil thought she had everything she wanted," I said. "Her husband dead, and someone to take the fall for it."

"Except one thing," O'Shannon said.

Charlie asked, "What?"

"The poor bastard was dead broke. Hadn't even paid the premiums on his life insurance."

"So what happened to her?"

"Disappeared," I said. "Nobody knows."

Mannie smiled and suddenly he had our complete attention.

"I introduced her to a guy," he said, "who'll teach her what real pain feels like."

So Pretty

Kevin Egan

Taped to the airbag, the photograph of the little blonde girl cartwheeled as Berk turned onto the treelined street. It was a grainy shot taken with a telephoto lens and blown up enough to reveal the girl's features. She was pretty, Berk supposed, in that unfinished, almost cartoonlike way that young girls were pretty. At the bottom of the photo, where the girl's pink sneakers skipped over the blur of a jump rope, the lawyer had scribbled a three-digit number in black ballpoint. Berk eased off the gas and oriented himself to the house numbers. The three digits matched a white Victorian with a wraparound porch. He tooled past, noting the empty driveway, the open garage door, and the brightly colored plastic play structures in a corner of the backyard. On the seat beside him were a box of baby wipes and a beanbag shaped like a dragon. He was half an hour early.

A block past the house, Berk spotted a woman watering her flowers with a garden hose. She was a shapely middle age, wearing cut-off jeans and a denim shirt knotted under her breasts to expose her stomach. Berk slowed his car, watching her tug at the hose.

That's it, he thought, bend over, bend over. There.

The image fixed itself in his mind.

Berk drove on, crisscrossing the neighborhood. He ran a calculated risk; someone might remember his car, no matter how nondescript. But the neighborhood straddled a ridge, and the roads connected in complicated fashion. He needed to scout the best route to the Interstate.

Some time later, the image of the woman with the garden hose overcame him, and he nudged his car to the curb on a dead-end street. This was stupid, he knew, even more risky than constantly tooling through the neighborhood. But the image was too powerful, so he gave himself up. Transported, he imagined himself approaching her from behind and cupping her breasts. As he held that image, he pinched his own nipples, feeling them tingle, feeling a glimmer of life in his crotch.

The earliest incident occurred in college, with a girl in his English Lit class. Berk caught her eye several times during the semester's opening lecture, and once thought she grinned before dropping her gaze back to her notes. After class, he tried to think of an intro line, some witty take on the professor's words. But words never came to Berk; he dealt only in images. He saw himself as in a silent movie, leading her by the hand to his dorm room, lowering the shades while she sat cross-legged on his bed, smiling demurely.

The girl lived in a nearby dorm, and everyday they took the same route across campus. At first, he tailed her at a distance, concentrating on the shape of her legs or the swing of her skirt. As each day passed, he closed the gap until he followed directly on her heels. He meant no harm, even when he stepped on the back of her shoe. He hoped that she would say something to show that she imagined those same images he saw so clearly in his mind. Instead she seemed horrified.

"Get away from me," she screamed, and broke into a run.

Two nights later, a group of fraternity brothers surrounded him in a remote corner of campus. One punched him in the stomach. The others dumped him head first into a hedge.

"Stalker," they called him, and walked away laughing.

The final incident occurred years later, after he sat next to a pretty young woman on a commuter train. They didn't speak a word, of course, but he felt the images cascade: leaving the train together, wending through the parking lot to his car, driving to his apartment. Over the next several weeks, he tried to meet up with her again, prowling the platforms at rush hour, taking different trains, sitting in different cars. Finally, his persistence paid off.

The seat beside her was occupied, but he found a spot a few rows away where he could watch her throughout the ride. She liked him, he could tell, from the way her eyes flicked toward him while she pretended to gaze thoughtfully out the window. When the train reached his station, he nodded good-bye.

More weeks of searching passed before he found her again, this time with an empty seat beside her. He plopped himself down and smiled his best smile.

"Remember me?" he said.

The woman excused herself.

"I'll watch that for you," he said.

But she took her satchel anyway. She hurried down the aisle and pounded on the conductor's booth. Berk, mystified, waited for her to return.

The police surrounded him on the platform when the train arrived at his station. A female officer held the sobbing woman in her arms.

This last incident led him to the lawyer.

"Stalking's a crime," the lawyer said. "Been that way five, six years now."

"I wasn't stalking her."

"Maybe. But whether we go jury or non-jury, either way you're cooked."

In the end, the lawyer brokered a deal that kept Berk out of jail. The downside was the psychiatrist.

"I just want to be friendly," Berk said.

"I know." The psychiatrist scribbled the court-ordered prescription. "You mean no harm."

The lawyer had summoned Berk two days ago.

"I call this clients helping clients," he said, and described a battle over Memorial Day visitation rights. "Dad owns a private jet. You'll rendezvous at the abandoned hangar at the county airport."

He gave Berk the particulars, the photo, the beanbag dragon, which he promised would lure the girl over hot coals. And the baby wipes.

"Mom doesn't keep the girl clean enough for Dad. You're to wipe her head to toe before handing her over."

Berk hesitated.

"Look, there's no time for me to go to court."

"Why me?"

"Because we're clients helping clients," said the lawyer. "And if you refuse, I'll speak to your probation officer about your medication."

Berk's timing was perfect. He swung onto the street

just as the girl and her playmate rounded the corner. There was no sidewalk, and the two kids made a game of walking with one foot on the road and the other on the curb. Berk drew even, leaned away from the steering wheel, and threw open the passenger side door.

"Hi," he said, and waved the beanbag dragon.

The girl froze, captivated by the toy.

The boy hung back, calling, "No, no." But the girl stepped closer, into the mouth of the open door. The moment she touched the dragon, Berk wrapped his hand over hers and pulled her inside.

The girl screamed. Berk groped for the door handle. Unable to reach it, he pressed the accelerator. The car lurched forward, throwing the girl back against the seat and swinging the door shut. The girl bounced up and slapped her hands against the window. Berk pushed her under the dashboard and drove swiftly out of the neighborhood.

On the empty Interstate, he allowed the girl to sit up. Dirt from the floor mat smudged one of her cheeks. He reached over, moistened his thumb with one of her tears, and wiped the smudge clean.

"I want to go home," she said.

"We're going to the airport. You're going to fly in a jet plane."

"I want to go home."

"Don't you want to fly? With your dad? In a jet plane?"

"My daddy's dead."

"No he's not. He's coming in a jet plane to see you. Spend the weekend with you."

"I wish he was. He'd beat you up." She broke down. "I want to go home. Take me home."

Berk turned up the radio to drown out her cries. He

exited the Interstate, then doubled back along a service road to a chain-link gate. Weeds sprouted through seams in the abandoned tarmac. In the distance, the control tower gleamed in the late afternoon sun. High up in the landing pattern, a glint of silver flashed in the blue.

Berk parked behind the old hangar and cut the radio. The girl was curled up, withdrawn, whimpering, clutching the dragon. Berk wondered, was her daddy really dead? It sounded like the kind of lie an estranged wife would tell a child. Well, what did he care? He had his job. Clients helping clients. Somehow, the lawyer knew he skipped his medication. If his probation officer found out, he would go to jail. He searched the landing pattern again. The jet was closer now, taking shape.

Berk opened the box of baby wipes. The girl didn't resist. He swirled the moist, pungent towelette across her forehead, then her cheeks, then the back of her neck. The wipe turned brown with little flecks of dirt. He tossed it into the back seat, peeled off another, and continued to wipe her with long, gentle strokes. A spot of blue marker disappeared from her elbow, a grass stain dissolved off her knee.

And then, when Berk finished, the girl did something totally confounding. She nestled against him.

The feel of the girl's little body electrified Berk. For years, he had tried to connect with women only to have them flee in fear or call the police. Now, this little girl curled beneath his arm. Her tiny ribs rose and fell with each breath, so delicate, so trusting. Berk instinctively knew what she told him was true. This *wasn't* any custody battle. Her daddy *was* dead.

The jet was alighting, its flaps huge, its wheels clawing for the tarmac. Berk ticked through ideas: dirt, mud, ink from a ballpoint pen in the glove compartment. No. The wipes would wash them all away.

Then he had it.

He lifted the girl aside and tucked her gently on the seat.

"Stay here," he said.

He sank into the weeds behind the car, hoping enough days had passed since he last took his medication. In the distance, the jet's engines whined as the thrust reversers kicked in. He pulled up his shirt and crept a hand toward his nipples. Images unreeled in his mind. Women he'd seen, women he'd followed, women he thought might have liked him if only they'd given him the chance. He settled on the woman watering her flowers, conjured her kneeling in front of him, her thighs pressed together, sweat on her cleavage. He heard her say "hi" in a sexy, smoky voice. He imagined her being friendly, very friendly, as he unbuttoned his pants.

Minutes later, he arranged himself with his free hand. He opened the door and called for the girl to come out. She'd been asleep and now stood blinking against the sunshine. She nuzzled the dragon.

The jet taxied closer, crushing weeds in its path.

"Here." He dipped a finger into his opposite palm and dabbed her hair. "It's just some glue. Like Elmer's. It will protect you."

The jet swung around broadside, its engines whining. The back door opened with a hiss, and a wiry man wearing a muscle shirt clomped down the gangway. The man sneered contemptuously at Berk, then took the girl by the hand. She hesitated, and Berk lifted his chin, telling her go on, it would be all right.

The girl climbed into the jet. She stood facing another man who was visible to Berk only by his feet and knees. A hand appeared, appraising her. The girl turned her head, displaying her hair. A thin finger touched it.

That same hand waved the little girl away. Muscle Shirt looked out the door, locked eyes with Berk, then said something to the man inside the jet. The little girl came down the stairs. Muscle Shirt stood at the top, waiting for her to clear. When she did, he swooped down, closed on Berk with long strides.

"You piece of shit," he said.

Berk never saw the punch that ripped a hole in his gut. One second he was looking past Muscle Shirt at the little girl; the next, the world upended. The clouds spun past until the second punch shattered Berk's jaw. The third crushed his windpipe.

Berk lay in the weeds as the jet rolled away. The girl crouched beside him, staring curiously. Struggling, Berk lifted a hand and stroked the spot in her hair.

"Told you that glue would protect you." Dry already, it crumbled in his fingers.

The girl started to cry.

"You're safe. They won't be back. You're so pretty, my little friend." Berk fought for his last breath. "So pretty."

Contributors

Tom Sweeney has published about three dozen short stories which have appeared in such diverse magazines as *Analog, Blue Murder,* and *Woman's World,* and in numerous anthologies, including *Mystery Street, The Mammoth Book of Legal Thrillers, Hardbroiled, Small Crimes,* and both *Fedora* and *Fedora II.* His stories have been nominated for the Pushcart Prize and the Shamus Award. The editor of *Reflections in a Private Eye,* the newsletter of the Private Eye Writers of America, he and his wife live in Portsmouth, New Hampshire.

Lee Goldberg is a two-time Edgar Award nominee whose many TV writing/producing credits include *Diagnosis Murder, Martial Law, Hunter, SeaQuest, Spenser: For Hire, Nero Wolfe, 1–800-Missing,* and *Monk.* He's the author of several non-fiction books, including *Unsold Television Pilots* and *Successful Television Writing,* and writes the "Crimetime Television" column for *Mystery Scene* magazine. His novels include *My Gun Has Bullets, Beyond the Beyond, The Walk,* and the *Diagnosis Murder* series of original paperbacks. He lives with his wife and daughter in Los Angeles.

Carol Kilgore's short fiction has appeared in *Blue Murder,*

TheCase.com, Futures Mysterious Anthology Magazine, HandHeldCrime, and in the anthology *Hardbroiled.* She also has a story scheduled to appear in *Bullet Points,* an upcoming anthology of flash mystery fiction. Her flash mystery, "Just a Man on the Sidewalk," received the Derringer Award, presented by the Short Mystery Fiction Society, for Best Short-Short Mystery 1999. She has completed three novels. A native Houstonian, Kilgore has lived in locations across the U.S. She and her husband currently reside in Corpus Christi, Texas.

George Wilhite's first novel, *The Texas Rodeo Murder,* was published in 2003 by Eakin Press. Two short stories were nominated for Spur Awards by the Western Writers of America. He has received numerous awards from national and regional press associations as a journalist. A former rodeo clown/cowboy and editor of *Rodeo News* magazine, he was named to the board of the Texas Rodeo Cowboy Hall of Fame in 2003. Wilhite is currently a writing instructor at Texas State Technical College in Waco, Texas, where he lives with his family.

J. L. Abramo's first private eye novel, *Catching Water in a Net,* was recipient of the St. Martin's Press/Private Eye Writers of America Award for Best First Private Eye Novel; introducing San Francisco private investigator Jake Diamond and published by St. Martin's Minotaur in 2001. The series continues with *Clutching at Straws* (2003) and *Counting to Infinity* (2004). Abramo lives in an old church in central Vermont where he is working on the fourth book in the Jake Diamond series.

David Terrenoire is the author of *Beneath a Panamanian Moon* and ghostwriter of *Man Down, A Broken Wings Thriller* by John Douglas. Terrenoire's short fiction has appeared in *Ellery Queen's Mystery Magazine, Blue Murder, Hardboiled, The Dead Mule School of Southern Literature,* and the anthology *Mystery in Mind.* Represented by Richard Abate at ICM, Terrenoire is currently working on a new ghost assignment, his fourth novel, and several new short stories. He is an editor, copywriter, retired actor, and full-time amateur blues musician. Terrenoire and his wife, Jennifer, live in Durham, North Carolina.

David Bart's stories have appeared in Mystery Writers of America anthologies, *Ellery Queen's Mystery Magazine* and *Alfred Hitchcock's Mystery Magazine.* One of his many stories published in *AHMM* was translated and reprinted in a Paris anthology. He recently completed a novel featuring the main characters of "Captiva" and is currently working on a suspense novel in addition to more short fiction. Bart is a member of Private Eye Writers of America, Mystery Writers of America and SouthWest Writers. He lives in New Mexico.

Bev Vincent's first book, *The Road to the Dark Tower,* an exploration of Stephen King's Dark Tower series, will be released by NAL in November 2004. He is a contributing editor with *Cemetery Dance* magazine and book critic with the *Conroe* (Texas) *Courier.* Recent short story appearances include *Borderlands 5, Shivers II, The Murder Hole, All Hallows, Here and Now,* and *Who Died in Here?* Born in eastern Canada, he lived in Switzerland before moving to The Woodlands, Texas, where he lives with his wife and daughter.

James S. Dorr's collection, *Strange Mistresses: Tales of Wonder and Romance,* is available as a trade paperback from Dark Regions Press. His work has appeared in *Alfred Hitchcock's, New Mystery, The Strand, Enigmatic Tales* (U.K.), and numerous other mystery, horror, SF, and fantasy magazines and anthologies including *The Best of Cemetery Dance* and *Small Crimes.* His story "Paperboxing Art" was a 1998 Anthony finalist. Born in Pensacola, Florida, Dorr has lived in New Jersey and the Boston, Massachusetts area, and currently resides in Bloomington, Indiana.

Chelle Martin is published in short fiction and non-fiction and is currently working on several novels in genres ranging from romantic comedy to mystery. She is a member of Mystery Writers of America, and the national and New Jersey chapters of Sisters in Crime and Romance Writers of America. One of her short stories appears in *Small Crimes.*

Dorothy Rellas's suspense novel, *Hidden Motives,* was published several years ago. Her short fiction and articles on writing have appeared in *Futures Mysterious Anthology Magazine,* and the anthologies *A Deadly Dozen, Hardbroiled,* and *Small Crimes.* She lives with her family in Pasadena, California.

Ann Aptaker continues to write crime fiction. She works for a private investigations firm in the San Francisco Bay area, and lives in the historic North Beach neighborhood in the city of San Francisco. One of Aptaker's short stories appeared in *Fedora II: More Private Eyes And Tough Guys.*

Nick Andreychuk is a Derringer Award-winning author and editor. His short crime fiction has appeared in *Crimestalker Casebook, Detective Mystery Magazine, Down These Dark Streets, Fedora: Private Eyes And Tough Guys, Futures Mysterious Anthology Magazine, Hardbroiled, Mystery Time, Murder By Six, Rex Stout Journal, Shred of Evidence,* and *Who Died In Here?,* among other publications. Andrechuk's work can also be found in *Bullet Points,* an anthology of short-short mystery fiction that he co-edited. Born in Ontario, Canada, he currently resides in British Columbia.

Michael Hemmingson lives in San Diego and has published numerous books, including *Wild Turkey* (Forge), *The Case of the Absent College Girl* (Blue Moon), *Borrego Springs* (America House), *The Mammoth Book of Legal Thrillers* (Carroll & Graf), and *The Lawyer* (Blue Moon). He is currently working on a critical study of William T. Vollmann for the University of South Carolina Press, another thriller for Forge called *Flyover,* and the completion of his *House of Dreams Trilogy* for Blue Moon. One of Hemmingson's short stories appeared in *Fedora: Private Eyes And Tough Guys.*

Graham Powell's stories have appeared in *Plots With Guns, HandHeldCrime,* and *The Thrilling Detective.* Originally from Shreveport, Louisiana, he and his family currently live in Fort Worth, Texas.

Fedora III editor **Michael Bracken** is the author of *All White Girls, Bad Girls, Canvas Bleeding, Deadly Campaign, Even Roses Bleed, In the Town of Dreams Unborn and Memories Dying, Just in Time for Love, Psi Cops, Tequila Sunrise,* and nearly 900 shorter works. He previously edited *Fedora: Private Eyes and Tough Guys, Fedora II: More Private Eyes and Tough Guys, Hardbroiled,* and *Small Crimes.* Bracken has received numerous awards for advertising copywriting and his short story, "Cuts Like a Knife," was nominated for a Derringer Award. Born in Canton, Ohio, Bracken has traveled extensively throughout the U.S., and currently resides with his family in Waco, Texas.

Kevin Egan is the author of a science fiction novel, *The Perseus Breed,* and short stories that have appeared in *Fiction Quarterly, Rosebud, Whispers, Small Crimes,* and on nylawyer.com. Writing as Conor Daly, he has published three mystery novels: *Local Knowledge, Buried Lies,* and *Outside Agency.* Two of these novels, *Local Knowledge* and *Outside*

Agency, received the Washington Irving Award for fiction in 1997. He lives with his family in White Plains, New York.

www.ingramcontent.com/pod-product-compliance
Lightning Source LLC
Chambersburg PA
CBHW020612310726
48979CB00008B/1454/J

* 9 7 8 0 8 0 9 5 8 9 4 5 6 *